DEDICATION

This book is dedicated to my loving wife Mary Ellen, who has always been there to support me.

This book is also dedicated to the memory of Reed Donovan, Gilbert Anderson, and Mary Doyle Keefe.

ACKNOWLEDGMENTS

I would like to thank my wife, Mary Ellen Keefe for her patient, careful and insightful reading and editing of the manuscript. This is my first fictional work and as such she had a large task in front of her to find and fix the scores of contextual, grammatical and punctuation errors littering all 350 pages. Managing the content was easy in comparison to her task. I am grateful to her for her efforts in that regard.

She also had to bear with me as I read each new chapter to her out loud! I learned she has remarkable patience and I'm indebted to her for putting up with me in the early mornings and late nights for these readings. Her plot suggestions were invaluable. I hope we can follow a similar process for the next book (which may be asking too much, but I'm hopeful).

I'd also like to thank our daughters, Sarah Soifert and Hillary Fortin, and my good friend Bob King for their reading of the chapters as I finished them. Their suggestions and comments helped me nuance some of the characters and formulate the plot. I know it was especially difficult reading an unedited book in an on-line document, chapter after chapter, for six months. They never complained even once and for that I am most thankful and appreciative.

Note from the Author

How does someone go from an avid reader of novels to a writer?

This novel started out as an experiment to see just how much work it would be to write and edit a 90,000-word book. I've heard it said one should write about something one knows about, and shade tobacco farming is something I know a lot about. I've lived with these thoughts quietly churning away in my head for 30 years. Writing about them now has been a true catharsis for me.

I admit hours and hours were spent at the keyboard over a six-month period. I wrote every day for an hour or two, early mornings before heading to my day job as a systems architect.

With this backdrop, a character, Jason Kraft, emerges who just happens to live a dual life; his real life and the "Scam" he is running as a DEA agent. He relishes the dual life he leads. Seeking justice, he can't (or prefers not to) do it alone, so he's side-by-side with a beautiful woman, Alondra, as their past relationship is rekindled.

Jason's biography parallels my own, but Jason's background is more flawless. His character was born from my own experiences as a systems contractor. I would go from job to job every other year and the first month or so I'd be scamming my way, trying to fit in and make a more permanent home for myself. Knowing I'd be finishing the assignment and starting a new one was always a bit scary, just like it is for Jason in his scams. Of course, I too have a beautiful woman, my wife Mary Ellen by my side.

My hope is you will enjoy this read, and discover what Jason does: some things aren't always what they appear to be.

Keith Bombard, November 2015

Preface

Jason Kraft, an agent in the DEA's covert operations group has just been assigned to infiltrate a large tobacco farm in New England. This farm is thought to be responsible for a special hybrid of genetically engineered tobacco, known to look and smell like normal tobacco, but it has the chemical component THC, having a similar effect to potent marijuana when smoked. It is critical that Jason finds the strain and destroys it before it hits the streets.

This assignment takes him into the complex world of Connecticut shade tobacco cultivation, to infiltrate the largest farm in the region where expensive cigar wrapper leaves are grown.

The FBI is also interested; they unknowingly assign Jason's former lover Alondra, to work the investigation with him. Their relationship is rekindled as they reunite for this common goal, to find the strain.

Alondra, of Puerto Rican decent, develops her own agenda: to fight for equality of pay and better working conditions for the large contingent of Puerto Rican workers on the farm. She works to bring labor unions in for the first time to help establish more wages, benefits, and a better life for the seasonal Puerto Rican farm workers, who for years have struggled and have been left behind.

They are both nearing their goals, but there's a dilemma: if they find the strain, the case ends and Alondra will lose the opportunity to establish unions and labor equality for the first time in the Connecticut tobacco industry.

Read this book to follow Jason's and Alondra's quest to find the strain, and to learn all about how shade tobacco is grown and how children and migrant workers have sacrificed for years to make Connecticut farmers wealthy.

The plot is contrived and the characters are fictional, but the descriptions of tobacco operations, activities in the fields, depictions of migrant farm labor and the plight of the workers in the Connecticut shade tobacco industry are 100 percent real.

Chapter 1

Cody Mason waited until dark to pull into the yard. The place was abandoned this late and that prerequisite would be met. He pulled on the mask Peter had given him. "Cody, when you do it, wear a mask just in case," he'd said.

With the mask on, he climbed out of the truck holding his backpack and made his way to the door. It was a warm spring night and he could hear the tree frogs making their mating sounds. They were loud and that's about all he could hear. The darkness was punctuated by a few luminescent green fireflies floating in and above the grass next to the house.

The door to the dark house was locked with a padlock. He knew it would be and he had the keys with him, but it was so dark he had to put the flashlight on the ground and prop it up with a small rock, enough to see the lock to use the key. Ten seconds later the door was open and he stepped in.

Using the small flashlight Cody carefully made his way all the way to the back of the house. He found the first platform on a beam in the center of the floor. He had to stand on one of the beds to work on the beam. Carefully reaching into his backpack he removed one of the devices and placed it on the beam. He armed the device and set the digital timer for its final countdown to eight minutes. With flashlight in hand, he repeated this operation three more times on his way out of the house, using two-minute intervals and carefully timing his exit, setting all four timers to go off simultaneously. By the time he finished, condensation in his mask was dripping on his face.

He exited the house and relocked the door, then ran back and jumped into the truck pulling off the mask. As he did so, the house behind him flashed three bright flashes in close succession, and then a fourth flash appeared a few seconds later.

Cody knew he would kill thousands that night.

He didn't feel too bad about it; if nothing was done early those tiny whiteflies could multiply exponentially and had the potential of ruining the new tomato crop. The pesticide bombs were guaranteed to rein them in.

He didn't need the pesticide mask after all. He wiped his sweaty face with his sleeve, started the truck and left the yard.

Chapter 2

The Drug Enforcement Administration (a.k.a. DEA) training academy's three-story building in Quantico, Virginia was typically reserved as the classroom for newly hired DEA agents. There, newbies were taught a number of basic skills including firearm usage, forensic laboratory methods and crime analytics using sophisticated computer software. For the past two years, completely veiled from the public, it was also where the DEA covert operation teams learned about their next assignments and received their orders.

I was there that spring day, a warm Monday morning in mid-April, to take new operation orders from the CC (a.k.a. Covert Operations Commander, and I know why they left out the "O" from the acronym). I was about to attend a briefing revealing background and details for the next covert operation.

The DEA covert operation teams are out in force, but very few people know about them. They really are covert.

These teams were established after 911, initially as a joint effort by the DEA, the FBI and Homeland Security, but more recently, within the past two years, the DEA was taking the lead role, calling in the FBI when needed, to work the financial or interstate aspects of a case. Homeland Security had bowed out and was no longer involved in covert ops.

I use the word "team" loosely here; in many instances, the team would be one individual, operating in the field completely in an incognito capacity, as an infiltrator. Their sole purpose was to build a case to take down the most serious drug offenders using a false identity from within, to gather evidence to support the prosecution. The "Operation Scam" could be short, a week or less or as long as several months if needed. The fact these scams were, as of yet, almost completely unknown to the public worked in our favor, and if they were designed and executed carefully, the targets would never understand what hit them. Not all scams resulted in indictments; the success rate was about 70 percent. This percentage was improving as the scammers, scam architects and handlers gained experience sourcing and implementing the scams.

I just completed an assignment (called operation FlightPath) which resulted in the indictment of a team of drug-running small-plane pilots in Pensacola, Florida. The flight school and several pilots were suspected of ferrying designer drugs using the small Cessna planes student pilots used for training. It was a four-month assignment, and I had managed my time wisely and attempted to 'fit in' by gaining a pilot's license from the flight school. The student pilot ruse turned out to be a perfect cover. I was older (34) than the young ex-military instructors whose average age was 26. They took me under their wing as the 'old guy' and I had no trouble integrating into the day-to-day activity flow. I waited until the day I took the check ride for the pilot's license to pull the plug and snap the scam, leaving the hangar at the airport just hours before a caravan of DEA agents driving black Ford Navigators rumbled in to perform the search, make the arrests and close the place down.

The difficult part was over. We had the hard evidence: receipts, bank statements, cash, tape recordings, and even sample product the flight teams were delivering all across the southern coast of Florida and Louisiana. The future courtroom battle was next, which would be difficult for me, as it had been in the past, having to abandon and turn against relationships (and friendships) I had crafted over the four-month duration of the scam.

The evidence was collected in a way that I would never be revealed as the source, but it still bothered me to see people I knew well, and in some cases liked a great deal, go down.

I always tried to get something out of the scam for myself; in this case it was a pilot's license. I rationalized this benefit, playing it against the inherent danger (and boredom) I faced daily in the contrived role.

Sometimes I wondered if I needed to be someone else, to live a different life where I could hide from myself. It came naturally; I craved it and considered it a worthy challenge. So far it had worked out for me and I was counting on that streak to continue.

The ops planning conference room was at the end of the hall on the third floor. It was a sizeable room with three large windows facing south, overlooking the parking lot. I figured they set it up this way so the view out the window was uninteresting enough to keep people from gazing out the window onto the beautiful park-like grounds on the other side of the building. I was seated in the middle of the large 20-foot rectangular conference table with a conference phone in the middle and small wired microphones at each end of the table.

Bill Sweeney the CC, sat directly across from me at the table. John Trane the assistant CC, was seated close next to me on my left, almost too close I thought. I did not know the CC well; met him only once before when he assigned me to the FightPath con. He was older, in his late fifties, balding with a beer paunch. He was a clear candidate for a low-carb diet.

John, Bill's assistant, had the file open and was prepared on cue from Bill, to physically pass and explain critical pages from the new case file to me. I had never met John, but our paths had crossed by way of field updates on previous cases with the case handlers. I finally got to put John's name with the face and was not disappointed; I had pegged him perfectly, down to his short dark hair, tall thin build and full mustache. He was impeccably dressed and detailed in appearance.

Bill made a weak attempt at introductions and small talk. In his mild south-Texas accent he said, "Jason, I assume you and John know each other; for the record, John Trane, this is Jason Kraft."

He continued, "Jason just finished an operation down in Pensacola; he did great work too. Shut down a designer drug transport operation there lickety-split. Did exactly what we wanted him to do. Congratulations Jason, nice work. The DEA and the country owe you one."

I really didn't believe I was owed anything; on the contrary, DEA had paid more than $12,000 for visual flight rules (VFR) training to my benefit. Bill, who was never that close to the details in a scam, obviously didn't know this, and probably would never have agreed to that spend if the case handlers hadn't authorized it at the onset as perfect cover for the scam. I was content to be out of the Flightpath scam and on to something different. That scam had gone on too long. My fault in part, as I was finishing the flight training and I needed it to last until I had accumulated enough air time on Uncle Sam's dime, to take the flight check for the license.

I had to admit, living the scam, as we call it, for extended periods of time was not an easy thing to do. It was important you kept as close to the truth as possible. This way the associated risk of being discovered was lessened. The 'acting' component was reduced and if you were living close to your real self, it was safer and psychologically better all the way around. We were urged in training to find 'opportunities of compatibility' in the scam role, especially if the role was for an extended time. The scam architects had extensive personality profiles on each of us, and it was their job to match the personality and skillset in the profile to the new scam. They got it right most of the time; for me they had anyway. It was important they got the correct match: the right person for the right scam. When they didn't, the scam was blown and the operation washed out. The DEA lost a valuable opportunity, sometimes lost for good. Some scams could be restarted with new operatives, but others could not and those were lost.

I looked up at the clock and saw we were six minutes into the meeting and the architects were not in the room yet.

"Bill, where is the architect team? They're late."

"They're coming in a short while," Bill responded. Staring right at me, Bill continued, "I'll call for them when we're ready. We're doing something different this time Jason. We're not letting the architects in on the most critical details of this plan. Too sensitive; we're trying to limit exposure. We decided this one is too important to broadcast and we're taking extra precautions to keep it tight. So, I also have to ask that you not communicate the details we're about to share with the architects, or anyone else on the team initially. Of course we'll keep the standard protocol for updates and you will share everything as always with your admin contacts, once we're underway and communicating in the field."

I wondered what effect there would be if the architects building a scam were in the dark on important details. This was out of the norm and I was not pleased they were not operating with me 100 percent on the case.

Bill continued, "So let's get on with it. John, can you give us a short summary of the first exhibit, the one with the background case info. You're going to love this one Jason."

John pulled a one-page document from his folder and studied it intently for a few seconds. I noticed the paper was light blue and I could see some of the text from where I was sitting, on John's right. He began his presentation by reading the document.

"On January 10, San Juan, Puerto Rico, 8:55 a.m., an individual named Roberto Martell-Valentin, a white male, age 25 and reportedly under the influence, was detained by the San Juan Police for suspicion of possession of a controlled substance and breach of peace.

"The officer was cruising in his patrol car, a 2014 Ford Mustang, when he noticed an individual staggering along the sidewalk. The officer pulled over closer to the curb to get a better look at the individual. As he did that, the man appeared to lose his balance and fell awkwardly onto the front hood of the police car, now parked next to the sidewalk. The officer exited the vehicle and attempted to aid the individual but was met with hostility and verbal abuse. A struggle ensued with the officer, resulting in the unarmed person being placed in the back of the cruiser. The man had ID. He was also smoking an unfiltered oversized cigarette, of a homemade variety. The cigarette was confiscated for analysis.

"The individual was driven to the Maria Street station for questioning. He was detained in a temporary holding cell, while a brief analysis of the cigarette was performed in the quick lab, on premise. Initially, it was thought the cigarette was some form of tobacco dosed with a cannabinoid or with marinol, as the subject was exhibiting behaviors of acute marijuana ingestion."

John stopped here to add this explanation, "Jason, I know you're an expert in designer drugs, but if you're not familiar with marijuana and related drugs, a cannabinoid is the generic term for the chemical compound found in marijuana and its oil can be extracted from the marijuana plant using solvents. This oil is then added to a tobacco cigarette to yield a marijuana cigarette. Marinol is similar, but it is the synthetic version of the ingredient in marijuana, THC, which yields the 'high' everyone clambers for."

I had basic familiarity with the topic and didn't need John's explanation, but I listened patiently anyway. I reminded myself that I had never smoked marijuana, and knew only one other person in my life besides me who also had not.

Bill sat there looking bored, obviously having discussed this all before the meeting.

I replied, "Thanks John. Keep going."

John continued reading the report, "The subject agreed to take a urine test, and subsequently tested positive for marijuana. However, initial analysis found no trace of cannabinoid oils or marinol or any other foreign drug substance in the cigarette; it was identified in the quick lab, to be unaltered tobacco, pure and simple."

John added a sidebar comment, "Well up to this point, nothing remarkable here. But further analysis revealed something very different, not seen before. I'll get to that later, but let me keep reading the report."

He continued, "When questioned later about the positive urine test and his behavioral state, the individual had no explanation for it and repeatedly denied taking drugs of any kind. He insisted the only addiction he had was tobacco and he had never had a drug problem and hadn't used marijuana in months. Yes, he had tried marijuana in the past a few times and liked it, but it was illegal and too expensive, so he could never be a serious user. When asked about the cigarette, he became excited and went on to describe a common practice he had to make his own cigarettes using leftover tobacco scraps where he works as a leaf sorter at the cigar manufacturing plant in San Juan. He insisted his supervisor knew about this activity, as these scraps were swept up and discarded at the end of each shift anyway. He went on to say that many workers are doing the same thing. After being detained for several hours, the subject was released and all charges dropped."

John looked up from his focus and looked across the table to Bill. Bill cracked a knowing smile and nodded for John to continue. John carefully placed the blue page he was reading from, face down on the table and went on to the second blue page in the folder.

Before he continued reading, he looked over to me and said, "You're wondering why the big deal. They need a better lab, right? Well I have more."

He then continued reading, "Results from the main lab were returned 14 days following the incident."

John stopped reading and looked up, "Apparently the process in Puerto Rico is to quick-lab all finds first but the sample, if there's enough of it, then gets sent offsite to the main lab, across town. This is done on a routine basis and this was done in this case. The main lab will confirm the results of the quick lab, and most often will add additional tests and results. I believe this analysis took longer than usual, because they did it twice. But I'll get to that in a minute."

He continued reading, "The sample in question looked and had the outward properties of tobacco leaf, and did not contain any external chemical agents, oils or modifiers. It outwardly tested as pure tobacco. The tobacco in this cigarette sample was unusual in that it was not the variety of tobacco normally found inside cigarettes or cigars. It was identified as cigar wrapper leaf. This tobacco exhibited the characteristic color, thinness and texture found in the tobacco industry's most expensive cigar wrappers."

The analysis provided by the main lab was consistent with what we already knew: the cigarette was home-grown made by the subject as a laborer using scraps of tobacco in the plant. What we didn't know was that the cigarette was crafted from a type of tobacco used for the outside wrapper on a cigar. I had no knowledge of cigars and what was in the inside or on the outside of a cigar.

John continued, "The source of these wrappers varies. Much of the wrapper stock in the San Juan plant comes from Indonesia, but in this case, we determined later

Roberto works in a separate assembly line where only premium wrappers are used to craft the most expensive cigars. These wrappers are known to originate from small tobacco farms in the Connecticut River valley in New England, most predominantly from the state of Connecticut."

"Wow!" I exclaimed. "I had no idea tobacco was grown in Connecticut."

"Ditto that," John responded.

"How did you find that out, I mean where it came from?" I asked.

"The FBI used an agent in San Juan to interview the plant manager and the subject who was arrested. They cooperated fully and gave us a baseline."

"Oh, so the FBI knows all about this too. Can you tell me who the agent is who went there?" I was hoping it was someone I had worked with before.

"Let's see."

John thumbed through his folder.

"They sent a young woman from the agent pool who speaks fluent Spanish, her name was Alondra Espinoza. You probably don't know her. She was down there anyway on a vacation visiting with her family so they tapped her for the case."

I hesitated, "I know her. She's very savvy. Worked with her some last year for a short time on a case cleanup."

John paused, then turned back to his document and read

on.

"This cigar wrapper tobacco is grown and harvested in large fields draped under cheesecloth netting. It is commonly referred to as *shade* tobacco. The shade cast by the netting makes the tobacco leaf thinner and more compatible with the equipment used to roll the cigar. This top grade tobacco, seen exclusively on the outside of the most expensive cigars, has a market value of up to $80 to $100 or more per pound when harvested, without holes or blemishes and if properly cured. Several hundred tons are produced each year by a small number of specialty farmers in Connecticut."

I was getting a little antsy wondering where this was going.

"John," I interrupted. "Do we need all this background? Something tells me this is not the punchline. Can we get to that? And what are you reading from? Certainly the lab in San Juan didn't come up with all these historical tobacco facts."

John looked up, clearly annoyed and let out an indignant huff, before responding, "Well it's very simple, the lab report was used to source my material and I put a brief description of the environment together for the session today. I thought you would want that. I also prepared a similar document for the architects, leaving certain key facts out as we discussed. I hoped you would find this initial background interesting; I believe it to be important and it will be of value to you in your operation."

As he shook his head, I could sense he was ticked I questioned the value of his material. I probably should keep my mouth shut.

"Okay. Sorry John. I do appreciate the info. Please continue," I said.

John continued, "So the lab continued the analysis, and did a burn test, measuring the smoke compounds and particulate matter using a mass spectrometer. They had an interesting result. I'll read this, but before I do, I want to make it clear that what I'm about to read is not to be broadcast to anyone, and that includes the architects."

John turned his attention to the blue page once again. I could see a middle section of his document was highlighted with a yellow highlighter. I assumed he was reading from that section.

"The sample was subjected to a level two burn test. The test revealed a significant concentration of THC, compatible in structure with the THC found in the most common species of marijuana, Cannabis sativa. Most remarkably, the burn sample looked, felt and smelled like tobacco, before, during and after the burn. As previously stated in the initial analysis, the sample was void of any external additive of THC or hash oil, either natural or synthetic. Note that THC yields vary widely depending on the strain of marijuana and if the flower, leaf or stem of the plant is tested. The burn sample THC yield was compared to the average leaf-based THC yield for marijuana. The THC present in the sample burn was thirty percent above the average concentrations found in the same volume test using the most common marijuana strain.

"A second test was ordered to confirm no external additives were present in the sample and care was taken to ensure an accurate measurement of THC content. The two tests indicated similar results."

John stopped briefly to loosen his tie. He continued, "So I know you're going to ask me about our own lab's view of the sample. Yes we did the analysis in our own lab. The sample size was small and we didn't have much to work with, but we confirmed the sample is for real. It shows positive for THC, in larger concentrations than average Cannabis. And no additives are present. Microscopic analysis indicates a cell pattern similar but clearly different than other cigar wrapper samples."

John stopped here and asked if I had any questions.

I responded, "Looks to me a very different variety of tobacco leaf was in that sample. If the lab is for real and nothing external has been added, then this is a really big deal. Someone has genetically manufactured a new strain of tobacco exhibiting properties of highly potent marijuana. I think we have a huge problem."

John turned to me and nodded agreement. All he said was, "Got that right Jason."

Chapter 3

The DEA Architect Team was most often two or sometimes three agent analysts. They were often working together and managing a case, way in advance of the operative agent (referred to as the principal or operative), sometimes as long as a month before the case was known and presented to the principal. This case was no different. They were charged with understanding the basic information and overall premise for the scam, creating a new identity, in whole, for the operative. It was critical the person 'fit in' to the new environment, as this individual had to live a new life basically, dropping into a new living stage cold turkey. Profiling of the principal was key. They needed to know everything about the agent's intelligence, personality, likes and dislikes and temperament, abilities, sex habits, past history and even future wants. Inventing a false identity that worked into a case was not easy and the more information the team could amass about the operative, the better the chances of a successful placement and end result.

Of course, the principal was almost always single and without family. Rules about that were evolving but it was generally understood an individual living with spouse and family could jeopardize the scam, as the temptation to communicate would be too great. Budding relationships were allowed, as long as the principal understood the long-term continuing relationship might inhibit them from taking future assignments. If the relationship became permanent, once the scam was completed the individual would be removed from covert ops and seek alternate employment in the DEA, or worse, if nothing was available, leave DEA employment altogether.

There were two architects assigned to the case: Roger Dupre and Jackie Turney. Their team name was the *RoJac* team and they had worked together before, building the FlightPath scam. This was good news; the exhaustive profiling was already completed on Jason, and they both knew him very well. Before joining the architect team, both Roger and Jackie, who were nearing retirement age, held high positions in other divisions. Roger was formerly an officer for DEA Intelligence where he was accountable for inter-agency communications. Jackie came from the international training group, where she had responsibility for operational planning and overview of international drug trafficking methods. RoJac was a uniquely qualified team, applying experience, analytical savvy, and laser focus, building the identity plan so Jason could hit the ground running (or at least a fast walk) in a carefully crafted new identity. The architects also enjoyed the responsibility of naming the new scam. After a short but lively debate, the name was born: ***TobaccoNet***.

For three long weeks, they had labored over the build, gathering critical background info for Jason, and sculpting the contrived role he would assume. They were ready to turn everything over to Jason and the administration team that morning at the intake meeting, in the ops planning conference room. The meeting started at 9:00 a.m. and they usually were in the room when it started but Bill, the CC, asked they hold off initially. They sat together in Roger's office waiting for the phone to ring that would summon them to the long-awaited work session. It would be a three-hour display where Jason would learn all about his new contrived role. The meeting would last all the way past the lunch hour. They would be called into the conference room within the hour.

Roger picked up the profile folder labeled 'Jason Kraft' and looked over to Jackie across the desk.

"Jackie, let's review Jason's profile while we're waiting."

"Okay, I'm pretty familiar with it but it couldn't hurt."

Roger skimmed through the folder and started reading out loud.

"Jason Ridge Kraft, single, never married, 34 years old, born in Bangor, Maine. Top of his class in high school, valedictorian, attended Bowdoin College, was president of Chi Psi fraternity, graduated summa cum laude majoring in government studies. Worked during summers on his father's potato farm. Has a striking resemblance to the actor Matthew McConaughey. Nickname in high school and college was 'Mattie'. After graduating Bowdoin, went to NYC to begin a career in banking at Chase Bank, focused in bank operations. Attended several external educational classes for bank management, and Harvard Business School's mid-management development program. Made VP in five years. Was assigned to head up mergers and acquisitions. Became disillusioned and left the banking business a year later; returned to Maine to work on the family farm for six months. Joined the DEA at age 30 in an office job, manager of covert operation coordination. Attended agent training and moved into the agent pool here two years ago. Case managers give Jason high marks; they classify him as a top agent. Most outstanding traits are memory skills. Highly coordinated and in excellent physical shape, his IQ scores are high, averaging 145 in math and verbal. No significant others; not in a relationship at this time and no children that we know of."

Roger looked up at Jackie and ended with, "Interesting. That's the summary. That's all we need right now I think. I expect they'll call us in any time."

Bill mentioned the reason for the delay was that he and John, the assistant CC, were clearing up a few dangling issues related to Jason's previous scam, FlightPath. Word was floating around FlightPath had landed some large unbudgeted expenses. They both assumed Jason was being questioned about it. The meeting would begin as soon as that discussion ended.

Right around 9:30 a.m. the phone rang in Roger's office. It was Bill asking RoJac to step into the ops conference room. They were cleared to begin the presentation.

I was anxious to get started with the architects. It was only 9:25, a half hour into the meeting, but it seemed much longer than that. I suppose just like a watched phone never rings, wishing for John to finish made it worse. He was not done until he was done. He finally finished up with some new information which made the wait palatable. He had mentioned earlier they had sent Alondra, an FBI agent I knew, to San Juan to interview the cigarette man, Roberto Martell-Valentin and his management at the cigar plant. They were interested in knowing more about the tobacco, its origin, was it abundant, etc. John went on to say they studied additional samples from the cigar wrappers Roberto was handling. Although they were unable to obtain a larger sample of the THC strain tobacco, they did determine the likely origin for the tobacco with reasonable certainty. The cured cigar wrapper batches Roberto was assigned to during that time had all originated from a tobacco co-op based in Hartford, Connecticut.

The Hartford Shade Co-op had been active since the 1930's. In the past, this co-op was owned and operated by upwards of twenty small to medium-sized family farms. More recently, as property values soared, many Hartford area farmers traded their tobacco lands for profits, selling out big to developers. The tradition of a New England family farm, being passed on to generation after generation was dying. Today the co-op owner list was down to three farms, two small farms, and one very big one. If this special strain of tobacco was indeed being produced in any quantity, it was likely it came from Hartford, and they had narrowed it down to one farm in particular.

I heard a quick double knock on the door and in came Roger, carrying the presentation materials in his big brief bag. He was the first to enter the conference room and took a seat at the end of the table by the door, followed by Jackie, who took the opposite seat across from Roger, on my side of the table. There was a built-in audio/visual control panel in front of Roger that accessed the overhead projector in the ceiling above the table. The room was recently renovated and upgraded with the latest audio/visual equipment. The ceiling projector displayed the computer desktop's screen image against the end wall using the whiteboard as a screen. The computer desktop's icons were now fully displayed on the large whiteboard screen on Roger's right and Jackie's left.

"Hey Roger, nice to see you again. Hello Jackie," I said and stood, as both he and Jackie stood up from the table and came over to repeat the greeting and to shake my hand. It seemed like much longer, but only five months had passed since I had seen them in the architect meeting for FlightPath.

They also greeted Bill and John, but with less fervor. They probably saw them all the time.

Bill started up his intro, "Good morning everyone. Apologies for starting off a little later than usual. We had some unfinished business to discuss and now that's cleared we can begin anew. As you know, I don't attend these sessions and I won't be attending this one. John will attend and cover any admin items coming up. So with that, I'll leave you to it."

Bill exited the room and closed the door carefully on the way out.

I reminded myself to be careful here during the presentation. We had info about the special strain that was not to be broadcast. I wondered what they knew and what they were going to tell us. I was about to find out.

I was surprised when Jackie stood up and started. Usually, Roger took the lead. This was different.

"Good morning everyone," she began. She then walked around to Roger's side and hit the lights to dim the room. Blinds were already down along the windows on one side of the room, so the room darkened a lot.

Jacqueline Turney, who preferred to be called Jackie, was a young 55. She was 100 percent Irish. She had beautiful thick red hair that was still its natural color (although it could have been dyed but didn't look it). She was stunning, very fit and also a well-proportioned woman who clearly turned men's heads walking in the hallways or on the street. Very intelligent and focused, she had an energy and confident air about her that men liked, and most women were envious of her physical and intellectual endowments.

Jackie was not married but still wore her ring. Her husband passed away suddenly in their home two years ago of a bleeding ulcer. She found him on the floor in their bedroom.

She was available, but hadn't started dating anyone. She wasn't ready to let anyone into her life just yet.

Her specialties were operational planning and international drug trafficking. One thing she was known most for: she talked really fast. She always had something significant to say but keeping up with her meant you had to listen carefully.

"Today we are presenting the background and plan for the upcoming case." As she said this, Roger pressed the clicker to start the PowerPoint presentation, and the word **TobaccoNet** flashed up filling the screen.

"We've named this project **TobaccoNet**. You will be hearing a lot of information today. This data was collected over a three week period by the collection team using a variety of sources, including internet, direct observations in the field, conversations with previous employees, up-to-date satellite imagery, the IRS and other methods, better left unsaid. I know you all know this, but I have to say it anyway. Following strict protocols, please do not take notes, and do not repeat what you learn today outside of the team staff. For obvious reasons, today's session will not be recorded. I'll start with the background info and Roger will take it after that, with more specific details.

"As you know, the original case identified an individual who discovered several batches of cured marijuana in a cigar manufacturing plant in San Juan, Puerto Rico. This individual and his company are cooperating with the PR police and the FBI to help us identify the source of this marijuana. We have strong suspicions on its origin and we can share those with you later. The case has merit and clearly warrants the covert ops engagement due to the significant potential for a large quantity of illicit product hitting the street."

I now understood how the internal cover would work. The special strain discovery was replaced with a large-scale marijuana discovery. RoJac would be in the dark on this critical piece. That works, for now.

She continued her presentation, talking with clarity and purpose.

"I'd like to move into the first part of our presentation and that is a discussion of the facts surrounding the production of shade tobacco in New England. Roger, next slide please."

Roger clicked to the next slide and the screen filled with a nice picture of a field of dark green tobacco plants covered with white cheesecloth netting.

She continued, "In Connecticut today, what you can see in this picture is a field of ripe tobacco plants, covered by the netting used to shade the plants. Notice how high and lush the plants are in this picture, with wide long leaves.

"The origins of tobacco in Connecticut date back as far back as 1640. In the early to mid-1800's the cigar industry was booming in central Connecticut. In the late 1800's, due to competition with growers in the south, the farmers added cheesecloth netting over the fields to provide a light shading on the plants and to increase the humidity in the field. The shade cloth would be strung over wires nailed to poles placed in the ground at regular intervals. The shade produced a thinner leaf while the humidity increased the yields as the plants and leaves grew larger. The result was the best cigar wrappers anywhere in the world.

"This tradition continues today, albeit at a reduced rate. From a production standpoint, the total acreage under cultivation has dropped more than 90 percent. Currently, the total shade tobacco acreage is less than 2,000 acres."

Jackie stopped and asked, "Any questions so far?"

John looked over at me and back to Jackie, shaking his head no.

I couldn't resist asking the big question, "So Jackie, you seem to be an expert on the topic, and I know we've just started to see what you have here, but let me ask it anyway... do you think the climate and growing conditions in the tobacco fields are good for growing marijuana?"

Jackie flashed me a cute smile and said, "Yes, I believe you are correct in your assumption Jason. The conditions in the Connecticut River valley are perfect for tobacco *and* marijuana. But before we get into that aspect I have more to share with you."

She continued, "Shade tobacco farming today is still a labor-intensive undertaking. That being said, I'd like to show you by giving you a review of the many stages of production. Jason, you may think this is, well, boring, but keep in mind we have all this for a reason. You will need this background for your upcoming assignment, so I would hope we have your undivided attention. Roger, next slide."

Before each section's explanation, Roger would click to the next slide, exposing a picture matching her description.

On the screen now was a picture of a crew of about 30 migrant workers, mostly men, inside a cavernous plastic-roofed greenhouse carrying wooden pallets of white plastic trays filled with brown dirt. In the middle of the house on the ground was gray metal piping running the length of the greenhouse.

"Here we have the planting of seed. The tobacco plants are started from seed in a greenhouse in late-April. Using a special vacuum machine built just for this purpose, individual pelletized seeds about the size of a BB are dropped into small rectangular plastic trays holding one inch pots of potting soil, 96 pots in each tray measuring 12 by 18 inches. The thousands of trays are laid out on wooden pallets in massive greenhouses. Trays are carefully watered each day by semi-automated watering devices."

The picture switched to a large field punctuated with brown poles. Men, standing on wooden sawhorses were pulling white cheesecloth bundles over the gray wires attached to the poles spaced at regular intervals. The rows and rows of poles in straight lines grew smaller in the distance; you could not see where they ended. It was a huge field.

"Fields are readied for planting. Fields are plowed, harrowed multiple times, sometimes limed, fertilized, and fumigated with a strong poison to destroy root-eating bugs. The cheesecloth netting is then strung on wires to cover the tops and sides of the field. The wires are suspended on thick wooden poles, placed in the ground at regular 33-foot intervals. The distance between each pole is called a 'bent'."

The screen flashed to a picture of a red tractor in a poled, netted field, dragging a large green five-row planter, with five men sitting in chairs facing backwards, evenly spaced across the back of the tractor. Each man had a white tray of small plants on his lap. They were feeding four-inch plants into the mechanism; you could see the five-row trail of seedlings left in the ground behind the tractor.

"The seedlings in the trays are then manually planted using special five-row tobacco planters hauled behind large slow-plodding tractors. The planter rides up one side of the bent and down the other, planting ten rows per bent with every other row spaced slightly wider than the adjacent row. Wide rows are 3½ feet wide, and the narrow rows are 2½ feet wide. This allows the tobacco plants to be serviced manually, with the person walking down the middle of the wide row, attending to plants on either side. Plants are separated by an average of twelve inches in the row when planted. The average small farm raises 50 to 75 acres, larger farms up to 200 acres. For a large farm, there will be three to six of these planters operating all at once, requiring crews of six for each tractor. Planting goes on for one to two weeks starting in mid to late-May."

The display switched to a picture of the men in the field walking down rows of tobacco seedlings, each carrying a plastic tray of plants in one hand and a small trowel in the other.

"Seedlings are replanted as necessary. Laborers walk up and down rows in the field carrying trays of plants replacing small plants that are dead or missing from the first planting. Crews doing this are comprised of migrant workers numbering from 50 to 100 and are driven from field-to-field in school buses leased for the summer."

I was impressed with Jackie's presentation, the level of detail and pictures. But it described a foreign world I had no knowledge of and hadn't known existed. My mind raced ahead to thinking about the new scam and what Roger might have planned. I was beginning to get that feeling of dread in my stomach as we approached Roger's presentation. I didn't even know what the scam was yet, but still I was haunted. That feeling gripping me now was fear; the fear of not understanding everything I needed to know to assume a new identity. The fear of just one slip that would give me away and crash the scam, and what that might lead to. At the same time, I was fascinated I would be tested once again. So much of my previous success was linked to my skillset. That knowledge calmed me.

"Jason!" she screamed. "Do I have your attention? I need you to stay with me. We put this presentation together for YOU!" Jackie was staring at me... I had drifted off and away from her and she knew it.

"Sorry Jackie... I was somewhere else. Won't happen again. Please continue."

The screen changed to a new picture of a large red tractor dragging a huge white cultivator, in the middle of a field of small tobacco plants under the cheesecloth. She went on.

"More Tractor work. The small plants are cultivated with large five-row rotary cultivators; the idea is to push the dirt up against the plant stems for protection."

Roger clicked and another picture flashed up of a whole crew of dark skinned men leaning on wooden handled hoes, hoeing rows of tobacco seedlings under the nets. There were more than 100 men in the picture, spread out over five or six bents, two men per row. Some men were way ahead of the others in their row.

"More Field work. Plants are hoed, to push even more dirt up around the stems of the young seedlings. This operation is repeated; the entire acreage gets manually hoed twice. This takes a couple of weeks."

Jackie then broke cadence by asking if we wanted a break.

"We're about halfway through my presentation at this time. This is a lot of material to absorb all in one sitting. Let's take a quick 20-minute break. Any objection?" No one responded. "So, I take that as a no." Jackie looked at her watch and said, "It's 9:55. Please be back here at 10:15. Thanks."

With that, she picked up her iPhone on the table, opened the conference room door and walked quickly out of the room. Roger stood up and stretched. "I'm going for coffee," he said.

"I'll follow you," I said as I stood up. "John, are you coming?"

John looked down at his folder and then back up at me.

"No thanks. I'll stay here. I had my allotment of caffeine already."

We walked in silence to the coffee room. I knew better than to try to pump Roger for info ahead of his presentation. He was water tight; I'd just have to wait.

In the small windowless breakroom at the end of the hall, Roger pulled out two mugs from the overhead cabinet and poured coffee into both.

"This stuff isn't very good, is it?" he said. "No it's not," I replied.

We always had free coffee on the training floor but it wasn't that good and I would have gladly paid money for better coffee, but management had it in their heads it was their gift. It was their decision about the brand to buy. I was sure the bean counter who made that cost-effective decision wasn't a coffee drinker. Management was on board with the free coffee because they thought classroom participation would increase if everyone was all pumped up on caffeine. That was probably true.

As we fixed our coffees, a woman with long, black, straight hair entered the breakroom. I couldn't see her face as she had turned into the counter and was pouring a coffee with her back to me. She was smartly dressed in black tights, black high heels, and a black above-the-knee skirt. She wore a shawl-like black and gray sweater that draped around her shoulders and arms. I was immediately attracted to her; just by the way she dressed and carried herself.

When she finally turned around, our eyes met. My heart skipped a beat.

"Hello Alondra. It's been a long time."

She didn't respond right away, she just stared at me. Her long straight black hair framed her dark tanned skin perfectly. Her eyes were so dark from six feet away, it looked like she had no irises, but I knew she did.

"Hello Jason. It's good to see you again," she said to me in her cute Spanish accent. I was always surprised she still had an accent. She had been on the mainland for 15 years, but it had not melted away yet. I hoped it never would; I was intrigued by it.

“I heard you were working down in Florida on a case. You must be finished if you’re back here now.“

“That’s true,” I said. “I’m on a new assignment starting today actually. I’d tell you about it, but I don’t know very much yet and this one is kind of under wraps anyway. It’s really good to see you.”

I paused and hoped she would respond with something similar. She didn’t.

“What are you doing now?” I asked.

Before she answered, Roger motioned with his mug in the direction of the door to tell me quietly he was going back to the conference room. I gave him a quick thumbs up, nodded to him and he turned and left. Alondra saw me and turned to watch Roger leave the room. Now we were alone. She turned back to me and answered my question.

“Oh, the usual thing. On small assignments mostly, traveling a bit now and then. The agency uses my Spanish. I’m okay I guess. I’m here today running a training class for non-Spanish speaking agents. They want me to focus on cultural aspects of the Hispanic population. They’re trying hard to boost agents’ sensitivity when dealing with the Latino community.”

I was always infatuated with her good looks. Alondra could have been a model; she was almost physically perfect. In public, she was often mistaken for the actress Naya Rivera and could have easily passed for her twin sister. We were close once, but we ended our relationship after several months. We were too much into our careers and we wanted different things from each other. I still cared a lot for her and I always thought of her as the perfect one whom I let slip away. We totally lost contact with each other when I was in Florida.

I was not surprised she never mentioned her sojourn to San Juan and the cigar plant. She was probably under the same gag order I was. She might be in the inner circle and know as much as I did, then again, that was probably not the case. The FBI wrote the book on compartmentalization and the need to know. She didn't need to know about the special strain to conduct an interview at the plant. I was not in a position to ask her about it, even if I wanted to. I made a note to myself to circle back to John on that question. He might know.

"That sounds just like you Alondra. Maybe we can catch up before I go under. I will call you soon, okay?"

"I'd like that too," she smiled.

I was still drawn to her and wanted to be with her again. With that small exchange, we both left the room, albeit in different directions.

They were all waiting for me when I walked into the conference room. I carefully parked myself and my coffee back in my spot at the conference table next to John.

Jackie continued her presentation.

"We'll continue from where we left off. The last bit of tractor work now; the small plants are dusted with bug poison."

The screen flashed to a picture of the field of small tobacco plants. In the picture was a dark skinned man riding a small red tractor under the nets with a contraption on the back of the tractor. It was a small box with five vacuum cleaner hoses snaked across a long piece of angle iron steel directing the dust down onto the tops of the six-inch plants in five rows. Tan colored dust was seen spewing from the hoses onto the plants. Some of the dust was drifting in the wind to the left behind the tractor. The tractor driver was not wearing a pesticide mask.

Jackie paused to let the scene sink in.

Before she started again, a new picture flashed up on the screen showing a large dilapidated gray building with second floor dormered windows across the front. In the foreground, a group of men of mixed color gathered around a picnic table and in various lawn chairs, smiling at the camera, holding what looked like beer bottles in small paper bags.

She continued, "Up until now, labor you've seen in the picture has been exclusively migrant farm workers, either from Puerto Rico or Jamaica. These individuals are from the local vicinity or brought in seasonally by the farmers. Housing, if you could call it that, is supplied in the form of a basic labor camp that's owned and operated by the farm. This has been common practice in the past but as farms have dwindled, the practice has ceased for all but the largest farms. Only the bare essentials are provided in the camps. The farmers supply non-air-conditioned sleeping quarters, usually four bunks per room, a communal hall for eating and showers, and a lunch meal to go for those who want one. A reasonable charge for staying at the camp is subtracted from the individual's weekly pay.

"One interesting fact few people know about is that back in the forties farms were employing college-age blacks from the southern states to work in the tobacco fields. In fact, Martin Luther King worked tobacco in the summers and stayed in a farm camp in Simsbury, Connecticut."

"I had no idea," I said. Jackie only smiled.

The picture changed and the camp picture was replaced by a shot of a field again; the bright green tobacco plants had grown about a foot under the cheesecloth netting. Spread across the field you could see boys sitting on the ground in the rows and tending to the plants on either side of the row. The children, no more than 14 or 15 years of age were predominantly white and dressed in brightly covered bandanas, T-shirts, and shorts. Some wore jeans. There were also two older teenage boys 18 to 20 years old, standing in the field in the middle of the children, with their arms folded. In the distance was a yellow school bus parked next to the field.

"The labor picture has changed. Once school is out, migrant farm workers are augmented by local children aged 14 to 18. School children working in the fields are paid less than minimum wage migrant workers. For example, the adult minimum wage is $9.15 per hour whereas the rate for minors between the ages of 14 and 18 is 85 percent of the minimum wage, which computes to be $7.78 per hour. Laws are relaxed in the State of Connecticut to enable family farms to pay children to work on the farms at a reduced child rate.

"The boys in the photo are suckering the small plants. Suckers are small unwanted shoots of new growth that form between good leaves and the stem of the plant. They are stripped from each plant by hand. The technique is to sit on the ground facing backward, suckering plants on either side of the row. The work is hot, dirty and tiring.

"Young girls also work, but they do other tasks in the field; I will discuss that in the next section.

"Older teens work there too as drivers or 'straw bosses', paid to manage the children and ferry the kids from field to field on the bus. These same buses are used to pick the kids up in the morning and drive them home at night.

"Large farms will field up to 100 boys the first week to sucker the tobacco. It's hot, laborious, backbreaking work, not for the faint of heart. The workforce thins out naturally to a crew of about 70 in the first week, and then again to 50 the second week. This is expected. Only the kids who can survive suckering stick around for the rest of the season. Next slide Roger. Thank you," she said.

Roger saw me raise my hand to get her attention. "Jackie, I have a question."

"Sure Jason. Go ahead."

"Does the local child population replace the migrant worker population? Or do they work together?"

She paused to think about the answer.

"It's my understanding the migrant and child crews are still in force at the same time, but working on different jobs. They are separated, and rarely, if ever, work side-by-side in any capacity. The migrant population works the entire season. As you'd expect the children work the middle of the season to accommodate their school schedule. The core crew is the migrant crew. Tobacco farms could not exist without them.

"There are some trusted older teenagers who attend private high schools and are assigned on occasion to work with the migrants. Others are in college and working summer jobs. These individuals have a longer summer schedule; they are eligible to work several weeks before and after the public school kids. It's not uncommon for the same crew of kids to come back year after year and gain expertise in their particular roles."

"Got it. Thanks."

Jackie nodded at Roger and the next slide popped up.

On the screen was a picture of girls under the nets in a field attending to 18 to 24-inch plants. This time they were standing in the rows, some were bending over and others reaching up. Each had a small ball of string attached around their waist with a cord. They were tying a thin white string to each plant and reaching up to string the plant to a small gray wire running directly over the plants down each row. Each girl wore a ring with a small curved knife blade which they used to cut the string.

She continued, "Plants are tied or stringed. This is done to prevent the plants from toppling over in strong thunderstorms. This operation follows directly behind the suckering. On most farms, the boys do the suckering and the girls do the stringing. In this picture, you can see the shriveled dead suckers cast aside by the sucker crew on the ground between the rows of plants. As you can also see, the leaves are getting much bigger and these plants will continue to grow fast, become more top-heavy and if not tied could easily fall over in strong winds. On large farms up to 100 girls will be hired the first week for stringing. This number melts down to near 50 by the third week.

"At this point, I'd like to take the next sections a bit differently. We are at the meat of the harvest now and it makes more sense to combine the next five sections and talk about them all as one section. I think this is better; you might be more attentive if you can see the whole picture. Roger, next slide please."

The display switched to a composite picture comprised of five separate pictures. Each small picture depicted a separate operation.

"Tobacco leaves are picked, dragged out of the rows in large plastic baskets and hauled to sheds on rack trucks. In the sheds, leaves are sewn onto strings held by four-foot wooden sticks called lath and hung in the shed rafters for curing. This cycle is called the harvest cycle. This is a huge production operation. In full swing at large farms, 120 school children and 100 migrant workers are employed for six to ten weeks. The boys and men do the leaf picking and dragging from the field to the trucks. The girls sew the tobacco onto the wooden laths. Boys or men hang the tobacco in the rafters in the sheds.

"Starting from the bottom of the plant and working up, the ripest two, three or four leaves are picked and the cycle begins. The entire acreage is covered in about five days, crews moving from field to field and shed to shed. When the acreage rotation is completed, it starts all over again for the next picking. Once a shed is filled, the operation moves on to fill the next shed. Upwards of 35 to 50 sheds are filled with tobacco in one season on large farms. The cycle repeats itself over and over again, seven or eight times. By the eighth picking, each plant in the field yields between 20 to 25 leaves.

"So to recap, the leaf harvest cycle is this: leaves are picked, hauled out of the field, driven to sheds, sewn on laths and hung in the rafters. Any questions?"

"Yeah," I interjected. "What happens when it rains? Doesn't that delay the cycle?"

"Well, yes and no," Jackie answered. "The workers are issued inexpensive raincoats, and as long as the rain isn't a downpour, they are often required to work in the fields in the rain."

"The workers? To whom are you referring? The men or the children?"

"Both groups work in the rain. They are separated and work in different fields," she responded.

"Are you kidding me?" I blurted out. "That's hard to believe. I understand kids are allowed to work on small family farms at young ages but based on the scale of the operation you're describing, the intent of those laws is being stretched pretty thin. Add to that a 'work in the rain' component, that's surprising."

"I have no answer for you Jason. As you know, we only present the facts. We have no interest in the social or political interpretation of events."

"I know. Still bothers me. Sorry for the emotional response."

"I know Jason, we can all empathize with the men and the children here. But you as well as anyone know the rules about letting your personal feelings take hold in a case. It's important you learn to separate those feelings and not get too involved with the mark. Remember *'straight face'*."

Straight face was the reminder phrase drummed into us in training. It meant whatever was going on around us, we should be careful not to get personally involved. I didn't like the term and I didn't like that approach. I also never told the case handlers how I felt. I was convinced the trainers never ran a scam, or at least not a long-term one. I found it almost impossible not to get personally involved with the people you met along the way in the scam. You were there living it; how could you not? *Straight face* meant non-involvement, and that, in my opinion was a recipe for failure. I purposely went out of my way to do the opposite; I cared about my life and the individuals I worked with. It had worked so far, but it was still difficult at the end. Leaving the life when the scam was over was always traumatic for me, and equally difficult on anyone close to me in the life I would leave behind. I was comforted knowing I'd be back in a different place soon after a scam ended; into a new life where I could make a fresh start, once again.

"Okay. So we have just a few sections left to talk about and then we'll break for lunch."

We had been grinding through her presentation for an hour and a half. I was getting a little antsy. We had covered a lot of material and most of it was new to me. After lunch, we'd hear from Roger, but before Roger started, I'd be asked to do the read-back.

Read-back was my specialty. I'd be asked to tell all I learned in Jackie's session, every detail. There were two read-back rules: no notes and the read-back had to be finished in six minutes or less. When finished, I would be graded. If I passed the test, all was good. This part of the session was designed initially for one purpose: to weed out operatives. If the operative couldn't listen carefully to two hours of new material and memorize it enough to spit it back, how could they be expected to assume a whole new identity? I always thought this test was a bit over the top, but I had no trouble with it as my memory was perfect and I had a knack for recounting minutiae. For me, it was never a weed-out test; it was a test of mental capacity and I looked forward to it.

Jackie started up again and began a description of the "tobacco firing" operation. This is how the tobacco is cured in the sheds. She went on to describe a grillwork of hundreds of small propane stoves resembling flat inverted funnels burning on the brown dirt floor.

A picture projected on the screen of these small burning stoves laid out in straight lines as far as the eye could see, in a darkened shed filled with green tobacco leaves hanging from the rafters.

She continued, "Large propane gas tanks or natural gas lines feed gas to the stoves. It takes three to four weeks of intermittent firing to fully dry and cure the tobacco. This is the more dangerous part of the production; sheds have been known to burn down from faulty stoves or leaky gas lines."

Just as she finished her sentence, a new picture flashed up. It was a dim grainy shot, taken at night, showing a close-up of a faded red shed. A brown-skinned man in a white T-shirt held a lighted flashlight as he entered into the black interior through a small wooden door. The door was wide enough so you could see past him and into the shed as he climbed over the foot-high threshold. Inside you could barely make out several rows of blue flames shimmering in the darkness on the dirt floor. These had to be the firing stoves.

She continued, “It’s common practice to use multiple one-man crews at night to make the rounds to service the burning stoves. Rotating shed to shed, each individual services up to ten sheds a night in the height of the curing season.”

She let this picture sink in before asking Roger to move to the next slide.

“So now we are at the end of our study.”

She paused briefly and then started up again, “The *takedown* operation is upon us. Taking down the dried tobacco in the fall and packing it into crates is a job for the migrant men crews. School is back in session and that precludes any kids from helping with these tasks.”

The screen changed again to a full shot of an enormous red shed in a field next to a pond, with fall foliage in the distance. Leaves on the surrounding trees had turned a bright yellow and orange; a clear indication the seasons had changed. The shed looked different too; it was covered on the front and sides with a translucent milky-white plastic, from the ground all the way up to the eves. The plastic was attached to the shed with thin wooden sticks nailed all the way around from top to bottom and at vertical intervals on the side of the shed, securing it in the middle sections.

Jackie pointed to the screen, ”Here in the picture we can see the plastic covering the shed. This is a critical part of the takedown operation. Tobacco must be sufficiently moist to begin the takedown. Smaller farms wait for moisture in the air from rain or fog in the early mornings. The larger farms, some with up to 50 sheds to take down, must pump steam into the air with industrial strength humidifiers. The plastic surrounding the shed holds in the moisture. The tobacco must be moist enough to feel like a soft sponge when a handful of cured tobacco is squeezed. Next slide Roger."

The screen switched to a daytime shot inside a shed with men carrying four-foot long sticks with brown leaves of tobacco hanging under the sticks from white strings. Others were standing over three-foot square wooden crates, packing handfuls of tobacco into the crates lined with an orange colored paper.

"The tobacco is stripped from the wooden lath and tied onto small bundles about the size of the straw at the end of a broomstick. Each bundle of cured leaves is called a *hand*. Hands are then packed tightly into wax-paper lined wooden boxes. The paper helps retain the moisture content in the tobacco prior and during transport. Depending on the size of the shed, a full shed will fill from 60 to 120 boxes, and each box will hold between 70 and 100 pounds of cured tobacco. The boxes are often stacked up in the corner of the shed and picked up later for transport to the co-op, for further processing.

"So that wraps up my presentation. Are there any questions before we break for lunch?"

Her question was met with silence. She hit the switch and the light came on. Roger shut off the projector, but the fan continued to run. The room had warmed a bit since we started. I stood up and stretched.

I looked down at John on my left, still sitting at the table. I said to him, "I'm up after lunch with the read-back."

“I know,” he responded. “I’m sure you can do it in six minutes. I can’t wait for the entertainment to begin,” he said sarcastically and smiled.

Chapter 4

I took 45 minutes for lunch and was the first person back to the conference room. I sat in my chair with my eyes closed, logging my thoughts for the read-back. This was my time now. Jackie had presented a boatload of information to remember and regurgitate. I had most of it down, but I liked to add my own twist to the material and some of this couldn't be done ahead of time; I had to do it on the fly as I presented it.

Sitting there waiting for the others to come back, I was reminded of a debate at Bowdoin College where I was the captain of the debate team for two years. The debate was about the supremacy of the British Empire. To make my point, I stood up on the podium without notes and proceeded for 10 minutes, to rattle off detailed material on all the British holdings around the globe for the past 200 years. We won the debate hands down.

Throughout my entire life, I used my memory and intellect in similar ways and life was easier for me because of it, no doubt; tests in school, work challenges in banking in an earlier career and now with DEA read-backs and covert ops. I didn't need to *tell* people around me I had a great memory, but I relished the opportunity to *show* them, and to use it to my advantage whenever I could.

But having a perfect memory wasn't always a good thing. I could use it as a skill to help maintain a different identity, this was true, but I also carried with me all the baggage of unpleasant memories. I had instant recall of all the good *and* all the bad memories in my life; I couldn't forget anything. There was a Catch-22 thing here; the more I tried to abandon the bad memories, the more I held onto them.

My father, when I was younger, used to tell me all I needed to be happy was a bad memory. I think he felt my dilemma, as he too was burdened by the same talent.

A few minutes later John came into the room followed by Jackie and Roger. They took new seats at the table across from me. Jackie and Roger had notepads and pens out; John sat back in the chair away from the table with his legs and arms crossed. He had a smile on his face.

Roger spoke first in a business-like tone, "Okay Jason, we all heard Jackie's presentation and we're here for the read-back session. You've done this before so you know the rules. You have six minutes or less to retell the information from Jackie's session, without notes or prompting from us. Jackie has her watch and she'll be timing you. Are you ready?"

I sat up close to the table with my hands folded in front. I was relaxed and stared straight ahead at all three of them sitting across the table.

"I'm ready," I replied. I had six minutes to present and it was going to be close. I started, talking quickly, presenting the material in a robot-like fashion.

"Cigar tobacco in Connecticut dates back to 1640. More recently in the 1800's shade tobacco flourished and became a specialty crop. Tobacco is grown under cheesecloth nets to simulate warmer climates in the south and grow thinner leaves. Large farms average in size between 100 and 200 acres.

"Shade tobacco is used as the outer wrapper on expensive cigars. It's costly to grow. It's machinery intensive (tractors and farm implements) and labor intensive. Farms use a mix of migrant workers (mostly men) from Puerto Rico and Jamaica, and local school children, ages 14 and up to tend the fields. Migrant crews are comprised of up to 100 men and child crews can go to 200 or more. Both crews pare to about half the original number for the harvest cycle.

"You mentioned some migrant workers live in camp housing provided by the farmers. Living conditions in the camps were described as minimal at best.

"Field preparation in the spring is normal; includes plowing, harrowing and fertilizing but with an added step, fields are fumigated too.

"Cheesecloth netting is strung over the fields on wires nailed to poles. Distance between each pole is called a bent. Distance between bent poles is 33 feet. Each square bent then measures 1,089 square feet. There are 43,560 square feet in an acre, so there are exactly 40 square bents per acre.

"I know you didn't mention some of these facts, but I thought it would be helpful for you to understand I was listening and have retained key elements of your presentation.

"Tobacco seeds germinate in greenhouses first. Pallets of trays with seeded pots are laid out in large greenhouses with piping running the length of the houses. Plants are transplanted into the fields from these small pots. I'll go back to the trays in a minute.

"Men riding on the back of tractors plant five rows of seedlings at a time. There are 10 rows in a bent, and if plants are spaced one foot apart in each row, then there are approximately 330 plants per bent. At 40 bents in an acre, that comes out to 13,200 plants per acre. For a large farm averaging 150 acres, that is 1,980,000 plants. That's a lot of plants!

"Back to the trays. You said 96 pots were inside 12 by 18-inch plastic trays. That means there were 96 plants for every 1.5 square feet of greenhouse space. For the 150 acre farm, there would be 20,625 trays needed to plant that many plants. If each tray takes up 1.5 feet square feet, the requirement for greenhouse space would be 30,938 square feet. If the average greenhouse is 300 feet long and 50 feet wide, the requirement would be for at least two, possibly two and a half greenhouses, accounting for aisle space needed to service and water the seedlings."

I continued to stare straight ahead. John was in the same position, still smiling while Roger and Jackie appeared to be jotting down notes on their pads, expressionless. They both finished writing and looked up at me waiting for more.

"Plants are in the ground now, so it's time to service them with the crews. Missing or dead plants are replaced manually. Tractors then dust the young plants for bugs and push dirt up against the stems of the plants. I think your word was 'cultivate'. Plants are then manually hoed, twice. Crews remove unwanted growth called suckers from each plant and tie each small plant to wires stretched over the rows.

"Next we're into the harvest cycle. Boys and men pick on average, three leaves from the bottom of the plant up and drag the leaves out to trucks for transport to sheds. Girls sew the leaves onto string held by wooden lath, to be hung in rafters in the shed. This rotation is repeated seven or eight times and as many as 25 leaves per plant are processed this way. I will spare you the calculation for the number of leaves per acre, etc.

"Once the tobacco is hung in the sheds, it is 'fired' or cured using propane or natural gas stoves. The firing can last from three to four weeks and is carefully monitored by night crews.

"We are at the final process. In the fall season, sheds are completely wrapped in plastic. Steam machines are used to increase the humidity to the proper levels so hands of cured tobacco can be prepared by men and packed into boxes in the takedown operation. Between 60 and 120 boxes per shed are produced and stored for eventual transport to the co-op."

I stopped and silence fell onto the four of us for 20 long seconds.

"Okay, I'm done," I finally said. "Did I make it in six minutes?"

Jackie looked at her watch, then up at me with a cute smile, looked down at her notes, and then back up.

She answered, "Nice job Jason, I have you timed at five and a half minutes. Timing-wise you're okay, but you missed something."

She was sitting directly across from me. I looked at her carefully, studying her and what she said. I was sure I didn't miss anything.

"What did I miss?" I asked without a bit of emotion.

She responded, "You completely missed the section about how tobacco plants are irrigated in the field."

"Oh yes, irrigation in the field. Let me see if I can remember that section." I was getting a bit agitated; I had expected fair play and not this. I wondered where this was going. Maybe she had inadvertently missed a slide in her presentation, as there was no mention of irrigation in the tobacco fields. Or maybe they were pulling my chain to see how inventive I could be. I chose the latter and decided to play along.

"Jackie," I started, "You're right. I missed that in the read-back. But I know why. I missed it because field irrigation was a topic you left out of your presentation."

John and Roger sat and stared straight ahead, frozen like statues. As Jackie looked at me, I registered a slight smirk on her face. Before she could respond, I quickly kept talking.

"Now, no worries, I can put that section back into your presentation for you. We can use one of the slides you already have. Maybe the shot with the men pulling the cloth over the wires; there was plenty of evidence of irrigation piping running along the poles and I distinctly remember seeing small irrigation pipe-heads popping up along those mainline pipes. In at least two other shots, we saw small ponds next to the fields and we can use those ponds as a water source. What do you say, Jackie? We have a deal?"

Jackie's face was smiling in full bloom now. I had chosen wisely.

"Jason, you did a marvelous job today; we are fully impressed, aren't we Roger?"

She looked at Roger and he managed a quick "Yes, that's right. Very impressive job Jason. I especially liked your numerical embellishments."

John sat with his legs still crossed, hands folded and just nodded his head in agreement slowly, a satisfied look on his mustached face.

Jackie continued, "Sorry about last curve Jason. You are correct, we didn't discuss irrigation in the fields, but we were hoping you could put two and two together with some creative thinking on your own and create a plausible solution. You didn't disappoint us. Roger, John, do you have any additional comments for Jason?"

John spoke up, "Just one. Jason, awesome job. Everything I've heard about you is true. I know why you've been so successful in your work. I've heard it said to be a good liar one needs an excellent memory. If a scam can be described as living a lie, you certainly have the tools for a long career here in covert ops."

Roger stood up and addressed the group, "Are we interested in taking a break before the next session? Or can we start? My presentation will take less than 30 minutes."

"I'm ready to go Roger, let's do it," I said. John and Jackie nodded in agreement.

I was anxious to see what Roger had in his bag of tricks. I wanted to get on with it and hear about my new identity.

Chapter 5

Roger Dupre was sixty-one years old, tall and had a long thin face. He looked and acted like a gray-haired Mr. Rogers. He always wore dark cardigan sweaters and had that distinctive calm demeanor. I was introduced to him last year for the first time in the FlightPlan presentation. I thought then his first name was fitting because his personality was so Mr. Rogers-like.

He walked over and hit the lights, dimming the room. He held the clicker in his right hand, but nothing was displayed on the screen just yet. Then he started.

"Thank you Jackie, for your presentation, and you too Jason for your recap. We all know a lot more about the shade tobacco industry in Connecticut. As you know, over the past three weeks, both Jackie and I prepared these presentations, but I will be presenting the bulk of this one.

"I would like to mention one thing about this case before we begin. Initially, the case review team wanted to initiate the scam from the Hartford co-op. As you recall, the batch of marijuana in Puerto Rico was found and traced back to the co-op. It was then determined to be tagged with origin to a specific farm in the region. Our scam initially targeted the co-op, but after a second review, the board decided to redirect the scam to the source farm and away from the co-op. At first, I didn't agree with the board's decision. I assumed we would have a shorter and more contained scam at the co-op. Their thinking was it would be more efficient to begin at the farm and kill the source, before responsible individuals in the co-op could communicate with individuals on the farm, potentially shutting down the source there. They thought if we could get to the farm source covertly first, we'd have a much better chance at cutting off the head of the dragon."

Wow, I thought to myself. Roger was presenting evidence RoJac was in the dark about the operation. That's consistent with the board's movement away from the co-op. RoJac was told the find was a straight marijuana discovery which would have had to pass through the co-op as recognizable marijuana, implicating the individuals there. In fact, the material we were after looked like normal shade tobacco, so it may never have been noticed in the co-op. In all likelihood, the co-op was not involved. So the review board must have overruled the initial recommendation for the co-op scam on that basis, to enable the scam to begin at the farm.

I understood this subterfuge with the board's decision about the co-op was necessary for the purpose of keeping the true nature of the operation under wraps, and to focus the scam at the farm. What was still puzzling to me was *why* the board wanted RoJac out of the loop and in the dark. This was unusual protocol.

"Today we'll be examining a specific farm where we think we have the best chance at discovery on the case. We'll attempt to match your profile, Jason, with specific responsibilities at that farm. We'll also attempt to drop you into this farm covertly, as a sole operative."

I was wondering just how they were planning to drop me into a farm in an active capacity. This should be interesting.

"Let's start with a bit of your profile."

I expected he would proceed to discuss my related farm background and how we could use it. This technique was common; stay as close as possible to reality in a scam and that lessens the risk of discovery.

"We know from your profile you worked on your family's potato farm in Aroostook County in northern Maine. You drove tractor and trucks for many years. Can you elaborate on that experience for us?"

"Well, there's not much to tell. As you know, my family owned a potato farm in northern Maine. We had a small farm, about 60 acres. I drove tractors mostly; we had four of them, two Fords, and two International Harvesters. Bucket loaders, scrapers, potato pickers, you name it, I drove it. We also had several aging trucks and lots of basic farm equipment to plow and till the fields. I learned to service the equipment in the winter when I worked during school breaks; got really good at it too. I did almost everything all through the school years each summer, and for a growing season after school too, before I started a banking career in NYC."

"So," Roger continued, "would you say driving is one of your skills?"

"Yes, driving is one of my hobbies. I love to drive. In my short life, I've owned and operated many vehicles. Anything that moves, I can drive it. This includes school buses, motorcycles, quads, snowmobiles and jet skis. I even fly small planes and have a pilot's license now."

"Yes, I heard about the pilot's license," Roger responded. "Let's keep our wheels on the ground for this one."

"Roger," I asked. "Judging by the questions you're asking, you're dropping me in as a driver on that farm."

"Maybe. We'll see."

The screen then flashed to a Google Maps satellite shot of farmland north and east of a large winding river. You could make out several large white fields, most in square and triangle shapes, dotted at regular intervals with brown dots. Arranged around the fields were rectangular reddish-brown sheds with gray-white roofs. The shot was at an angle giving the buildings recognizable perspective. These sheds were quite long, some positioned in groups of two or three in parallel. Dirt roads surrounded the fields and the sheds. A few small black ponds could also be seen nestled in between the white fields. In the foreground were five large greenhouses side-by-side, partially out of view of the shot.

"People, at this time, I'd like to introduce you to the farm of interest in this case. This is the Treadwell Enterprises farm in Sunbridge, Connecticut.

"This farm was identified as the most likely candidate for us to investigate. Let me take just a few minutes to review the reasoning and critical factors leading to this identification.

"First and foremost is the marijuana found in Puerto Rico came from batches of tobacco from Hartford Shade Co-op. This co-op has declined in recent years and is known to have only three members left, Treadwell being the largest participant by far.

"A second critical factor is the management environment in place there today. Harold Treadwell is the principal owner and manager of his farming enterprise. He is also a gentleman and one of the nicest people you will ever meet.

Today he is managing his multi-million dollar farm at an arm's length by proxy. A savvy foreman and up to six mostly college-age, seasonal, and highly-experienced employees are running this farm. Harold Treadwell is often absent from day-to-day operations, traveling in Europe or vacationing at one of his homes in Boca Raton, Florida, or Sonoma, California. The farm's properties have been in the Treadwell family for five generations, but this might be the last, as Treadwell is close to retirement and he has no offspring working on the farm now to continue the business.

"A third factor is the sheer size of the operation." Roger pointed to the display of the farm on the screen.

"Treadwell is currently farming between 150 and 200 acres of shade tobacco. Due to the heavy snows this year in New England, their greenhouse operations have been pushed back a few weeks. As a result, we're still trying to determine the exact size of this year's readied tobacco crop.

"In addition to tobacco, Treadwell is growing 100 or more acres of pickle cucumbers, and two large greenhouses of tomatoes. The cucumbers are destined for the pickle markets in Massachusetts while the tomatoes will be sold to local food stores and farmers' markets.

"We believe it is highly likely, marijuana is being grown here right under the nose of the absentee owner. Getting you in there Jason, is our best shot. Any questions so far?"

"Wait, are you implying this nice guy is innocent and doesn't have a hand in it?" I asked.

"Well, Treadwell is a very wealthy man. He's in his sixties. His company owns mortgage-free land holdings, worth by some estimates, 30 to 40 million dollars. Holdings are fairly liquid as well; most of the farmland property is prime real estate. Two years ago he sold a 15-acre field to a housing developer netting the company 1.8 million. He pays himself a small salary and drives around in a Volkswagen Jetta (presumably for image), but his tax returns tell a different story. His annual bonus, depending on the quality of that year's crop, averaged $850,000 for the past five years. In the winter months, he lives in Boca Raton or Sonoma, beautiful properties he owns outright, mortgage free. Let me ask you, why would someone who is so well-off and successful risk it all to grow marijuana? Can you see my point, Jason?"

"How do you know marijuana hasn't been a staple for years and that's where his money is coming from?" I blurted out this question quickly; too quickly. I cringed.

I hadn't thought it through before asking the question. Paid income taxes must be showing a valid trail of income from legitimate sources. Treadwell's taxes paid to the IRS, had to be the DEA's source of information and it was unlikely proceeds from marijuana would ever show up in his tax filings. Besides, RoJac didn't know the truth, that this case wasn't about Treadwell growing marijuana. It was a silly question.

Before Roger could answer, I said, "Forget I asked this question Roger. I get it."

Roger smiled back at me, "No worries. Any more questions?" he asked. Jackie and John were shaking their heads no. I was quiet so Roger continued.

"Let's move on to the next topic. And that is getting you in there Jason."

Roger clicked to the next picture, showing a fog-filled early morning image of a grassy yard filled with farm vehicles. There were many different trucks and tractors, some old and new, facing forward, all lined up in a row from left to right forming a semi-circle. The camera for this shot had been in the center of the circle about 30 yards away. Parked in the center of the circle and closer to the camera, was a tan colored Ford 150 pickup truck and a small crowd of men and boys, mostly teenagers surrounding the front of the truck. There was a slightly older man, who looked to be in his thirties sitting in the truck. He appeared to be pointing to one of the tractors. On the left in the distance was a red barn marked with a number “2” stenciled in white paint, on the front side just under the roof’s peak.

“You guessed it earlier Jason; the basic premise we’re going with here is the operation will need drivers, tractor drivers and truck drivers. This is especially true if a key staff person leaves unexpectedly.”

I knew from previous scams sometimes things happened to create breaks. These ‘things’ just didn’t happen, but circumstances were sometimes helped along and given an ever-so-slight nudge to uncover opportunities we could make use of.

Not holding anything back I asked, “Okay Roger, what did you do to set me up?”

Roger continued, “On the way to answering that good question Jason, I want to fill you in on some critical staffing demographics. In this shot you see the farm foreman, Peter Roscoe sitting in his pickup handing out the day’s assignments to his key staff. As you can see, most of these individuals are of high school or college age, but a few key staff are older, say 26 to 30 years of age. These individuals are teachers, who return every year on summer break to work as drivers or in management. Some of the teachers drive the tractors, and others help to manage the large throngs of school children working in the fields and sheds.

"That being said, your cover Jason will be that of a teacher, on summer break who is looking for part-time or full-time summer work. We think this approach has the highest probability of success. The foreman, Peter Roscoe, has been known to hire teachers on the spot, especially if there's a need. We'll be talking more with you in the next few days, at the logistics session. You know, more on living arrangements and what you can expect, etc."

"How are you creating that need for me?" I asked.

"I want you to take a look at this person right here." With that, Roger walked to the screen and pointed to a tall man with longer hair and a goatee. He was a sophisticated looking individual clearly older than college age, perhaps in his late twenties, wearing jeans and a bright red striped long-sleeve shirt.

"This is Wesley, a.k.a. Wes Ackerson. During the school year, he's a history teacher at The Loomis Chaffee School in Windsor, Connecticut. He is an intelligent individual with a high IQ, well-liked by everyone and an excellent teacher.

"Wes works the summer break at Treadwell. He drives tractors, trucks and is a boss in the fields during the harvest cycle. He's had five years working in this capacity. Jason, we are hoping you can take Wes's place in the operation this year."

"Right. So I'm assuming Wes will not be there. Where's he

going?" I asked.

"Well, we're not 100 percent sure, but we're working on it. We hope he'll be traveling within the next few weeks to Moscow, Russia, to accept a new teaching position at the America school in the embassy compound. For the past two years, Wes has applied to work there but has been turned down each year. His fortunes are changing, but he doesn't know it yet. He'll find out in the next few days a new position at the embassy teaching American History just became available, and it even includes airfare and upscale living quarters for him and his family.

"It's amazing what friends in high places can accomplish, don't you think?" said Roger as he made his way to the door and switched on the lights.

Chapter 6

At 6:15 am, Peter Roscoe, the Treadwell foreman, pulled up with his tan Ford pickup in front of the last greenhouse, marked with a large '#5' on the front of the house. The seed house was different than the others. It was smaller and it had a more highly pitched plastic-pillow roof. A small blower forced air between the two plastic sheets separating them to create an insulating pocket of warm air. This house had toughed out one of the worst winters on record in New England and it was that roof that had made the difference. The warm air insulated the house and melted the snow.

The sun was up, but in mid-May there was still an early morning chill in the air. As Peter neared the door, he noticed the padlock was unlocked and the door was ajar. No other cars were parked there. Seeing this and thinking it rather odd, Peter went inside.

As he entered the house he noticed the grow lights were on. The gas furnace in the corner of the house groaned with its familiar rumble, blowing warm air from the large round openings on the top of the furnace.

"Marco?" He yelled out. "Marco, you in here?" Peter looked down the center aisle of the house; large green tobacco plants on either side of the aisle were stretching up to the roof. Tops of the plants had tangled in the grow lights with new leafy growth. Many plants had flowered-out with the traditional small yellow trumpet-shaped flower. Some had fallen off onto the dirt floor. The stalks on these mature plants were two inches thick. The leaves were big and had grown so far into the middle he had to take care not to damage them as he made his way down the center of the aisle.

As he continued walking, he saw Marco in the distance at the back of the house, standing on a footstool reaching up to the top of a plant to the right of center. As he got closer, he could see Marco, wearing white iPod wires dangling from his ears, was tagging a plant with a red tag. Black characters were scribbled on the tag. A sweet cigar smell permeated this section of the house.

“Marco,” he said loudly. “I had no idea you were in here. I didn’t see your car out front.”

Marco removed his earbuds and pulled the unlit cigar out of his mouth and couched it between his fingers.

“Good morning Peter!” he said in an overly friendly tone. “My car is in the shop today; a friend dropped me off. I was just tagging the latest strain, listening to Bach. I love Bach. I find it soothing.”

Marco Pinto was Italian, in his mid-fifties, short in stature and balding. He had tiny corn-like teeth, badly stained from cigars he sucked on constantly.

Peter and Marco just barely got along. Marco was a tobacco geneticist, or so he said. Peter thought Harold had made a huge mistake hiring him. But here he was, for the past two years, demanding more and more support for his genetic program. The entire greenhouse was devoted to his strains; what Peter considered to be a lame attempt to find the best seed, the biggest tobacco leaves with the best combination of leave color, thinness and weight. Tobacco was sold by the pound; a ten percent increase in leaf weight was worth hundreds of thousands. In defense of himself, Marco had repeated this mantra over and over and Peter was sick of hearing it.

He climbed down off the footstool and asked, "Peter, did you find more red tags for me? I'm down to my last few. Got to keep the tagging on track you know."

"No, sorry Marco. I'll get them this afternoon."

"Good. You may want to check the thermostat, too. It felt cold in here this morning. Heat was on, but I still think there's an issue with the timer.

"And I could use some help in here. Harold promised me I'd have help with germination and the tagging. There are more than a thousand plants here. I can't do all this alone. If you pick one of the men, he's got to speak good English. The college kid I had last year was great, but he's probably still in school. I can't remember his name. Smart guy, going to UMASS for some marine thing." He put the cigar back in his mouth and chewed on it vigorously.

"All right. I checked the thermostat last week, it's fine, but I'll check it again. As far as your help goes, I'm working on it."

Having said that, Peter turned and walked quickly away from Marco, back toward the front of the house. He passed the thermostat on a middle pole and gave it a sharp slap with his hand, but kept walking. Marco couldn't hear Peter talking to himself as he walked out through the gantlet of large green leaves. "Pain in the ass," he muttered. He could still feel the furnace blowing warm air as he left the house.

Chapter 7

"Nice to have you flying with us today Mr. Kraft. Can I get you something to drink?"

I was surprised to find the aisle seat next to me in first class empty. It was a short flight from Dulles to Hartford but sitting in first class had its advantages. I had no problem taking service before the plane was pushed back from the terminal.

"Sure," I replied. "Tanqueray and tonic. Mind if I have two?"

"That would be fine," she answered and smiled back at me.

"Ice?"

"Just a little," I replied as she set the glass down on the small armrest and handed me two small bottles of Tanqueray.

I didn't really enjoy flying in big planes. I felt I was a total captive and I didn't like the fact my life was in the captain's hands. I understood the safety stats, that I had a better chance getting hurt crossing the street. Made no difference. For that short flight, I was not in control of my destiny. I could not shake that feeling. Just last year a co-pilot on a Lufthansa flight had locked himself in the cockpit and flown a plane and all 150 passengers and crew into a mountaintop to their deaths. Incidents like this had motivated me to earn a pilot's license a few months ago in the FlightPath scam. I craved my own destiny.

Right now, I had no control so I numbed myself with the ritual of a double gin and tonic. It always helped.

The logistics meeting with Roger had gone well. That guy I was replacing accepted the position and was bound for Russia, leaving on May 23rd. Today was Friday, May 15th, so that meant his departure was one week and a day away. He had already notified the Treadwell foreman Peter Roscoe he was headed for Moscow and would not be working on the farm this summer.

My cover would be I was a history teacher looking for a teaching job in the area. I would say that I had three schools on the hook, two private and one public, and a job was imminent so I decided to move into the area. School wouldn't start until fall so I had to find summer work. I could sell my experience driving a tractor and working on the potato farm as a youth. Roscoe was known to hire potential drivers on the spot. All I had to do was to rent a car at the airport, drive 21 miles to Treadwell Farm, look for Roscoe's tan pickup and offer myself up as a farm hand. The thinking was he'd be trying to replace the vacancy ASAP. I was more skeptical than the planners this would work as designed, but here I was on a plane about to take off to Hartford's Bradley International Airport. A lot depended on me selling myself into the job.

The gin began to work even before the plane took off. I found myself thinking of Alondra and the evening we spent at dinner the night before. I was smitten again; there was no doubt about that. I knew it might be months before I saw her again so I took a chance she would say yes to dinner with me at my favorite restaurant in D.C., the Old

Ebbitt Grill. She did not disappoint. We had a wonderful time together, as we had always had. She filled me in on goings-on in the FBI and I was purposefully quiet about my new assignment. She understood I couldn't discuss my work. We promised to keep in touch. We didn't have a romantically intimate evening last night, but we were both kidding ourselves if we thought it wouldn't get to that point once again if we kept seeing each other. I hoped I'd see her again soon, but we had no plans.

As the plane accelerated quickly down the runway, I was pushed back into my seat. Feeling the effects of the second gin and tonic now, I was overly careful not to spill it. I was amazed how big the plane was and how quickly we accelerated. I couldn't imagine anything this big making it into the air. If I was the builder and my charge was to conceive and build the first aircraft to fly 300 souls, flight would never have been born. I was just not creative enough to envision what needed to be done to build anything this big and functional.

I looked out the window to see the green grass next to the runway dash away below in a blur. The engines were whining as the nose of the plane angled up and the wheels thumped off the tarmac.

The flight went quickly; I was in a gin fog the entire way which was okay by me. I was coming out of it when the plane landed. With no checked baggage, I walked through the exit doors and out to the bustling street where cars, taxis and buses of all types were pulling in to receive arriving travelers. I spied the Hertz bus and made my way to it.

I packed light with only my backpack and clothes for the

first few days. One of the perks in this job was the living allowance. It was significant at $4,000 per month. That was meant to cover everything; hotel, food, long term rent, a car, even a new set of clothes. Gone were the days of receipts.

Hertz rental was a two-minute bus trip and I was soon on my way to Treadwell Farm in Sunbridge driving a brand new black Prius. I figured the conservative approach would be the best. A hot Mustang or that new Hot Wheels Camaro, even though I was dying to drive one of those cars, didn't project the right image for my chance meeting with Peter Roscoe.

The GPS in the Prius worked fine and I arrived at the farm headquarters just after 4:00 p.m. I pulled into the gravel yard and parked in front of the left side of the building.

I recognized the barn-red equipment shop in front and the large plastic covered greenhouses behind the shop from pictures Roger shared in our logistics meeting. I asked him then where this picture and all the other color pictures had come from in Jackie's presentation. He said someone had written an eBook called _Tobacco Road_ filled with black and white pics of Connecticut tobacco farms. They contacted the author and she was kind enough to share all the original color shots. Some of these were from Treadwell farm. Lucky for us.

The shop was a converted barn. It had three large garage door bays in front, with a small entry door on the right side of the building. One of the bays was open and I could see the back of a red tractor in the open bay. Over the center bay and nailed up on the side of the shop building was a distinctive white sign with large black lettering announcing

Treadwell Farm.

No other vehicles were in the front yard, so I decided to wait in the car hoping Roscoe would show up. It was an overcast day in the low 60's; the new buds on the trees were just beginning to pop; some had already. I tried to imagine what was going on in the greenhouses behind the shop.

In less than 10 minutes, a tan Ford pickup pulled into the gravel yard and parked quickly in front of the shop bay doors. Peter Roscoe stepped out of his truck and looked over at my Prius. I opened the door and climbed out facing him.

The scam was on.

Chapter 8

Peter Roscoe looked up at me from 20 feet away. In his late thirties, he had a strong powerful frame, brown hair, and a large square shaped head. I also noticed his large hands; clearly beefed from all the farm work.

I walked over to him with an outstretched hand, we shook and I quickly introduced myself, and he did the same.

"Glad to meet you Peter. I heard you were the foreman here at Treadwell."

Peter eyed me carefully, and with a quizzical and somewhat skeptical look asked, "What can I do for you?"

I explained my situation, that I was a teacher on summer break and was looking for new employment for the coming school year, and until then needed summer employment. I told him I had three pokers in the fire at schools in the area and I was sure one would come through. I then went on to tell him about the potato farming experience in my youth, and about the tractors and driving the potato trucks on the farm in northern Maine. That softened him up a bit and he began to relax. He started asking me farm questions.

"Can you drive a tractor?"

"It's been a while but I did it for years and it will come right back I'm sure."

"What kinds of tractors did you drive on your farm?"

"We had four tractors, two International Harvesters, and two Fords."

"How long has it been since you've driven one?"

"Last time I was on a tractor was about five years ago. Went to visit my dad on the farm, he's retired now. He needed some tractor work so I jumped on it. No trouble at all. Came right back to me."

"How many blades on the plows there?"

"We have two plows on the farm, one's a three blade; use the Fords for that plow. The other's a four blade. The big IH has no trouble pulling that, as long as the frost is out of the ground."

"And you can drive trucks too, all kinds? What about school buses?"

He was obviously having fun now and trying to catch me with something I couldn't do. I knew I would surprise him with the bus license.

"Yes, I can drive almost anything. Pretty good at backing up trailers, too. I also have a bus license."

"Tell me why *you* have a bus license."

"Not much mystery there. My mother was a teacher at the small grammar school in our town and she was also the bus driver. She wanted some backup for morning pickups so the school board agreed I could drive the bus when she couldn't do it. They paid me 23 dollars a round trip. That was a long time ago, but I'm sure it will come right back to me."

"Okay. So far so good. Last question. Do you have any experiences milking cows?"

That was a surprising question. There was nothing in Jackie's presentation about a cow farm. He asked one I couldn't say yes to. But it worked in my favor anyway; he had me and he was proud of it.

"No, I have to admit I've never milked a cow and have no experience doing that."

"That's okay," Peter replied. "We don't need any help up at the barn anyway. Just curious."

These questions formed the basis of a job interview. I was hoping I passed. I'd know in a minute.

After a short pause, Peter said, "Looks to me we may be able to use you. I didn't ask any hard questions, but I can see you've had some farm experience and look strong and able bodied so I suppose I can take a chance with you.

"I can't start you more than minimum wage though. State keeps raising it but today it's $9.15 per hour. As we get going and I see how good you are with the tractor, I can raise that up a buck or two but that's all you can count on.

"We're going to be short a driver and a field boss this year. A guy who works here every year just called and told me he's not working; got a teaching job in Moscow of all places. That creates a vacancy you can help fill.

"We have a great seasonal crew here. Most all of them come back year after year. Keep in mind most are high school and college age, younger than you, and if you share info on wages, you'll find we're paying at least four of them more than we're paying you. I won't say how much, but you understand the others are experienced and highly skilled. They keep the place running smoothly. The pay isn't much, but the hours are unlimited. Their checks are bigger than my check most weeks.

"By the way, you mentioned you're from Maine, potato country. Where did you go to school?"

"I went to high school locally, and then stayed in Maine for college. Small school named Bowdoin College in Brunswick, Maine. Majored in government studies."

"I know about Bowdoin. Neighbor's kid tried to get in there. Nice school, and near impossible to get in. Expensive as hell, too."

"Yeah, nothing's changed since I was there twelve years ago. I was lucky enough to qualify for a full scholarship, with good grades and being from Maine. My parents, far from wealthy, could never afford to send me there without a scholarship."

"When did you say you were available?" Peter asked.

"I can start Monday. Is that too soon?"

More for effect than anything else, Peter brought his right finger up to his chin as if in heavy thought, and folded his left arm under his right elbow. "Let's see, today is Friday, I think I could be ready for you on Monday. I can't promise what you'll be doing exactly, but I have something in mind."

"Well thanks Peter. I want to thank you for the job."

I reached out and we shook hands. Of course I knew his last name, but it would appear more genuine if I asked.

"Sorry Peter, what did you say your last name was?"

"Roscoe, Peter Roscoe. My friends here call me just Roscoe. We're not exactly friends yet, but you can go ahead and call me Roscoe."

"Great. I'll see you..." I hesitated, "at what time on Monday morning?"

"Oh, that's right, how would you know? We start at 7:00 a.m. sharp, right here. See you then. Oh, almost forgot, I'll have some tax paperwork for you to fill out and sign next week."

With that, he climbed back into his truck and drove out of the yard taking a right on the main road and up the hill.

I slid into the Prius and pushed the start button. I had to find a temporary hotel now and some permanent housing for the long term. And work clothes. Getting started was always difficult, but exciting, too. Beginning anew. I wondered what I'd be doing on Monday.

I selected 'Hotels' from the search list in the GPS. There were several less than a mile from me. I liked the Marriott and had accrued huge points there. Why stop now? It was also really close, good for the next few weeks, or as long as it took me to find a condo or a small furnished house to rent. So I drove just a half mile up the hill on Night Valley Road and came to the Sunbridge Marriott hotel on the right. I pulled in and noticed the happy-hour sign. Time to find a seat at the bar and continue the conversation I started earlier on the plane with Mr. Tanqueray.

Chapter 9

"We could have done this on the phone at our weekly status. Why are you here?"

Becky Sadler quickly glanced around the restaurant scanning for anyone she recognized. Then she focused on the bar. Satisfied no one was watching them, she relaxed a bit, pulled on her neat scotch, then continued her rebuke.

"This is a stupid place to meet. Too many people here. Anyone can see us," she said.

"I thought it would be best if we saw each other again. I need to tell you a few things in person. And this is a perfect place. You live in this hotel don't you? Anyone sees us, tell them your brother came in for a visit."

"I don't live here anymore. You should know about that from reading my status reports, *if* you read them that is. I have my own place now, and you don't look like my brother. My brother lifts weights and has two kids, and I know that's not your shtick."

"Let's not get nasty Becky."

"Okay John, but didn't you tell me your guy's coming this week? What if he pops in here? He doesn't know me, but he knows you."

"No worries. He's staying at the Marriott down the road, that's where his points are. He won't be popping in here. He doesn't like Hiltons."

Becky was clearly getting upset. She started to raise her voice, "Don't be so sure. And you're acting kind of smug. And why are you bringing him in anyway? The deal in the beginning was I would be on my own and the fewer involved the better. Why the turnaround? It's like you don't trust me."

John put down his martini and stared at his glass and not her. "Becky, you need to calm down. Things changed. A lot is at stake here and the seniors are worried."

A waiter arrived at the table, smiled and politely asked if they wanted another drink.

Becky looked at John and asked, "Another round?"

John replied, "Sure. Why not? I've got a while before I leave for the airport."

Becky took her pocket mirror out of her purse and checked her hair. She was in great shape for her mid-forties age and some people said she resembled an older-looking Jennifer Aniston.

John watched the waiter leave and then continued, "I tried to talk them out of bringing in another agent, but I couldn't. They wanted the new asset in here and I sold them on keeping you here too.

"Look at it from their side. If that strain hits the street, we'll have a huge problem. A weed source like that passed around in plain sight, undetectable; it's just unthinkable. That will set us back years. Just thinking about it makes me sick. We need to find the seed to that strain and kill it ASAP.

If we allow that to go live, we are totally screwed."

John then finished the first martini, holding the glass up high to get every drop. Before he continued the waiter arrived with two more drinks.

He started up again, "Jason's one of our elite. He's got incredible skills and a farming background. We're dropping him right in there. He's our best shot. You keep your thing at the experiment station going and don't over communicate with him; make sure you keep your cover. We'll hit this with both barrels independently. He can't know about you either, at least not right away. He's got a big ego and he'll be pissed if he finds out you're here and we didn't tell him. You're in the know, he's not; that should make you feel better.

"Your work so far has been good. We'll continue to make progress and we'll find the strain, I'm sure of it. We have to continue with the plan and do it carefully, in black."

In black was the DEA term meaning completely under cover, with no possibility for discovery. He took a hit from the second drink, and thoughtfully put it back down on the table.

"Can we count on you?"

"Of course you can count on me," she shot back.

"Okay. Before I head back I want to review the suspect list with you. I'm canceling tomorrow's weekly update; we'll do it now."

He reached into his breast pocket and withdrew a small yellow pad of Post-it notes. He carefully thumbed the pad and cut it like a deck of cards at a predetermined spot to reveal an internal page with writing on it. He peeled the single page from the pad and turned it around and placed it on the table in front of Becky so she could read the contents. The writing was small so you had to be up close to read it.

Becky looked closely at the small note on the table.

She looked up and said, “I have no changes to the list or the status in the case.”

John looked up at her and very quietly, but pointedly said, “I still think you need to refocus your efforts on Marco Pinto. He’s the geneticist. If anyone’s doing something with tobacco strains, it’s most likely him.”

Becky replied, “I know you think that John. We’ve had this discussion before. He may be a geneticist and a nice guy, but he is not a rocket scientist. There is no way he’s responsible for creating this strain. I don’t think he’s smart enough. I’ve worked in his seed house. There’s nothing there, I’m telling you. I’ve looked at all the strains; spent hours with him discussing leaf sizing, light dispersion, cross-pollination, seed pelletization and God knows what else. He’s a pretty lonely guy and he wants attention. I gave him some and he opened up his whole professional life to me. I’ll keep trying, but I think we’re wasting our time focusing on him. He may look promising on paper, but I don’t think he’s your man. I even took leaf samples from every plant group and looked at them myself under the microscope back at the experiment station. There’s nothing but run-of-the-mill shade tobacco growing in that house. If something’s going on, it’s somewhere else.”

Becky finished emphatically, “I think we should look at the

owner. I know he's never there, but he has access to everything and it's his farm. He has the most to gain from this."

John nodded his head deliberately in agreement and finished the second martini. Becky watched him reach down slowly and take back the Post-It note. In one motion, he slid it into his water glass. As he did so, the ink on the note began to dissolve, darkening the water. In a few seconds, there was nothing left to read, as the note was completely blank.

"Hmm," Becky said, watching the note in the glass. "Interesting tradecraft. I guess this means we're done with the update."

On the way back to the airport driving the rental car, John dialed his iPhone.

An automated woman's voice answered, "Please enter your security ID."

John spoke a ten-digit number into the phone, "1 2 2 3 1 1 4 7 9 0."

The automated voice then prompted him for his name. He responded, "John Trane."

The voice came back with, "Please enter Target ID now."

He replied with a five-digit number, "9 8 9 1 0."

She responded, "Target ID accepted. Connecting your secure call."

After three rings, Bill picked up.

"Bill, it's John."

"I hope you have better news for me," Bill stated quickly.

"No, I don't. This is turning out to be more difficult than we thought. Becky continues to find nothing in the seed house. She's even convinced Pinto has nothing to do with it."

"Damn it, John. If we don't want the FBI bigfooting this on us, we better find that seed and I mean now."

"Well, our hands are tied Bill, not a whole lot we can do without creating a huge incident and blowing the whole thing wide open. You know that's out of the question."

"I know, I know. I don't want to use strong-arm either.

"Is your new guy in there yet? Did you meet with him in situ?"

"No. He doesn't know I'm here. He also has no knowledge of Becky. He starts on Monday at the farm. I have complete faith in him. I know this will work. Let's give him some time."

"Well, it better work. I want you to update me on a regular basis. I want some good news."

"Got that. Talk to you soon," said John, but Bill had already hung up.

As John hung up he pulled into the rental car drop-off. Exiting the car, he glanced at his phone and saw a text from Jason. It was a simple coded message.

"The weather is looking better for the next few days," was all it said.

That meant there would be no communication for the next several days, and all was well.

As he walked to the shuttle bus, he couldn't help thinking about the long, hot summer ahead and the serious mess they were in now; but he had to have patience and let Jason go to work.

I sat at my desk in the hotel, staring in a trance at my laptop screen. A friend in the server room had given me a highly classified program that connected to my iPhone as I made calls or sent text messages. The program used satellite triangulation methods to display my exact location as well as the person you were calling or texting as long as that person was using an iPhone too.

The screen displayed two small windows of Google Maps, one window with a green and the other with a red blinking dot. The green dot was no problem; it was my location in Sunbridge at the Marriott. The red dot was John's location, and that was reported to be only 20 miles from me, less than a half-mile away from the Bradley International Airport in Windsor Locks, Connecticut.

That's odd; John is at the airport here in Connecticut and that was news to me. What's he doing here? And why am I out of the loop?

I wanted to text him again, but I had just sent a message that I wouldn't be communicating to him again for the next few days. It would be unusual to break communication protocols and I'd also be putting him on the spot; not a good thing either. If he wants me I'll hear from him, but with no notice? Makes no sense, no sense at all.

I shook off the dark-side thoughts for now. I'd just ask him about it next time I saw him; or maybe not.

My attention swung back to the women's basketball game just starting on ESPN. I turned up the volume to watch the tip-off. It was a great game; there was a ton of hype about it. UCONN women were playing Notre Dame and this game was for the national championship and their tenth title. It was a replay from the game five weeks earlier. I was tied up and missed the real game, but they were showing it tonight again. I meant to watch from the bar downstairs but lost track of time. I'd go down at the first timeout. I loved to watch UCONN women play. They're pure winners; I felt connected to the team and their accomplishments. This was going to be a great game.

Chapter 10

I spent the weekend driving around getting to know my new surroundings, shopping for work clothes and work boots. There were several nice malls in the area and many good restaurants to choose from. I always thought it was a good idea to use the first few days to acquaint myself with the area before interacting with others in a scam. This time was no different.

Monday morning came quickly as I found myself standing in the equipment yard behind the shop at 6:45 a.m. Several others had pulled into the yard and parked in the gravel space to the left of the building. There was room there for 10 or more cars.

Men and boys were gathering into two distinct groups in the center of the yard; one was obviously the migrant worker team, and the other group belonged to the high school and college-age kids. The migrant workers were smoking cigarettes; well most of them were anyway. No one was smoking on the kid's team.

They were all wearing hooded sweatshirts and jeans. Most wore dirty sneakers, but a few had on above-ankle work boots. They appeared to be fidgeting, hands in pockets and bouncing back and forth in their spots, in an attempt to stay warm. It was in the low fifties, no wind, but there was a damp chill in the morning air. I looked behind the yard equipment and could see the A-frame greenhouses about 150 yards in back of the shop. The spaces between the houses were drenched in a wispy gray fog that was beginning to lift now that the sun was peeking over the trees on the east side of the houses.

I watched a large green school bus pull into the yard from the main road. It roared quickly past us and down the gravel path leading to the greenhouses. It stopped in front of the middle house and the door opened. At least 40 men exited the bus and made their way into the middle house. I could see that the houses were labeled in front with numbers, but they were too small to read from this distance. If I had to bet, the houses were numbered from one to five from left to right. I couldn't be sure until I was closer. I would find out soon enough.

I thought I'd have more luck conversing with the kids, so I walked over to their group extending my hand in a welcoming greeting.

As I approached, a tall, good-looking college student who resembled a twenty-five-year-old Omar Sharif, saw me walking toward them. He stepped out to meet me and we shook hands.

"Hi, I'm Cody Mason," he said with a vigorous handshake and a broad grin. "You must be new here."

Cody Mason wore clean blue jeans and a green checkered long sleeve shirt. Over his shirt, he wore a baggy gray sweatshirt with UMASS printed on the front. I could tell by his forward and friendly introduction that Cody had a great personality.

"Yup, first day. I'm Jason Kraft."

"Well, you're in for a treat then Jason. Peter Roscoe, the

foreman will be here any minute; he'll blast into the yard like a white knight, the curtain goes up, and the Peter show starts."

"The Peter show?"

"Yeah. I saw the same show every day last week; you're bound to see it today too. Bet money on it."

"What's that like?"

"He blows in here in his tan pickup truck, real fast, slams on the brakes, throws the truck into park, and skids to a halt on the grass right there and before the truck even stops he's climbing out," he said dramatically as he pointed to the empty grass in the middle of the yard between the two teams.

"He has this deal where he uses his right foot for the gas pedal and his left foot for the brake. I've watched him do it more than once from inside the truck. Makes for quick stops.

"Now he's out of the truck and pointing to each one of us, dishing out the daily assignments in a loud military voice, one by one until we're all gone; dispersed to the various trucks and tractors you see here. He has military experience I think. It's quite a show, impressive actually."

Cody finished talking just as an old mustard colored Caprice left the main road and turned into the yard, gliding slowly past us and up the path to the greenhouses.

I knew it couldn't be Peter so I asked Cody, "Who's that?"

He replied emphatically "That, my friend, is Marco Pinto. You can see him headed for greenhouse #5, what we call the Seed House. That man is one looney tune."

"What's a seed house?" I asked.

"That's where all the latest and greatest shade tobacco is genetically engineered. We call him Marco the Man. I was lucky enough (or unlucky enough) to be paired up with him for about four weeks last year, right about this time, in fact. I was his grunt. I did anything he wanted me to do and it wasn't a whole lot of fun. But I did learn a lot about plant pollenization and pest control, fertilizers, and growing greenhouse shade tobacco."

"So you'll be working with him again this year?"

"No way, José. Not me. Peter's got me working with the men stringing cloth and prepping the fields for irrigation. I don't mind the field work; keeps me in shape.

"I told Peter if he wanted me back this year, he had to keep me away from Marco. Working with him once was enough. So far, promise kept. Grapevine says Marco's looking for help already. Don't quote me but I wouldn't be surprised if that's you. He always picks on the new guys."

"Interesting," I said. Cody was a great source of information. I wanted him to keep talking before Peter arrived, so I kept prompting him with simple questions.

"Who are the men you referred to?"

"See that green bus in front of the middle house?" he pointed to the greenhouses. "That's the men's bus. The men come mostly from Puerto Rico to work the farm each year. Same guys come back every year. They live here on the farm."

“The farm has a hotel or something?”

“Not exactly. They call it a camp. Real basic place. Actually, it’s a dump but they keep coming back because it’s all they have. We don’t have time here now, but we’ll have plenty of time to talk later and I’ll fill you in.” As he said that he winked.

“So you’ve been working here for a long time? I mean every year in the summers?”

“Not me,” Cody responded. “This is my second year doing this. I have three months left of summer employment, and then I’m out of here. I have a B.S. in marine biology from UMASS and I’m attending Tufts Veterinary School in the fall.”

“Really? That’s great! Congratulations. How did you get the job here?”

“See that guy over there with the dark hair and the mustache?”

Cody pointed to the group of kids about 15 feet away. I could see a guy matching his description talking with others in the group.

“That’s Kevin Bomard. Kevin is my good friend and was my college roommate senior year at UMASS. We sang acapella in a barbershop singing group together at the university for two years. We also studied abroad together in Vienna, Austria. It was his idea that I come to work here. Not such a bad idea either. It’s fine if you’re not afraid of a little hard work and the money’s good too, mainly because we can work as many hours as we want.

"Kevin's a lifer; he's been here every summer since he was thirteen. He's a trusted member of the Roscoe inner circle. I am too, in association with Kevin. Kevin knows everything there is to know about raising tobacco and working here at Treadwell. Get him started and he'll tell you everything you want to know."

"What does being in the 'inner circle' buy you?" I asked.

As I asked the question, Peter Roscoe drove in and skidded to a halt in the center of the yard, just as Cody promised. Cody, smiling now, pointed at Peter climbing out of his truck. He answered my question in a deep thespian voice, imitating Darth Vader: "Wait just a minute my son, your primordial question is about to be answered."

Chapter 11

The Peter show didn't disappoint, and Cody was exactly right.

Once all the others around me were dutifully assigned to their trucks, tractors or greenhouses, I was left standing in the middle of the yard. Peter, in silence, then motioned for me to join him for a ride in his truck. I climbed up and onto the passenger side of the bench front seat. I was surprised not to find bucket seats, but then again, it made sense that a real farm truck would be chosen for utility and not riding comfort.

He didn't say a word, not even a good morning, as we drove up the greenhouse path, past the green bus to the number five house. Peter parked the truck right behind the Caprice blocking it in. I got the feeling he would not be parked there long and that I was staying.

As the truck stopped Peter said, "There is someone I want you to meet. You'll be working here in this house for at least the next two weeks."

We both exited the truck and made our way to the door. Peter carried a small cardboard carton with him into the house. As we approached the door, I noticed an open padlock. That was odd; I could see that this was a wooden frame house covered with double-layer plastic, one layer on the outside of the house, one on the inside. Anyone breaking in could simply cut the plastic with a knife and slide right in through the hole in the plastic. The padlock was no deterrent.

The roof on this house was also different than the others. This house had a much higher, rounded plastic roof and looked like a large milky-white pillow sitting on top of the house.

We entered the greenhouse full of tobacco greenery. I was hit with a blast of warm mildly fragrant air; it was humid like a tropical paradise.

The large leafy plants in straight rows grew all the way up to the fluorescent light strips about nine feet up. The bright green leaves grew progressively smaller toward the tops of the plants. You could see small flowers at the top, tangled in and around the light fixtures.

A stocky, round-faced, balding man came walking toward us from the rows of plants with a cigar in his mouth. He extracted the cigar and said, "Good morning Peter. Who did you bring me?"

"Marco, this is Jason Kraft. Jason this is Marco Pinto. Marco is responsible for Treadwell's genetic program. Here in this house the finest shade tobacco is born. Jason is a teacher, and he'll be working with us this summer. I'm assigning Jason to work with you for the next few weeks Marco. He's all yours. Oh, and here are the red tags you wanted."

Peter handed the small cardboard box to Marco. Marco turned to his left and put the tags down on a small table next to a warm-air furnace that was running in the corner.

"Thank you for the tags Peter, and thank you for the compliment. I didn't know you felt that way about my work here." Peter only smiled. He pushed open the door and walked out of the house. The plastic covered door banged shut on spring hinges.

As we stood in silence for a few seconds, Marco stared at me smiling, rolling the chewed cigar around in his mouth.

I could not believe my luck. The very first day of work, I was paired up with the most likely candidate responsible for the strain, or at the very least, someone close to him who may have been responsible. I'd have the next couple of weeks to delve into the problem and figure it out. I wanted to text John right away to pass on the good news, but it could wait.

I was left to fully introduce myself to Marco, standing there in front of the tall plants.

Marco put me right to work watering the plants by hand. The rows of plants were fitted with a drip irrigation system comprised of black plastic tubing, but he didn't trust that technology and preferred to water the plants manually.

So back and forth I walked up and down the aisles of plants, with a garden hose connected to a brass wand-like contraption that resembled a shower head on a stick. Care had to be taken not to break any of the large leaves as I moved up and down the rows. The idea was to water each few plants in a predefined group. These groups of plants were marked with labeled stakes. I assumed these groups represented the distinct strains of tobacco. There were ten rows of plants in the house, and judging by the size of the house, I estimated more than a thousand plants, made up of approximately fifty strain groupings. I could see that each plant was tagged with a red, orange or yellow tag. The same alpha-numeric markings on the plant tags were written on the stakes in the ground. Marco had created an elaborate system to propagate and track numerous strains of tobacco. There must be a spreadsheet file on a computer somewhere; no way anyone could support this many strains manually.

As I made my way down through the rows with the hose I noticed the back wall of the greenhouse wasn't draped in plastic, like the sides or the front of the house. It was made of light gray barnwood and so was the back door. Marco was up in the front of the house, out of sight, so I thought I could risk a peek out the back door. I turned off the water nozzle, opened the door and stepped into the darkness. I was surprised to learn that it didn't open to the outside, but to the inside of a small, dark, dirt-floored barn. It was noticeably cooler, less humid and there wasn't much light. I peered up into the rafters and could make out empty wooden lattices made of 2 by 4's and larger beams. Light was streaming in through tall slits in the side of the barn. As my eyes adjusted to the dark, I could see bundles of four-foot long sticks piled neatly in one corner. The barn was physically attached to one end of the greenhouse and was clearly a taller structure than the house, but shortened lengthwise.

Without my knowing, Marco snuck up close behind me and said loudly, "This is our seed shed. It's where we cure my strains."

He caught me completely off guard. I jumped back startled, turned half way around quickly and faced him. He was standing in the threshold, but the bright light from the house blinded me so I couldn't see his face.

"Oh sorry Marco, I saw this different door, I thought it opened up to the outside. Guess not."

"Not a problem Jason. I can see curiosity written all over your face. You must be new to the shade tobacco business?"

"Yes," I answered. "This is the first time I've worked on a farm like this."

"Well, I can understand your quest for knowledge being a teacher and all. You finished with the watering?"

"Uh, not quite. I have another pass on the left side of the house; I mean the west side of the house." I had to remind myself that many farmers were in love with the points of a compass and often referred to objects in reference to the sun. The 'north east' corner was always better than the 'left front' corner.

"Maybe I can spend some time this afternoon explaining things to you. In the meantime, please finish the watering. That will take you right up through lunch. If anyone needs me, I'll be in the #3 house. The men are seeding some of my strains today and I have to label the trays as they come off the line. If I don't watch them closely, they'll mess it all up and we won't know where anything gets planted."

"Right. Well, I sure appreciate you helping me to understand things here. Sounds fascinating," I said.

Marco put the cigar back in his mouth, turned around and walked back through the door leaving me standing there in the shed. The wooden door leading back into the house remained open. Unlike the front door of the greenhouse, there were no springs on it to swing it closed.

I finished the watering just before lunch. I was all alone in the house so I decided to walk around a bit on my own with no specific agenda. For thirty minutes, I dragged the water hose around with me as a cover in the event Marco came in. This wasn't really necessary; the growth in the house was so dense I was completely hidden from view less than ten feet into the house, but I took the hose with me anyway.

There was nothing in the house except tagged rows of plants, lighting fixtures, a furnace and the drip irrigation piping Marco wasn't using. I went back to the front of the house and secured the hose by winding it in large loops on pegs nailed against the front wall. When I was finished I noticed a narrow beaten path on the dirt floor behind the furnace, along the side of the house near the corner. As I walked around the furnace I bumped into a small steel file cabinet that was hidden from view. The front of the cabinet was facing inward and it was the same color and height as the furnace so you would never notice it unless you knew it was there and knew where to look.

Before opening the cabinet, I thought it best to check the front of the house first to see if I was really alone. I went to the door and slowly pushed it open. No cars out front, so I knew I had at least 20 seconds; I was sure I could hear tires on the gravel road if anyone pulled up to the front of the house.

I went back behind the furnace and quickly pulled open the cabinet. It was filled with Pendaflex file folders. The file tabs were labeled with the familiar strain markings I'd seen on the tags and wooden stake markers. There were at least forty folders there. The code pattern was similar; a number followed by two letters, followed by a dash, then two more letters, then four sets of numbers each separated by dashes.

15BB-NE-3-4-1-96

Scanning the folders, I noticed one in particular in the back of cabinet. A labeling pattern on this folder didn't match the others. Instead of a number followed by two letters, there were four 'X' letters, followed by the normal set of numbers and letters.

XXXX-NW-8-4-2-192

Just then I heard tires crunching on gravel outside the front door. I quickly closed the cabinet and dashed from behind the furnace over to the water hose. I fumbled with the hose and pretended I was looping it back up on the pegs. I glanced at my watch; it was 12:33 pm.

Peter Roscoe walked quickly into the house. The door behind him slammed shut on its spring hinges.

"You all set with lunch Jason? Where's Marco?" Peter asked.

"I don't know where he is; no wait, he said he would be in the #3 house. He left me here to water the plants. I just finished."

Peter saw the hose next to me and asked, "You were watering the plants with the hose?"

"Yes. It wasn't too bad. Got kind of hard to pull it along, especially down to the far end of the house."

Peter looked at me and shook his head in disbelief. Then as he pointed to the black plastic tubing running down each row of plants he said, "We spent a ton of money fitting this house with drip irrigation, just so we could water here without having to drag the hose. That system even has a computer timer on it so it waters automatically six times a day."

"Marco said he doesn't trust that system. He wanted me to water manually. Takes a while I must admit."

"You tell Marco when you see him he's a pain in my ass," Peter said loudly, turned and pushed through the door. The door slammed shut and I heard the truck start and make a wide circle back down the gravel path toward the shop.

I was by myself again in the house. I looked over to the furnace. Question was how long would I be alone?

Chapter 12

In less than a minute, Marco came through the front door of the house spoiling any thoughts I had about the file cabinet. He needed my help in the #3 house where the seeding operation was underway.

For the rest of the afternoon, I was assigned away from the seed house and asked to work with the men in the #3 house, learning all aspects of tobacco tray seeding. There was no opportunity to dash out for lunch so I was going to be hungry the rest of the day. I had my phone with me, but I would hold off communicating with John until after work. It was ahead of schedule, but I was sure he would want to hear about the seed house.

As I remembered from Jackie's presentation, the seeding operation was a multi-step assembly line, comprised of men, trays, potting soil, seed, machines, and pallets all working in harmony. Two crews operated to fill the floor of the house with seed trays; there were ten men in each crew working from opposite ends of the house.

The first step in the process was to fill the empty white plastic trays with potting soil. Each 12 by 18-inch tray held 96 one-inch soil-filled pots. The crews then used a special machine to lay 96 seeds into each tray all in one shot. The machine had a vacuum apparatus attached to a Plexiglas plate with 96 tiny holes spaced to perfectly match the pot pattern on the tray. Pelletized tobacco seeds about the size of a BB were poured over the plate. The rolling seeds stuck to the vacuum holes and were then released into the pots, all at once, just at the right time. The completed trays were then transferred to 4 by 5-foot wooden pallets, 8 trays per pallet. The pallets were laid down on the floor of the house starting from the middle and moving toward the ends.

I worked in the assembly line filling tray pots with potting soil for about an hour before Marco called me over and introduced me to his strain seeding operation. Marco was working with special pink colored trays which were seeded by hand from small batches of strain seed he held in small plastic pill bottles. He carried the bottles in a small satchel he wore around his waist.

He decided to abandon the vacuum machines because it was too intrusive to the production flow. For the small number of trays he would be seeding that afternoon, dropping the seeds into the small pots by hand was fine.

We worked together at a separate table, seeding the pink trays manually. He did the labeling and I did the seeding. We'd seed from one to four trays with one strain, before switching to the next. For each strain, he would hand me the next pill bottle. The bottles were labeled on the white plastic top with a strain number. He labeled the trays with a black magic marker, on the top edge of each tray, using the same code pattern I'd seen on the folders.

He was working from a print-off of some sort, so I was right; this info was in a computer somewhere.

Two men worked with us, loading the pink seeded trays onto pallets and carrying the pallets down into the house and into place on the floor. One of the men was friendly and spoke English reasonably well; he introduced himself to me as Julio Rodriguez. It was clear to me that he had worked with Marco before; he knew exactly what to do with the trays and there was an unspoken familiarity about the way they communicated with each other. It was too early for me to start a real conversation with him, but I planned on doing that in a few days once I gained his trust.

The strain coding method was revealed to me that first afternoon. It was a labeling code he invented which was nothing more than a way to track the exact location of the strains planted in the fields.

The perfect audience for him that afternoon, I quickly became a great listener. He jumped at the chance to tell me all about it.

If he labeled this code: 15TH-SW-10-2-3-288, it broke down this way:

15 - The first two numbers were the strain number.

TH – These two letters represented the first two letters of the field name where the strain was planted. All fields were named. Treadwell has 20 fields, and 12 of them were prepped for shade tobacco this year.

SW – These two letters represented a beginning compass reference point from the corner of the field. For example, SW stood for the southwest corner. This was the starting point reference for the next four numbers in the code.

10 – The first number represented the number of bents into the field from the corner location referenced by the two previous letters. In other words, SW-10 meant go to the southwest corner of the field and walk in 10 bents.

2 – The second number represented that number of bents

away from the outside edge of the field. So SW-10-2 stood for go to the southwest corner of the field and walk in 10 bents, then stop and walk at a right angle, left or right whichever way meant walking into the field.

3 – The next number represented how many rows of tobacco were represented. In this case, there were three rows. It was also an indication of how many trays of that strain were planted.

288 – This last number indicated the number of plants that were planted for that strain. This number was always a multiple of 96; in fact it was the previous number times 96, as there were 96 pots in a tray.

As we worked in silence, I kept thinking about that folder I'd seen with the XXXX coded label. Why would Marco label a strain without a strain number and without a field name? I certainly couldn't ask him about it. I didn't think to memorize the rest of that label which might be helpful if I could compare that sequence to some of the other sequences and perhaps get a partial match for field name, based on the corner location. I had to wonder, that might not work as the starting point could be any one of the four corners for the same field. Best bet was to go back to the seed house without being detected and read what was in the folders. That might be difficult if the house was locked each night with the padlock. Maybe it wasn't locked. I'd have to find out. I started to hatch a plan.

Chapter 14

Living out of a hotel was something I enjoyed, as long as the stay was not too long.

Happy hour here was over at 7:00 and it was 7:15 before I made my way down to the bar after a long hot shower. The bartender came over to the corner where I was sitting and slid the side of fries next to my plate. I thanked him and he retreated back to the other side to service a new couple who'd just seated themselves at the opposite corner. It was late for the bar crowd on a Monday night, and most had left.

When I arrived at the hotel last Friday, the manager agreed to a 20 percent reduction off the regular room rate if I paid up front and guaranteed to stay a minimum of two weeks, non-refundable. I thought this was a safe bet; I would be here for a while. Now I wasn't so sure. On the very first day, I made tremendous progress and felt this case could be over quickly if my luck continued.

Then again, I knew nothing about the strain's whereabouts and probably wouldn't until I became a more trusted member of the team. That would take time, days, in fact, to build the level of trust so it would become natural for others to feel comfortable enough to begin to share openly. It was critical that I didn't rush it; I needed to be patient and let that trust develop.

I also needed to consider all the possibilities. As was often the strategy, I needed to keep my head down, learn as much as possible by keeping my ears open, and not make waves that might cause anyone to suspect my agenda. Marco was the obvious choice here, but I'd learned from past experience that the obvious choice wasn't always the correct one. Was he acting alone? Was he taking orders from the owner? So far, I had only some unanswered questions about an oddly labeled strain, which was really nothing yet.

The bartender appeared in front of me and struck up a conversation as he polished the granite counter. "I saw you here on Saturday and Sunday. You sticking around for a while?"

"Yup. I'll be teaching history in the fall so I got a job for the summer working on a farm near here."

"That must be Treadwell farm. They're the only farm close to here really. How long are you staying in the hotel?"

"Just until I find more permanent digs. I can't afford too many more nights here; I made a good deal with the manager for the first couple of weeks. After that, I'm in trouble." I smiled as I said it.

Pointing to my drink I said, "Might as well bring me another one if you wouldn't mind."

"Sure thing," he said and grabbed another glass, filling it with ice.

"Hey, go easy on the ice this time."

"Got it," he replied and immediately dumped out half the ice into the sink.

I was in a relaxed mood; pretty satisfied I had survived and prospered in my first day of the scam. The small bar was about a quarter full; two couples and three business types in suits. A TV was positioned above the bar on each side. One was set to a golf tournament, the other was a women's basketball game; a WNBA game. Volumes were off on both, but the captions were on.

He brought the glass over and carefully set it down in front of me on a small square napkin.

I kept the conversation going. "So how long have you been a bartender here?"

"Been here for about a year now, since the place opened. Here's a coincidence you'll get a kick out of; this hotel and bar stands on property previously owned by Treadwell farm. A guy who works there and comes in here a lot told me about it. He said this entire hill was called Greenhouse Hill. Old man Treadwell sold out to the Marriott and the Hilton about two years ago. He relocated the greenhouses about a quarter mile down the hill behind the red Treadwell building on the corner." As he said that he pointed to his left in the direction of the shop down Night Valley Road.

"Cool. That is a coincidence. Is that guy you talk to here tonight?"

He looked around the bar and the surrounding tables in the lounge and said, "No, he's not here now. He comes in here about once a week; used to be alone, but lately he's with a lady friend."

"That guy's name wouldn't be Marco would it?" I asked.

"Yeah I think you're right. Marco. Know him?"

I paused. I was onto something. Marco had a friend he frequented the bar with. I was anxious to ask more and thought it unwise to be so blatant with my questions, but I couldn't resist. I would try casting some bait to see where it went.

"As a matter of fact I do know him. I worked with him all day today. He's a tobacco geneticist. I haven't met the woman he works with yet; I mean if she is someone he works with."

Before he volleyed anything back I quickly said, "Sorry, I don't mean to share personal information, and I totally understand if you feel you have to protect the privacy of your customers."

"No worries," he said. "I really don't know if his relationship with the lady is professional or social. I do see them sharing a glass of wine and reviewing paperwork now and then. My guess would be that they're working together, but sometimes they've been purely social, if you catch my drift," he said and winked.

"Do you want another one?" he asked pointing to my drink.

"Nah, I've had enough to eat and drink. I'm all set thanks. You can bring the check. Here's my card," I said as I handed him my Amex.

"Sure thing," he said.

A minute later he was back with my card and the receipt. I signed it and put a ten on the bar for the tip.

"Thanks Jason," he said as he picked up the ten and the signed receipt. "See you tomorrow?"

"You bet," as I slid off the stool, turned and walked to the elevators across the room. As I rode up the elevators to the fourth floor, I felt a bit guilty that our exchange was so one sided. He had provided some great info and I didn't even know his name. I'd fix that tomorrow.

At exactly 8:00 p.m. my cell phone rang with the familiar automated voice announcing a secure call from John Trane. I accepted the call with the passcode and John's voice boomed into my Bluetooth earpiece.

"Jason, good to hear from you so soon."

"Hello John, I hope all is well in Washington."

I remembered I needed to ask him about his whereabouts on Friday when I texted him. Wasn't sure how I would ask him, but I wanted to do it tonight.

John responded, "Everything's fine here. When I saw your message to call I had a feeling that it must be important enough for you to break protocol and contact me ahead of schedule. So what can you share with me tonight?"

"You won't believe my good fortune, John. They had me working today alongside their tobacco geneticist in a greenhouse they call the Seed House. The guy's name is Marco Pinto. I think following him around may prove helpful. As it stands right now, I may be working with him for the next few weeks."

"That's great news, Jason. From the environment you just described, your 'prove helpful' could easily escalate to 'hit the jackpot'. You think he could be responsible for the strain?"

"Well, I think he's the most likely candidate, or perhaps someone who works with him. I have a few connections to work through in the next few days and I hope to know more by Friday."

"Can you give me any specific details now Jason?"

"John, I've only been here one day. When I have something definitive, you'll be the first to know, I promise. Maybe you can jump on a plane and join me here for our next update, provided I have good enough material that warrants a trip here."

Before he responded, I asked him the question, "Have you ever been to the Hartford airport, John?"

There was a pause and then he said, "No, well maybe once or twice, years ago but not recently. Why do you ask?"

"Oh, well nothing really, except I think you'll really like this airport. It was recently updated to be more efficient, so getting in and out is a real pleasure, especially when you compare it to Baltimore and Dulles."

"Okay, I hope to have more good news from you soon Jason and I look forward to joining you in Hartford for that update."

I agreed to keep him apprised of my progress and we hung up.

I was stunned. It was only 8:10, too early for bed, so I decided to walk back down to the lounge, take a table and order another drink. The lounge was practically empty for a Monday night so the waitress came right over. It wasn't long before I was sipping that Tanqueray and tonic with ice.

There were a couple of things bothering me about this case and I needed to mull it over to try to reach an understanding.

I learned about the first issue back in the training session. The project executive board was keeping the true nature of the problem hidden from the scam architects. They were provided different but similar information; it was important for John and Bill to keep that one critical detail under wraps; the new strain of tobacco with a highly potent THC component genetically engineered into the plant.

Treadwell farm could be growing marijuana, or a special tobacco strain and the architects would still prepare the scam in the same way. I got that. I also understood compartmentalization and the 'need to know' were often employed at DEA and other government agencies. This was at times exercised to the extreme, even to the point of assigning false names to individuals within the agency itself, to protect real identities. But this was different. The scam architects were a chosen few who were trusted individuals. To keep them out of the loop and feed them falsehoods about the scam they were engineering was highly unusual. In my case, I was okay and I could work this scam either way, marijuana or special strain. But the more I thought about it the more annoyed I became.

The second issue was John's lie (or untruth) to me about not being at the Hartford airport over the weekend. I had no plausible explanation for why he was here and didn't confide in me. I even gave him a nice opportunity to come clean and he chose not to.

There was an undercurrent of distrust flowing here and the

current was getting stronger. I had the feeling that I had to get on top of that current or I would be swept under by it. I had only two options: to confront John directly, or to do my job and continue to wait it out, hoping something would break.

I began to suspect the two issues might be related. I didn't believe in coincidences, but it might be a stretch to lump these two anomalies together into some bizarre imagined conspiracy; at least not the very first day of the scam. If I confronted him directly on either issue, I wasn't convinced he wouldn't just lie to me again. No, I had to play it out without challenging John in any way; pick my spots for the challenge, if it went that way. I loved this job and I needed to be a team player and not rock that boat. I needed to figure it out on my own. At least for now, I'd have to play *Straight Face* with this one.

Chapter 15

The next day Julio taught me how to water the trays in the #4 greenhouse. Peter assigned both of us to this task from the yard. He also mentioned they would be using the drip irrigation system in the seed house from now on, so I didn't need to water there. That spoiled any opportunity I had, to easily review the files behind the furnace. Marco was nowhere to be found.

The #4 house was planted ahead of the #3 house and small quarter-sized bright green tobacco plants were already sprouting in the trays. Some were as tall as an inch or two. The task was to water the thousands of plants walking up down the main aisle, slowly pushing an unwieldy apparatus; a watering wand which was basically a long plastic pipe fitted with spray nozzles spanning half the width of the house. A water hose was threaded to the center of the pipe and the whole contraption was attached to a rolling dolly with grooved rubber wheels riding on a narrow train track.

As Julio was the trusted one, Peter gave him the responsibility of mentoring me in the fine art of tobacco tray watering. Julio was a great teacher. He quickly took me under his wing to show me the ropes.

He had a twin machine, same as mine, and his job was to water the other half of the house. We paced each other and conversed as we inched along side by side, from one end of the house to the other, spraying a fine mist of water on the budding plants. The house was huge; it must have been 250 to 300 yards long. It took a full hour for us to inch all the way to the back of the house then we repeated the process moving backward toward the front.

It wasn't difficult work and I was glad for the opportunity to converse with Julio. He spoke English reasonably well, but it took me a while to get used to his thick Spanish accent. It didn't take long for us to establish a bond and for him to open up about Treadwell farm. We had reached the end and were headed back toward the front of the house when we started really communicating.

"Julio, you say you've been working here for five years?"

"Yes, five years. I live in the camp, come back and forth from Puerto Rico to work."

"What kind of work do you do here?"

"Now I work in the greenhouses, sometimes in the field with cloth. Last year I worked with Marco the Man helping him plant his plants. After that, I work in the sheds and hang tobacco."

"You must work a lot of hours."

"Not so many. Carlos, the boss stops us to work if we have too much. Only 45 to 50 hours per week. I make more than other men, one dollar more than minimum wage. I know this; men talk. Not enough. They take 140 dollars out per week to live in the camp, more if you buy food. Then taxes and my checks are small, say 350 dollars. I send most of money to my wife in Puerto Rico. I have a cell phone, but is a cheap plan; I can only talk to her once a week with Carlos's phone; he has a good one and I use that. We have two childs, a boy and a girl. I miss my wife and my kids.

Many men do this. We have a slang saying in Puerto Rico. It means to work for your wife's lover."

I paused to let what Julio said sink in.

I knew the answer to my next question but asked anyway, "I bet you don't have unions here."

"Unions? No, no here." Julio shook his head emphatically. "Never. Once last year a guy came to the camp with papers about unions. Carlos stopped him, almost had a fight. He left. I know we need unions. Cody and Kevin say that. They know a lot. You talk to them. They tell you, but not when Peter there. Kevin's Peter's favorite; they's always together. You talk to Kevin alone. Kevin's very smart. Maybe someday things change here."

"How do you like living in the camp?"

"Is okay, not too bad. I used to it. Some guys drink all night start fights you know. Not me. Sometimes men come in cars from Hartford bring in girls. I don't like it. Sometimes bed bugs and cockroaches in the showers and kitchen. Peter sprays. Some nights cold. Cost twenty dollars per day to stay in camp; not bad."

We had just finished our second full pass and were back at the front. I looked down the length of the house we had just watered and before me lay a sea of green-filled white trays. All the trays were white; no pink trays. Marco's special seed trays were all in house #3.

It was getting hot and I noticed I was sweating heavily. Two large box fans built into the front wall of the house suddenly kicked on. They were attached to louvered doors and were sucking the hot air out of the house, pulling in cool outside air from open louvers at the far end. It took about a minute to feel the cool air pull through the house from the opposite end. After about ten minutes, the fans shut off. The house was noticeably cooler after that.

We made one more watering pass down and back and by then it was lunch time.

Julio left to find his lunch on the men's bus and I quickly ate the box lunch I remembered to bring with me from the hotel. After I finished eating, I walked quickly down the watering track and made my way to the back of the house. I opened the back door on the right and peered out over a grassy field. In the distance behind the field, I could see single-family homes in a residential neighborhood. I looked up to the right and behind to the northeast and I could see the roof of the back barn section of the seed house. That structure was not as long as the house I was in, so in order to see the back of the seed barn, I had to walk out around the back corner of the house and look back up toward the front of the houses. I quickly saw what I expected to see; a small wooden door at the bottom right corner of the seed barn. Jackie had presented a similar doorway in the discovery session.

I'd been away long enough so I went back into the house and walked to the front and out the front door. Julio was not back from lunch yet, so I walked over to the #5 seed house and noticed the front door was locked with the padlock. Now I understood what the expression 'locks were for honest people' meant. A dishonest person would have no trouble slicing the plastic with a knife and stepping right into the house. A padlock on a plastic greenhouse was a modest constraint keeping most of us out.

Peter and Julio came driving up together in the truck and Peter announced to us both we would be watering in the #3 house all afternoon. I looked at my watch and it was 12:31.

That afternoon Julio and I watered together, side by side up and down the house mostly in silence. The spray nozzles on the watering machines in this house were adjusted to spray an even finer mist of water onto the trays. This was to prevent the spray from knocking the BB-sized seed out of the small pots, as many had not yet taken root into the soil. As I made my way slowly down the track pushing the watering machine, I could see an occasional pallet of pink trays we had seeded by hand the day before.

I had lots of time to think. I thought not so much about Marco and the strain, but about this whole scenario I found myself in. Here was this huge farming enterprise owned by a very wealthy man who was never here, run by a proxy foreman in a pickup truck. The employees were migrant workers making minimum wage, skilled high school and college-age kids who were experienced and also making a minimum wage, and school children, ages 14 and 15 who were paid a child farm wage (so I learned from Jackie). I hadn't seen any kids yet, but I remembered the screen shots from Jackie's presentation vividly. No unions, no health benefits, poor working conditions, poor pay, yet operations like this were purely legal and normal for this industry. The thing getting to me the most was the inequity. I couldn't help thinking the owners of places like this had a free hand to ride off into the sunset with all their profits while the poor men and young children doing all the hard work were slaving in miserable conditions for peanuts. I knew we were living in modern times, but here, this place and this industry in Connecticut was a holdout from another era. I was not in a position to do anything about it; I had my job to do. Alondra would have a field day if she were here.

It took four hours to make the two round trip passes with the watering machines. I was tired; I would never have imagined how much energy was expended by purposefully walking slowly. Shooting a glance at the seed house, I climbed into the Prius to head back to the hotel. The idea was to shower and make my way to the bar for dinner, then wait for the darkness of night. I had big plans tonight which meant no gin and tonics for me, until afterwards. Maybe two or three afterwards if all went well.

Chapter 16

My Prius had a feature that would serve me well tonight. It was a plug-in. If fully charged, the car would run silently on battery mode for about 12 miles. I needed the car to run from the battery tonight. Earlier I had no trouble finding an empty parking spot with a ground plug near the front entrance. The battery was fully charged so I unplugged the charge cord, coiled it and stowed it away in the back of the car.

I glanced at my watch; it was 9:40. It was a very dark moonless night, cool in the low 50's with no wind. The stars were out. If all went well I'd be back in 20 minutes.

The plan was to drive slowly back to the shop and park near the vehicles in the yard. I would continue up the gravel path by foot to the #4 house where Julio and I were working that morning. I would enter the #4 house and make my way to the back and out the door, circle back around to the rear of the seed shed and enter it through the small wooden door. That door and the one inside the shed that led into the seed house were lock-free; at least I didn't remember seeing locks on either door.

I was taking a big chance, but felt it was worth it. If I didn't take action I might be waiting for days to get back into the seed house. Those files might hold the key, especially the XXXX folder. It was definitely worth a shot.

In the covert training classes, instructors frowned on these kinds of engagements. The whole idea was to behave within normal parameters in a scam. For me to be sneaking around at night with a penlight was way outside the norm. James Bond activities were discouraged because the price of discovery was too high. So the rule was if these kinds of activities were inevitable, you needed a cover of some sort in the event you were exposed.

My cover for tonight would be that I had lost my wallet. If I was caught in the #4 house, I lost it that day during lunch. If I was discovered in the #5 seed house I could say that I lost it the first day and hadn't noticed it because I was really tired and charged dinner to my room that night. Both versions were flimsy at best, but I was confident no one would notice a black Prius, parked in the yard near all the other vehicles, especially on a night as dark as tonight.

It took just a minute to drive down Night Valley Road to the shop. I turned quietly into the yard and immediately killed the lights, coasting to a stop in front of a Ford tractor parked in the yard. Before climbing out, I took my wallet and placed it under the seat. I didn't want it on me in case I was caught and had to use the cover story. I also turned off the dome light so I could open the door without the light coming on in the car. I sat in the dark car for a full five minutes with the windows down listening and searching for movement. Nothing. When my eyes were fully adjusted to the dark, I opened the door, stepped out and carefully shut it so as not to make any noise.

I wore my blue windbreaker and dark jeans. I was pretty sure no one would notice me walking up to the houses in the pitch black night. I followed the path up to the greenhouses and decided to walk past the #4 house up to the seed house just to make sure the door was locked first.

It was, so I doubled back quickly and entered the #4 house. It was very dark, but I could make out the darkened water track between the mostly white trays. I just had to walk on the track, keeping in the middle all the way to the end of the house. I walked slowly and carefully so I wouldn't trip. The door was on the back wall to the right. I found it easily and opened it slowly making sure I was alone and clear to exit. All looked good so I exited and moved around the house and made my way through the grass to the back of the seed shed about 50 yards away.

The shed was a dark red color that looked black in the darkness. I had to use my penlight to find the small door. I saw the hinges first. The door had a wooden button clasp that turned in a grooved flange on the shed, and that clasp kept the door closed. The small penlight flashed a tight beam and cast enough light, but having never seen anything like this clasp, I fumbled with it for a few seconds before the door finally swung open. Before I stepped into the shed, I crouched down and listened intently. No sounds other than an intermittent tree frog and an occasional faint swoosh of a car on Night Valley Road some 200 yards toward the front of the house.

Although I was cleared to go, I had significant doubts. I could turn back now and cut the risk of being caught. I was tempted. John and the review board would be livid if I was caught and lost this job. Then again, I needed to act and was sure I could get in and out of the house without a problem.

So I went for it. I stepped over the foot-high threshold and into the deep blackness of the shed. I was immediately swallowed by a damp musty darkness. I switched on my penlight again and cupped it in my hands carefully so the beam shot only a small spot of light on the brown dirt floor in front of me. I crouched down low and was sure the light could not be seen from outside the shed. I made my way slowly through the darkness toward the greenhouse door. I noticed gray metal piping was laid down through the shed in the center and open hose fittings were spaced regularly in the pipe. This must have been for the gas lines carrying the propane or natural gas to the stoves that heated the tobacco for curing.

Before long I was at the end of the shed and looking at the wooden door in the center leading into the seed house. I went up to the door and examined it carefully with the penlight. I noticed it was slightly warped and not shut tightly against the jam. I could see only a crack of darkness in the seed house. As I thought, there was no lock on the door, so I opened it slowly and slipped into the house.

The air changed from a cool musty to a warm fragrant humid. The dark green plants in the house made for an even stranger picture, as the penlight cast shadows from the large leaves into the dirt rows in front of me. I found the first wide row between the first two rows of tobacco on the east side of the house where the furnace would be at the other end. I took that row and began to walk in a low crouch brushing up against large tobacco leaves on both sides. I used the penlight sparingly, as some faint ambient starlight was filtering in from above through the clear plastic roof.

As I approached the furnace I heard its familiar rumble gradually growing louder. The furnace was on, but what I heard was mostly the fan noise. Then I was upon it. I took care to stay low and circle around the back side of the furnace to keep away from the front of the house. I was soon crouching on my knees in front of the file cabinet.

I quietly pulled open the cabinet and used the penlight to carefully play the tight beam across the folder tabs. I recognized the same folders I saw the day before. This time with an understanding of the coding, I quickly eyed the labeling pattern present on the top of the folders. The folders were numbered in order from 1 to 48, except #13 was missing. There too was the XXXX folder in the back of the file, next to the #48 folder.

I had three specific goals tonight once I got to this point. One, I would see what was in a normal folder and two, review the XXXX folder. I also needed to know if the folders represented the data for the seed planted and harvested in years past or for the current planting season.

I selected a middle folder, #25, and dropped it onto the floor, open in front of me. Kneeling on the dirt floor and carefully spraying the penlight onto the open pages, I reviewed the material for a long five minutes. These folders pertained to the past two years' strains.

There was what looked like a standard template form used to describe features of the strain. A date section indicated the date of seeding, planting, all pickings and firing dates; the last date being the date the tobacco was taken down as cured tobacco. There were checkmarks and comment space for leave size, thickness, aroma, taste, weight, stretch, color and cure. There were also designations for total hands of cured tobacco, total weight and the shed number where the tobacco was fired. It looked like pretty standard stuff.

I replaced the strain #25 folder back into the cabinet, and pulled out and examined folder #26. More of the same.

It was evident from the data in the folders the strains had been labeled with the same codes each year. That meant the strains were planted in the same field location the past two consecutive years in a row. It was conceivable then, the strains Marco was raising for this year's crop would also be planted in the same field locations.

I replaced the strain #26 folder and turned my attention to the XXXX folder. I reached into the back of the cabinet and pulled it out, placing it on the ground in front. I opened it to find the same template form, but it was blank, except for this code sequence, written in black magic marker near the top of the form:

13BL-NW-0-0-2-192

The XXXX folder referenced the #13 strain. It made some sense then, for the #13 strain to be missing from the ordered sequence of folders. But if that was the case, where was the real #13 folder with all the information for this strain? Unless there was no #13 strain folder and no information for it because it wasn't a normal strain.

The 'BL' designation represented the first two letters of the field name. I needed to learn where the 'BL' field was as there was a strong probability this special strain might be planted in the same location this year. I needed to ask Julio or maybe start a discussion with Kevin. They would know where this field was. If we couldn't find the seed, maybe we could find the plants.

I was done here. I looked at my watch; it was 10:07. I carefully replaced the XXXX folder back in the file and silently closed it. I stood up and walked around the front of the house, choosing the middle aisle to walk back this time because it was wider than the side aisle. That was my mistake.

As I crossed the center of the house toward the middle aisle the overhead grow lights suddenly clicked on, filling the whole house with bright fluorescent light, as bright as day, blinding me momentarily.

"Oh crap," I said out loud.

I froze there. I stood motionless for what seemed like forever, but it was only five seconds, thinking what's the point, you're out in the open totally exposed. Whoever turned on the lights knows you're here. But nothing happened. Not a sound was heard except the rumble of the furnace fan. No one was here. I looked back at the front door and then I saw it, to the right of the door. There was a motion detection switch that activated the lighting if someone entered the house at night. Didn't think of that.

I had to get out of the house fast. Leaving the lights on I dashed in a panic the length of the house, being careful not to break any leaves. I dashed through the back door into the seed shed. The shed was in total blackness as my eyes were no longer accustomed to the dark. I used the penlight openly now and ran back through the shed quickly and out the small door. Finally outside, I abandoned the #4 house exit idea. Using the penlight to guide my way, I turned back and ran through the grass between the shed and house #4 up to the front of the houses. The lights in the seed house were still on and I hoped no one saw me running past the front side of the lighted house. I jogged down the gravel road back to the Prius, jumped in and drove silently out of the yard on battery power, lights off.

As I headed back to the hotel on Night Valley Road, I looked back and stole a long glance at the seed house. Just at that moment, the lights in the house snapped off. Lights must be on a short timer I thought; *no motion, no light.*

That's exactly the way I felt.

Chapter 17

Marco Pinto lived in a red cape at the end of a private gravel road in the town of Granby, Connecticut. From the outside, the house was unremarkable but inside it was quite different. The interior of the house was authentic post and beam. Marco didn't have many visitors, but those he had would marvel at the beautiful pine timbers and the oak bracing throughout the house. Marco was proud of his home and eager to show it off. The contrast between the plain cape exterior and the beautiful wooden beams inside always prompted robust reactions and unique conversation.

He would have another opportunity for show and tell tonight because he had invited Becky Sadler from the experiment station for dinner. Marco had given her detailed driving instructions to find the house. GPS systems only worked as far as the mailboxes at the top of a half-mile gravel road. That road had a few twists and turns through the woods but if she followed the directions she would find the house.

He was reluctant to admit to Becky he hadn't cooked the meal. He was only warming it up; a caterer had dropped it off earlier with warming instructions. He had already set the table with the best china and silver. Marco hated cooking, but he was anxious to show Becky his house and maybe, if all went well, some of his experimental plant work in the basement.

He had known Becky for almost two months and was

becoming very fond of her. They had formed a much closer bond in recent weeks at the experiment station; she seemed eager to learn more about tobacco straining and that pleased Marco to no end. Finally, an attractive and intellectually stimulating woman was interested in his work. He wasn't sure where this would lead, but he thought there might be a possibility it could be serious. She was ten years younger and that in itself was a compelling reason to wonder if their friendship could be more; finally an eligible woman was in his life with the potential to rekindle closeness and sexuality. He wasn't sure he could trust her with everything, but tonight he would take a step in that direction.

With the chicken cordon bleu, side vegetables and rice safely in the oven, Marco took the stairs down into the finished section of the basement and walked across the game room to a side door. He opened the door and entered his basehouse.

The basehouse was Marco's name for the greenhouse in the basement. As he entered he was greeted by the sweet smell of plants and the warm humid atmosphere of the tropics. Florescent grow lighting completely covered the eight-foot ceiling casting a day-bright green glow from the light reflecting off the plants. Lush bright green vegetation was rising from 30 foot-long hydroponic beds running the length of the room. Filtered and nutrient-laden water bubbled through an elaborate piping system adding an acoustical ambiance to the tropical scene.

There were six separate Plexiglas troughs on the left side of the room for tobacco and on the right side were two additional troughs for marijuana. Marco found the step stool and climbed up to reach the top of one of the tobacco plants. With a small clipper, he quickly cut off the tops from the flowering plant making a small hand of the trumpet shaped light-yellow flowers. This would be for the table setting.

At that moment, he heard the loud driveway alarm. He looked over to the PC screen on the table next to the door to see Becky's Subaru pulling into the top of the driveway.

Living in this house at the end of a half-mile gravel road meant he was living in seclusion. To counter that he installed the driveway camera and had it linked to his Wi-Fi. He had screens in his bedroom, the kitchen, the basehouse and even could view cars entering on his iPhone.

He jumped off the step stool and ran up the stairs to set the flowers in a small vase before she could walk around to the back door. He set the vase with the bouquet of flowers in the center of the table.

He had a front door, but he never used it. The back door was the main entryway for the house because that path to the house overlooked a 20-acre field just next to the back yard. Not to use the back door deprived visitors of a beautiful view of the field and a small mountain in the distance. In another minute, she was at the back patio door ringing the bell.

She greeted him smiling as most first-time visitors did. They shook hands and after a moment's hesitation hugged warmly.

"Marco, it is beautiful here! And I love the post and beam," she said looking around the room. "Here, I brought you a bottle of wine. I hope you like it." She handed him the wine.

"Ah, thank you!" Marco replied as he took the wine from her and set it on the table. "You didn't have to do that. I see you brought a red, a Pinot Noir. This will go well with what we're having tonight. How did you know I like Pinot Noir?"

"I think you mentioned it once a few weeks ago. It smells so good in here. What have you cooked for us?"

"It's a surprise. You'll find out soon enough. Should I open this?" he asked holding up the bottle.

"I'd like that. Pinot Noir is my favorite too."

Marco went to a small drawer in the corner and took out a corkscrew and proceeded to crank open the wine. He looked at the label as he pulled out the cork. "Mark West. Don't think I've ever had that," he said.

The post and beam house had one giant room on the first floor, separated by furniture into four distinct rooms. The corner they were standing in was a newly renovated kitchen, surrounded by green granite and cherry cabinets.

"I love your house. It's beautiful; so different with all the wood. I love the granite too." Becky eyed the stove in the island and saw the temperature was set to only 200 degrees. She also saw nothing in the sink to indicate any food preparation had taken place.

Marco took two wine glasses out of the cabinet and said, "Let's go to the living room with our wine." He walked across the room to the opposite corner and placed the glasses down on the wooden coffee table in front of the couches. There, two green leather couches were pointed at a large flat-screen TV set diagonally into the corner of the room. Becky took one couch and Marco the other. He poured the wine into both glasses and handed Becky a glass.

They sat and chatted while sipping the wine. Marco liked the way Becky held her wine glass. She wasn't overly attractive, but she had a certain feminine quality when she smiled that reminded Marco of his first wife.

It wasn't long before the topic of strains came up in the conversation.

"So how did you get involved with tobacco straining?" she asked.

"About three years ago I was at an agriculture conference in San Francisco and I got to know Harold Treadwell, the owner. He was interested in crossing several of his top tobacco strains. I came out here on a small project at first. I had to prove myself I suppose; but right after the seed house was set up, under my supervision of course, he liked what he saw and made me an offer I couldn't refuse. Took a while for results; a whole growing season, in fact, but that didn't bother him. Have to admit I was pretty bored that first season. Then he started doing some other things and I helped them get started; greenhouse tomatoes and wholesale bromeliads, all different varieties. He even got heavy into pickle cucumbers; you know the small ones you can buy in a jar in the grocery store. Bromeliads are his latest thing and the tomatoes and cucumbers are still going strong."

Marco stood up and said, "I think the dinner is ready. Let's eat and after dinner we can continue our conversation."

Marco served the dinner which came out of the oven a little on the dry side as it had been warming for almost 30 minutes. It was still good though and Becky liked it.

"Marco, the cordon bleu was excellent; did it take you long to prepare this?" Becky smiled as she asked, wondering if Marco would come clean and admit the meal was brought in.

"Actually, I have to admit to you I'm no cook. Dinner tonight was compliments of a great chef at a restaurant called *Metro Bis* in Simsbury. I've had this dish before there and I thought you'd enjoy it too."

"Well thanks for telling me. It was delightful and I enjoyed it very much." With that, she reached over and put her hand on his. "The flowers, the place settings, and the food; this is really nice. Thank you so much for everything."

He rolled his hand over and they held hands and smiled warmly at each other for a few seconds before she pulled her hand and eyes away. He didn't want to rush things; he thought sharing a tender moment would be awkward, but it wasn't at all. It was then Marco knew this could be the beginning of something deeper.

Marco stood up from the table and said, "The wine was excellent too. Thank you for bringing it. Here, let's finish it." And he poured the remainder of the wine evenly into the two glasses.

"But first, I have another surprise for you," he said. "Follow me." He put his wineglass back down on the table and motioned her to follow him into the basement. She followed his lead and they both walked down the finished stairs and across the game room to the door of the basehouse. He stopped and turned back around to her.

"Becky, what you're about to see very few have seen before. I hope I can trust you to be discreet and not to broadcast anything you see tonight to anyone."

"You can trust me," she said with a big smile across her face. Still smiling she added, "And I hope I can trust *you* as I follow a handsome man into his basement on a treasure hunt."

"Good point," he smiled as he opened the door and they both stepped into the basehouse.

Becky was immediately awed by what she saw. She was familiar with hydroponics, but had never seen anything this professional or on this scale before.

Marco proceeded to give a guided tour of the hydroponic ecosystem explaining the complex feeding system built into the plumbing. The grow-lights were on computer-timed dimmers emulating nature; starting out low in the early morning and increasing in intensity, fully ON during the day then reversing the cycle in the evening. The humidity and temperature were regulated with day and night settings to match the perfect growing conditions for tobacco and marijuana. He strolled like a tour guide through the aisles of tobacco as he described the nuances of the various strains, with Becky following close behind.

Stopping next to one of the marijuana beds in the center of the house, he pointed to the ceiling and to the cheesecloth netting hanging between the lights and the tobacco plants.

"And here we have another element of realism added to emulate the truth. Cheesecloth nets provide just a bit of shade so we can test for proper leaf thinness, just like in the field."

Becky turned her attention to the beds of marijuana. "I see you have other interests besides tobacco."

"Yes, this is true. You see, Harold Treadwell is a realist. Marijuana is about to be legalized in the state of Connecticut, just like it was in Colorado last year. The General Assembly is voting on some amendments in a few weeks before the summer break. If those amendments pass, Harold will be in a great position to move into a new and more profitable business. What you see here are ten strains of marijuana, the most likely strains to thrive in the tobacco fields."

"But isn't all this highly illegal?"

"Well, it is and it isn't. Connecticut has a big medical marijuana program now and it won't be long before they approve recreational marijuana as they have in five other states. But today, Harold is willing to take a risk. You see now how important it is this secret stays a secret."

Marco turned to Becky, facing her and gently brought both hands up and touched her shoulders. He looked down at her affectionately and looked into her eyes for a long moment. She returned the stare. All they could hear were the bubbling hydroponics. He leaned down to her and kissed her gently on the lips. She didn't disappoint him in his affectionate moment; she kissed him back.

They parted, but he continued to hold her shoulders with both hands, "You also see it's not just Harold taking the risk here. This is my house and these are my plants. For all intents and purposes in the eyes of the law, if it ever came to that, I am taking the major risk here. You also need to know I think a lot of you Becky and I would never have brought you down here to share this if I thought for one second you would betray that trust."

Marco stepped back dropping his hands. He thought it might be better to change the topic and get to something lighter.

"So have you ever smoked marijuana?" he asked with a smile.

"Yes, but it was a long time ago." She played along, "Do you have any?" She smiled as she said it.

Marco answered, "Actually I don't have any ready to smoke. But maybe I should. We haven't experimented with curing it yet, only growing it."

"So what's the purpose having all these strains if you never smoke them to see how potent they are?" she asked.

"Well, it's like this. We hope to find the strain that grows best here in the Connecticut River valley. That means a number of criteria for us to look at. Take this one for example."

Marco went to the closest marijuana plant and reached in and fondled a handful of green leaves. "This strain is full and lush, but it's short and takes longer to grow than that one." He pointed across the aisle to a taller bush in the next bed.

"If marijuana sells by weight, we need to experiment to determine which specific criteria will yield better outcomes. That will help us decide which strains to grow in production, when the time comes. For example, do we need bushier growth, or taller growth to produce the best weight yield?"

"Well, I still think the potency of the strain is critical."

Marco replied, "I agree. We think we'll be able to charge more for more potent strains, but we have other methods to verify potency; we don't need to smoke samples to figure that out. Follow me."

Marco led the way to a large workstation nestled in the corner. Becky followed closely behind. He pointed to several instruments and other paraphernalia piled onto the workstation.

"This is our analysis station. We use the instruments and materials here mainly for marijuana analysis; occasionally with tobacco to measure pesticide content and absorption."

Becky eyeballed the station intently and pointed, "This is a mass spectrometer. That's a Vitamix high-speed blender, and that's a centrifuge. I think this rack holds solvents." She avoided comment on the computer and printer.

"Nice Becky. I would expect your familiarity knowing your line of work at the experiment station. We measure the marijuana's THC content and it gets a bit tricky accounting for volume and weight equality across the different strains, but I think we have that issue licked now."

Just then the driveway alarm sounded and Marco moved quickly back to the front of the room to the PC screen near the entryway.

"What's that?" she asked following him to the screen.

"Driveway alarm. Someone is coming down the driveway."

As they both looked at the screen a large black bear walked into view at the top of the driveway.

"It's mid-May; it's bear time. They're still hungry from

hibernation. I see them a lot in the spring. Looks like a big male. No worries. He'll cross into the back yard and walk across the field into the woods."

"I think that's so cool. Look at the size of him. This is the first bear I've seen in the wild," said Becky.

"You have excellent security here too."

"Yup, I need that because it's so secluded here. Let's go back up and finish our wine."

"Marco I really should be going. It's been wonderful. The dinner was super and your surprise here was definitely that, a real surprise."

"Okay. We're both working tomorrow so let's call it a night. I'll walk you out."

Once they were sure the bear was gone, Marco walked Becky out the back door and to her car at the top of the driveway. He faced her and gave her an affectionate hug.

"I hope I didn't scare you away. I'm very fond of you Becky."

"I'm fond of you too Marco. I hope we can see each other again soon," she said as she reached up and kissed him on the cheek.

She climbed into her car, started it, backed out of the spot and headed back down the wooded driveway. It was almost 8:00 p.m. and the sun was setting. Marco smiled and waved as he saw her lights flash on before she drove out of sight at the bottom of the driveway. He knew she hadn't seen him wave.

Chapter 18

As soon as Becky returned to her condo she went to the wine rack in the kitchen, opened a new bottle of Mark West Pinot Noir and treated herself to an exceptionally large pour. She then went straight to the music center in the living room and put on Jeff Beal's *House of Cards* soundtrack CD. She sat in her favorite spot on the living room couch, almost in the dark listening to the haunting music, thinking about the evening with Marco, what she learned, how she felt and what it all meant.

The third song of the album was playing: *I know what I have to do*. Tonight was her communication night; she texted encrypted status messages to John every three days.

She picked up her iPhone and sent the secure code to John Trane's private number in D.C. A confirmation number came back quickly meaning she was clear to send her message. She spent just a few seconds typing. When she was done she reviewed the text: *"Hope for sunshine to continue for the next three days. No change in the weather here*." She pressed SEND and the message was gone.

The message told John all was well and she would communicate again in three days' time; nothing had changed. She lied. The landscape had most definitely changed.

Chapter 19

I parked the Prius back in the same spot near the entrance in front of the electric plug I used earlier to charge the battery. With almost a full charge remaining, I decided not to plug it in. I was really tired and still a bit shaken from my adventure; I just wanted to get to the bar for a drink and call it a night. Before I exited, I remembered to retrieve my wallet I'd hidden under the passenger seat.

Not much activity was in the bar or the lounge on a Tuesday night at 10:15. I was all alone except for one middle-aged couple sitting at a booth in the lounge. The bartender was acting as the wait staff; the other staff was off duty. I needed some time to think about what I'd learned tonight and what the next steps were.

I made my way to the bar and sat and ordered a double gin and tonic, asking the bartender for a large glass, ice and tonic on the side and no lime. I wanted the gin almost full strength. Straight gin had a way of calming me down and I needed it tonight. I was not what you'd call an alcoholic, but I was known to be in the category of a stress drinker. From time to time in moments of extreme stress, like being captive on a commercial jet, or like a few minutes ago, snooping around at night in a lighted greenhouse, I was comforted by a quick hit of alcohol flashing through my veins gently numbing my brain; I could feel the stress dissipating. My problems were still there but in that state I could relax and push them back to deal with them later. The present was okay again, I could unwind and life was good.

As I sat I could feel my stress melting away as the double hit of gin began to do its trick. My thoughts about substance abuse were well known to me. I guess I was not alone in my use of alcohol as a stress reliever. I read somewhere 30 percent of Americans abuse alcohol. That's a big number. Was life becoming so complex for some of us, we just can't take it anymore? Think of all the productivity in the workplace wasted, the medical problems caused by the overuse of alcohol leading to billions wasted in health care and the drunk drivers who take innocent victims.

In covert training, they warned us what a scourge drinking was, that every day in America, almost 30 people are killed in drunk-driving related accidents. Thirty people every day. Hard to believe, but as I thought about it, maybe not. Say I had another drink or two, and I didn't live in the hotel. I'd climb into my Prius, now a lethal weapon and I'd weave my way home. Better not get in my way; if you do, tough luck for you. I bet that happens a lot. Too much in fact.

So they warned us to stay away from booze while running a scam because it clouded your thinking and that could lead to discovery, and other things. They were probably right but in this case, I was safe, my day was over and I'd soon be in bed.

I couldn't get away from my drinking tonight and the irony of this case. Here I am legally consuming this notorious substance called gin *that is known to be killing people*, while at the same time searching for an *illegal* strain of tobacco containing a marijuana-like substance that is thought to be less harmful than alcohol, and in many cases medicinally beneficial. What's wrong with this picture?

This was just another inequity in life I would never take personal responsibility for. I liked gin, it was legal, and I liked to drink. As far as the marijuana strain went, I had a job to do, was well paid to do it with an expense account to boot. I was taking care of me and that's all that mattered, right? Why should I feel responsible to right every wrong I happened to bump into along the way? The problem with this was too many of us were thinking the same way and we'd become, in a way, morally void of compass as a result; everyone in it for themselves.

It was getting late and I was getting depressed thinking so much. I signed the tab charging it all to my room, stood up from the bar and made my way across the lobby to the elevators.

I walked past the front desk and saw the night clerk I'd seen on duty the past four nights. He waved me over smiling so I stopped and noticed his nametag as I remembered it the previous times.

"Good evening Mr. Kraft."

"Hi Brendan. Were you waving me over?"

"Yes I was. I wanted to tell you your wife arrived and I gave her the key to your room."

"My wife?" I asked, careful not to show my surprise.

"Yes. She said you weren't expecting her until later, but she took an earlier flight. We knew you were out of the building; I had the bellhop look for your car in the lot."

I was intrigued. I was never married and didn't have a wife. I wanted confirmation on a hunch so I played along.

"Ah okay. Hey tell me something, my wife has really long black hair; at least she did last week. She's been thinking about cutting it. Did she?"

"No sir. She still has really beautiful long hair. She is a very attractive woman; I hope you don't mind me saying so."

"Not at all; she does have a way of turning heads. One more question, how long ago did she arrive?"

"About 30 minutes ago."

"Okay great. Thanks Brendan."

I turned and made my way to the elevators. I was instantly less tired and more awake than I was before, filled with a growing anticipation. Alondra was here and waiting for me in my room. I couldn't believe it.

The elevator opened to the fourth floor and I made my way to my door. Using the card key, I swiped the lock and heard the two soft beeps and the green light on the panel tell me the door was unlocked. I opened it only to be stopped by the security latch on the inside of the door.

"Hello!" I called out loudly. "Anybody home?"

"Just a minute," I heard her answer in that beautiful Hispanic accent. Next the latch was removed, the door swung open and there was Alondra standing before me. She still had her coat on. She was beautiful. I could not believe my luck.

"Hello sweetheart," she said with a tiny smile. "I hope you don't mind, but I told the young man at the desk I was your wife. He slipped me a key when the manager wasn't looking. Is a wonder what you can get away with for twenty bucks these days.”

“Some wishful thinking on your part? I mean the part about being my wife?” I smiled.

“Maybe,” she said. “We’ll have to find out won’t we. Why don’t you come here and say hello to me?”

I knew saying hello meant kissing her hello.

“I will, but why are you standing here with your coat on?”

“I just got here and I haven’t taken it off yet,” she responded. “I’ll take it off, but first I wanted to tell you this is not purely a social call. I’m here on official FBI business. I’ve been assigned to the TobaccoNet case too and we’re working together on it from now on.”

“Nice of the board to tell me, don’t you think? No one thought adding you to the case with me might be a conflict of interest? I mean based on our past?“

“I’m sure they know nothing about our past Jason. And I certainly wasn’t going to tell them and spoil it for us. I was the obvious choice for the assignment as I’d already done work for the bureau on the case in Puerto Rico. They were on the fence about it, but I pushed for it and here I am.”

I actually was pleased I was working with Alondra again on a case but it was rather unusual that one, no one at the DEA communicated this and I was the last to know and two, Alondra sneaks into my room like a spy without any advance warning; although I didn’t really think this was a negative and I was glad she was here, but it was still strange.

“They didn’t tell you because this was decided late this

afternoon by the ops coordinator in Quantico and it was after 7:00 and most had gone home so the DEA hasn't been fully informed. Your handlers don't know yet. I took it upon myself to take the first plane out of Dulles so we could be together tonight before my morning briefing. So you can blame me. Feel any better? Now are you just going to stand there in the doorway or are you coming in?"

I walked into the room and the door closed behind me. We stood facing each other in the small hallway between the door and the room. She reached up and put both hands on my cheeks. Her small hands were warm. Her naturally tan skin and flowing black hair were just what I remembered.

"You look great. Say hello to me," she said softly.

Our lips touched and I found myself sinking into her warm embrace. She pulled away and quickly released the top button of her coat. In less than one second her covering dropped away and she was standing before me naked. So that's why she had her coat on and she didn't just arrive, as I knew from the man at the desk. I held her tightly again and I walked her silently backward toward the bed.

In another hour she was asleep but I lay awake silently watching her breathe, thinking about the last tender hour we'd shared, the day's events, and where I was going in my life in general. Living a scam meant living in two distinct worlds, my own true world and the one I was infiltrating. Only two days into this scam; I'd made great progress and picked up yet another world along the way. Now there were three realities I needed to make sense of. I needed to close my eyes; 6:00 a.m. would come fast.

Chapter 20

The next morning in the hotel came and went with Alondra waking just enough to give me a passionate kiss good morning. I was alone in the breakfast room at 6:45 to grab breakfast and the box lunch.

At 6:55 I pulled into the yard and parked with the other cars just as Peter Roscoe pulled in with his truck and did his classic slide and stop trick. He was out quickly and as Marco was AWOL again, I was anticipating another day in the greenhouses, watering seeded trays. When the others had dispersed, he looked over to Kevin and called both of us over.

"Jason, you get a reprieve today from the greenhouses. Kevin, I want you and Jason to take the green truck to Broad Brook and pick up the machines.

"Kevin, sorry, have you met Jason yet?"

"Nope," Kevin said. "I've seen him around, but we've never met."

Peter responded, "Kevin meet Jason. Jason is a teacher working with us for the summer. Jason, meet Kevin. Kevin is my right-hand man."

We shook hands.

Peter turned to Kevin, "You remember where the machine company in Broad Brook is, right?"

"Yup." Kevin responded.

"You'll need to take three trips. There are 39 machines and the truck will hold 13 each trip. I want you to put the machines on poles in the #2 shed. This will take you all morning. I'll check back with you around lunchtime. All set?"

"Got it," Kevin said.

"Kevin, one more thing. Did you leave the seed shed doors open yesterday? I found both doors, the outside one, and the inside one wide open this morning."

"No sir. I haven't been in the seed house at all this week. I have no idea who was in the seed house yesterday. Did you ask Marco?"

"No, he's been spending time at the experiment station and hasn't been around. Okay, must have been the neighborhood kids then. I didn't think we needed to put locks on those doors, but I guess we do."

With that, Peter got back into his truck, exited the yard and drove up Night Valley Road, leaving Kevin and me standing there all alone in the yard.

We made our way to the green truck parked in the yard, Kevin taking the driver's side and me as his passenger. As we climbed up into the truck we had to wipe the morning dew away from the vinyl-covered bench seat and the windshield with our sweatshirt sleeves. Someone had left the windows open the day before. The green truck was basically a small dump truck with foot-tall wooden sides that could be removed to create a flatbed truck. It was one of the newer trucks in the fleet and was in decent shape.

Kevin turned the key, started the truck and we lumbered over to the side of the #2 shed that was behind the yard.

“First we have to dump the sides off. We need the flatbed.”

We both climbed out of the truck and each took ahold of one end of the wooden side on the driver’s side and lifted it off the truck, dumping it onto the ground. We repeated the action for the other side of the truck. Climbing back in, we lumbered off through the yard as Kevin shifted through the gears.

We were on the highway headed for Broad Brook before I started up with my questions for Kevin. I had no idea what we were doing, having no notion of ‘machines’ Peter had referenced earlier. So I asked him.

“Kevin, I have to admit I have no concept of where we’re going or what machines are. Where is Broad Brook? Can you fill me in?”

“Sure,” he said. “Broad Brook is about 20 minutes from here. The machines are these very expensive Swedish-made sewing machines the girls use to sew the tobacco leaves onto string attached to four-foot wooden sticks called lath. The lath holding the tobacco gets hung in the shed. Every winter our machines are cleaned and serviced by this small company in Broad Brook. I drive them there in the fall and pick them up in the spring. Been doing it for three years now.”

“Cody told me you’re a lifer.”

“I guess you could say that. I started here when I was 13 years old picking tobacco. Kind of graduated through the years to the assistant foreman position, but Peter will never tell you that; there is no such position. I'm a senior in college now, so this is my last year, or maybe next year will be after I graduate. Haven't decided yet."

We were off the highway now bouncing along on a country road driving east. The visors helped some but not enough. There wasn't a cloud in the sky this morning and it was difficult to see as we drove eastward into the sun. Today would be a warm day; especially in the greenhouses.

"What are you planning on doing after you graduate?" I asked.

"I want to go to medical school, but that depends on the financing, I mean the scholarships. My parents can't afford to send me on their own so if I go, it will be on me, almost all of it. Don't know if you know anything about medical school tuition these days but it's huge, like 80 plus thousand per year. Not sure I want to quadruple my student loan debt which is already big. I'll have a BS degree in molecular biology with a minor in plant genetics, from UMASS."

I saw an opportunity to poke so I took it.

"So you minored in plant genetics. That's cool. Have you had a chance to work with Marco yet with any of his tobacco strain development?"

"Yeah, I have. We all have in fact. I spent some time last year in the early spring with him, but my involvement was limited. Cody spent time with him too. Marco's a weird guy you know. He has this plan to create the best tobacco in the valley. His goal is to increase Treadwell's cured tobacco weight by 10 percent. If he succeeds, Harold will pay him a huge bonus. He never confided in me what it was, but I know it's substantial."

“I took biology in college a long time ago, but I have no direct knowledge of plant genetics. But seeing some of this in action is intriguing,” I said.

“Well, you’re not really seeing it in action. If Marco was a bit more out in the open with his strain crossing program you’d be seeing more. Fact is, what you see in the seed house is only the resulting strains. He doesn’t do any interesting work in the seed house; no pollinating or anything like that. He only grows the final strains there.”

I felt I might be onto something so I kept at it.

“Well I don’t really care, but if the seed house isn’t where the real strain work is, then where is it?”

“That’s an interesting question,” replied Kevin as we bounced along. We had been traveling now for almost 10 minutes so I figured we were about halfway there.

Kevin continued, “At first I thought he was crossing strains at the experiment station. But later I found out, and please don’t tell him I told you cause he’d probably freak out and never trust me again, that he has a hydroponic garden in the basement of his house. He must be doing some pretty sophisticated strain crosses there.”

“Wow, that’s cool.”

My response belied my true feelings about this discovery. I remained quiet so not to appear too anxious.

We continued to bounce along on a country road now. It was obvious to me Kevin was an excellent driver, and handled the big truck perfectly. We had turned north so the sun was no longer in our eyes.

"Yeah and that's not all I hear. I've never been to his house, but I've heard from more than one source he has marijuana growing there too."

"Really. Recreational marijuana is illegal in this state isn't it?"

"Yes, but probably not for long. Medicinal marijuana is already legal.

"Remember Marco doesn't do anything unless Harold authorizes it. Harold's got a pretty tight leash on things even if he's never here. So he's probably getting ready for the day marijuana gets legalized, and he's got Marco growing some pot in preparation. Doesn't take a rocket scientist to figure that one out."

"Do you know if Peter's ever been to Marco's house?"

"I don't know, you'd have to ask Peter that one. I did tell him about his basement and he wasn't happy about it. Peter hates Marco, has from day one. Tried to talk Harold out of hiring him back in the beginning. Kind of a competition going on between those two for Harold's attention. Marco will definitely win that battle, and that really pisses Peter off."

"Why do you say that?"

"Harold thinks Marco holds the key to future; I've heard him say it, more than once. It doesn't matter Peter is doing ten times the work Marco does. Marco gets away with doing almost nothing; runs back and forth between here and the experiment station like a prima donna tending to his seed house. And get this, they make the same salary!"

"Of course this conversation is just between us Kevin, but I gotta ask, how do you know that?"

"No worries, I'll tell you. Harold has an office in his house in the basement. One day last spring Peter asked me to take his snow tires out of his garage and put them in the basement. There was a ping-pong table there and lying right on the table was a big ledger book of some kind with all the salaries written in. It was lying on the table wide open. I couldn't help but notice that Marco and Peter's salaries were the same."

"Do these two guys ever really go at it?" I asked.

"You mean as in a fight?"

"Yeah."

"No, Marco just keeps being Marco and that pisses Peter off. Peter's always griping about small stuff; Marco really gets under his skin. Nothing serious, but Peter has a temper and one of these days he's going to explode. You can count on that. I try to stay out of it and just do my job. They're both considered to be my manager so I have to answer to both really, but Peter has the overall authority and Marco never really challenges Peter. Marco is kind of a wuss and I see him totally backing down if there is ever any real confrontation. Peter just thinks Marco's contribution is small and brings such little value we'd be better off without him."

"What do you think?"

"I don't know. I guess if Marco succeeds and makes his 10 percent weight and quality target improvement, it might be worth what to Harold... say $500K? That's a lot more than he makes so I'd have to say it might be worth keeping him around. In any case, measuring that will be difficult."

"That's a good point. Thanks for sharing this with me Kevin." I was impressed with Kevin's knowledge, his opinions, and his communication skills. Julio was right, Kevin was very smart.

"No problem Jason. I have a lot of time to think working here."

We continued on for a while in silence until Kevin said, "Here's the machine building up ahead on the right."

Kevin pulled the truck into the small parking lot and proceeded to back the truck up to a closed garage door. He left it running and just as he climbed out he said to me, "Wait here. The staff usually loads the truck; they take responsibility for the tie-down. We may not have to do anything here."

He shut the door and soon the garage door opened behind me. Watching from the side mirrors, I could see several men carrying the strange looking metal objects on black frames, which I assumed were the machines. Each machine was at least ten feet long. They slid them one by one onto the back of the flatbed, lashing them together and tying them to the truck with a thick rope. In about ten minutes, the truck was completely loaded and Kevin was back in the driver's seat.

"Okay, now we drive back, but this time we drive more slowly. Precious cargo aboard. Each one of those machines costs 15 thousand dollars."

He put the truck in gear and eased away from the building.

"Ever had any trouble driving these machines back to the farm?" I asked.

"Not me, but a few years ago Walter was driving this very truck with a load of machines. He went over a large bump. The dump engaged and the back of the truck came up on him while he was driving. He dumped the whole load of machines on the road. He kept driving for about a hundred yards before he realized it. About half those machines were ruined. Good thing it was Walter and not one of us."

"Why do you say that?"

"Walter is Harold's uncle. Peter was ripping mad, but it really wasn't his fault. Walter was in his late seventies at the time. You can still see him around doing odd jobs around the greenhouses and in the fields, always with a cigar in his mouth."

Kevin was driving much slower with the load of machines now. This would add to our travel time which was fine with me. We were driving southwest so the drive was much more pleasant without the sun blinding us.

"I remember Harold was all upset because insurance didn't cover the machines and he had to spend a fortune fixing them. I think five or six had to be replaced; kept the broken ones for scrap parts. That would have broken some small farms, but not Harold. That man has real deep pockets."

"What do you think he's worth?"

"I have no idea, but it's a lot. The farm has about 300 acres in and about Sunbridge. Then you can't forget the property he owns too. There are five houses here on the farm he owns and rents out. Then there's his own house in

Sunbridge center, a beautiful old colonial, one of the nicest houses in town. After that, let's move on to the two vacation homes, one in Sonoma, California, and the other in Boca Raton, Florida. I know for a fact the house in Sonoma is incredible."

I was being prompted to ask for more so I did. "How do you know about the Sonoma house? Ever been there?"

"No, but a good friend of mine was, Reed O'Bannon. He's not with us anymore; he died last year of a brain tumor."

"Oh, sorry to hear that. Were you guys close?" I asked.

"Yeah we were. We grew up together and were best friends since we were twelve years old. We used to work together here on the farm. He went to UCONN and I was at UMASS, but every summer we'd work on the farm together. It was really sad here last year when he passed away. I lost my best friend.

"That last week we all chipped in, each donating three hours of our pay so Reed could stay home and rest. He died that Friday night and I gave Pam, his fiancée, the check at the wake. I visit his gravestone in the center of town quite a bit. I miss him a lot."

Kevin was silent for a few minutes; I looked over and could see his eyes tearing up. He quickly snapped out of it.

"You wanted to know about the Sonoma house. I'll tell you. Before he died Reed and his fiancé Pamela took a cross country trip. I think Reed knew he didn't have much time left; the chemotherapy wasn't working and this was their last chance to see the country. Harold knew about the trip and was kind enough to give Reed and Pam the keys to the

Sonoma house before they left. So they drove all the way out there and stayed at the house. It was supposed to be secret, but I found out after they got back. He described this incredible property to me; must be worth a fortune. Not only that, the house was filled with period antiques. Mr. Treadwell is doing just fine; cigar-wrapper tobacco is a cash crop and Treadwell's got all the cash."

"I'm sorry for your loss Kevin."

"I've been doing all the talking and you've been quiet. I know this is your first week because Cody told me, so tell me, how do you like your first week here?"

"I've become an expert watering plants in Marco's seed house and with the watering machines in the #3 and #4 houses. That's the extent of my experience here, so far."

"I'm surprised Peter has you doing that. We all guessed you'd be with Marco pulling seed and logging strains in the seed house. Peter usually reserves the watering operation to a few trusted men."

"Oh, you mean Julio?" I asked.

"So you know Julio already? He's a great guy. So full of positive energy and smart too. He'll go far if he ever gets a job in the real world."

The truck was bouncing over some rough spots and Kevin carefully slowed, making his way around some dips in the road, undoubtedly left over frost heaves from this year's horrible winter.

"Julio and I were discussing unions yesterday in fact. He said I should ask you about it."

"Unions? Don't get me started. Unions will never get in here, and that's not to say they shouldn't. Every year they try and fail. They have no organization, no way to fight. Every time someone tries to organize from within, the owners squash them."

"How do they squash them?" I asked.

"Simple. They fire their ass, toss them out and bring in replacements. Momentum lost.

"My dad works in a big manufacturing plant. They have unions, a Human Resources department, rules and regulations, you name it, they have it. Protection. They just can't get rid of people.

"These men here, most of whom don't speak English, are lucky to have a job at all. They pay them minimum wage and they're here by the grace of Carlos the men's boss and Peter. That's it. There is no personnel department, no HR, no second chance, no nothing. If they don't like you for any reason you're out.

"I remember once it was raining hard and it was cold, and the men were suckering the small tobacco plants. They'd given the men some cheap vinyl raincoats that were totally worthless. I was driving the bus that day, sitting in the driver's seat and one of the men came out of the field and got back on the bus. He was a big tall man and his raincoat had torn and he was soaking wet and covered with mud. Peter drove up in his truck, saw the guy, got out of his truck and came up the stairs into the bus and demanded the guy go back to the field. He refused. Peter fired him right then and there, stomped out of the bus and got back into his truck. I was watching the man behind me in the curved overhead mirror as I sat there. The guy covered his face with his hands and started sobbing. I will never forget that. That's one example why I see a need for unions here."

"Did you say anything to Peter that day?" I asked.

"Are you kidding me? I learned a long time ago never to question his authority. Peter is mostly a good guy and a pretty straight shooter. But he's got a military background and he expects you to jump on his command. I wanted to keep my job that day and every day, so I keep my mouth shut. Another reason we need union oversight.

"In that particular case, no harm done really; the guy showed up two days later and Peter gave him his job back. Peter has a heart. He must have been having a bad day."

I was quiet and Kevin kept talking.

"They have what I would call the perfect cycle here. School kids come in just long enough to make money, stick around three to five years to learn the ropes and become trained employees, then cycle out and get real jobs. No one is here long enough to make or demand any real change. Parents are happy because their sons and daughters are out of the house in the summer and making a few dollars. They don't realize what these kids are putting up with, though. Most parents think working tobacco builds character. Sometimes true, but for the most part, that line is bullshit."

"So in your opinion, Julio shouldn't bet on unions here."

"Not anytime soon. Not unless there's a coordinated effort from the outside looking in. Maybe not even then."

I was amazed at Kevin's insight. He obviously had an experience set very few others had and at a very young age.

We drove along in silence for a while, both of us deep in thought. I started thinking about Alondra and what she would say about what Kevin had just told me. I would tell her later at dinner. I wondered what she was up to; she had a morning briefing, but that left a lot of time afterward with nothing to do. She would find something; she was resourceful. I still didn't know how she was going to fit into the scam and what her expectation was. We hadn't discussed it.

We went over a rough bump and the machines slammed down hard on the back of the truck. Kevin flinched as he stole a glance in the side mirror.

"Suspension on this truck sucks. You can feel every bump," he said.

I figured I would carefully inch toward the questions I had about the strain coding. I wanted to find out where the #13BL strain was planted.

"I was working in the #3 house seeding the pink trays manually on Monday with Marco. He introduced me to the labeling mechanism he invented for marking the trays."

Kevin shot me a glance and said, "He told you *he invented* the labeling mechanism? Right. Why am I surprised? Truth is, I invented it. Two years ago, he wanted to track the strains after he planted them, so we could watch them grow in the field and mark the leaves later with tags. So I came up with this simple code where we could track the field and the exact location of the plants. But you have to be careful handling those trays; you have to plant those plants in the right spot. You know, follow the tractor in the field and give the crew the pink trays at just the right time. I'll bet I'm coordinating the strain planting again this season, five days from now."

It was as good a time as any to ask about the field names so I asked him, "I know the first two alpha letters in the code mark the field name. How many fields are here on the farm?"

"Not sure exactly, but Cody worked with Marco last year on the labeling and he printed a list of field names. I think there are about 20. I think he still has it somewhere. I'll get you a copy."

"That would be great. Thanks a lot."

"No problem." As he said that the iPhone in his pocket started ringing the marimba tone. He reached for the phone and with some difficulty, pulled it out of his pocket.

"Peter's calling. It's his ringtone," he said.

I listened to the one-sided conversation.

"Hi Peter. Yup. Nope, haven't gone by it yet."

There was a long pause while Kevin listened attentively. Then he started talking again, "In about two minutes, you called just in time. Sure. Okay, that works. Will do."

He ended the call.

"That was Peter. He wants me to stop at the experiment station on the way back and drop you off there. It's on the way; we're almost there. Marco needs you this afternoon. He's there now and you can ride back with him. I'll pick up Julio at the greenhouses and he can help me unload the machines."

I said, "Okay. What does Marco want me for, did Peter say?"

"He didn't say actually. I haven't got a clue."

"I've heard the term experiment station, but I don't know what that is. Can you tell me?"

"Yeah. It's a state-funded organization open to the public in support of all things agricultural. They have a branch in Windsor; we'll be there in a minute. They analyze soil samples and do analysis on pests and plant diseases, that kind of stuff. As long as you're a resident you can use them. My mother brought them a tiny deer tick she found on me once; they tested it for Lyme disease. Marco spends a lot of time there these days. Rumor has it he has a girlfriend who works at the station."

That Marco had a girlfriend was consistent with what I learned from the bartender.

I wondered what Marco wanted me for. I'd find out soon enough as Kevin announced, "We're here," as he pulled up to the front of a small white nondescript building with a sign over the door: *Connecticut Agricultural Experiment Station – Windsor Branch*.

"Thanks for your conversation Kevin. I didn't do anything to help you."

"No worries; some days are like the military: hurry up and wait. I'll make sure you get a copy of the field names, hopefully tomorrow. Good luck with Marco the Man. Don't forget to take your lunch."

As he said that he gave me a quick military salute. I grabbed my lunch bag, opened the door, slid down from the high seat and dropped to the curb. I closed the door and Kevin slowly rumbled off with the machine load.

I walked up the stone walkway to the door and it opened before I could reach for the latch on the screen door. Marco greeted me in the doorway, behind the screen.

"Hello Jason." Standing next to him was a woman in a white lab coat. Marco, grinning, made an introduction. "Jason I want you to meet Becky, my assistant."

She quickly punched him affectionately in the shoulder and said with a smile, "I am not your assistant."

I opened the screen door and reached in to shake Becky's hand. I took her hand and as I looked into her eyes for that quick second something registered, way back. She looked familiar, but I couldn't place her.

"Nice to meet you Jason," she said with a warm smile. "I've heard a lot about you."

"Nice to meet you too Becky." I didn't return the smile but kept a straight face.

Chapter 21

John Trane sat at his desk with the phone in his hand staring out the window at the park-like lawn. His computer was open next to him and displayed on the screen was an email he'd just received from the FBI team, sent late last night.

"Judy, come in here please."

In less than three seconds Judy Sparks, his executive assistant, pranced in from her outer office holding a steno pad and a pen. She wore a short blue skirt, black tights, and four-inch pumps with raised souls which made her six inches taller and gave her an awkward stride. She needed to walk this way to keep her balance.

"Notes not necessary Judy, I just want you to get me Bill Sweeney's number. I need to reach him ASAP."

"You know he's on vacation in Scottsdale. He does this every year."

"I know, I know. I just tried his cell. It must be turned off; it just rolls to his voicemail."

"He's probably still sleeping. I think Scottsdale is three hours behind us. So it will only be 5:45 in the morning there."

"Yeah. I'll try to reach him at the hotel. I don't think he'll mind if I wake him up for this. He'll be more upset if I don't call him. Do you remember where he's staying?"

"I think I remember Betty telling me he stays in the same place each year. Let me call her. I'll find out."

Four minutes later she came back in with the phone number for the Fairmont Scottsdale Princess Resort hotel.

"Here it is."

John took the number and punched it into his phone. The front desk answered the call immediately. "Yes, can you connect me with Bill Sweeney? He's staying at your hotel. Yes, William Sweeney. Thanks."

Bill was sleeping peacefully until the three phones in his room rang in unison. He didn't hear the phones until he felt his wife punching him in the shoulder. Reacting quickly, he jumped up and grabbed the wireless phone on the nightstand. The phone continued to ring, but he wanted privacy before answering so he made his way across the darkened room in his pajamas and slid open the curtains and the balcony door underneath. The sun had just come up. Closing the door, he found the phone's 'ON' button and pressed it.

It was John. "Good morning Bill. We're on a secure line. You know I wouldn't be calling you if this wasn't important. Sorry to wake you but I'm sure you'd want me to."

"No problem John. You did the right thing. What's going on?"

"It's TobaccoNet. We've got real trouble I'm afraid. The feds are into it now."

"How? Tell me more."

"I got an email this morning from the FBI team assigned to governance on the case. The unit leader is a guy named Nick Parsons."

"Yeah, I know him. He's a pain in the ass."

"In his email he says they've activated an agent on the case, an active field agent, a woman in fact."

"Damn it, John," Bill said. "I was afraid of that. I had a conversation with him late last week in our update meeting and he told me they were on the fence and they were getting close to making a decision about jumping in. I begged him for more time and he said he'd speak with the other committee members and would try to get them to hold off. I told him we were placing a new resource in the field and we were expecting excellent progress. I honestly thought I'd convinced him to hold off."

As Bill talked he looked down from the fourth floor at the South Pool of the resort. The balcony looked out through the tops of several tall palm trees. Looking through the large palm fronds he could see the mountains in the distance. The sun had just come up and a hotel staffer was hosing down the brick walkways next to the pool. It was already 70 degrees and today was projected to be hot with a clear sky, an excellent pool day.

John responded, "Well they're jumping in. They're using the same agent they used down in Puerto Rico, a woman named Alondra Espinoza. I don't know how Jason will react to this, but I need to get to him right away. He knows this woman; he worked a case once with her a while back I think. We've got to get him on board and let him know before he finds out on his own. He'll start to suspect something if he runs into her before we can tell him first. He won't be too happy about it I'm sure."

John continued, "When you talked with Parsons last week, did he give you any info about their agent and what they're planning? There's nothing in the email. I don't see any angle for bringing in a woman on this case."

"No John, nothing like that. We didn't get into any case details. You know this really pisses me off. Somebody on the committee really has a bug up their ass and they pushed for this."

Bill watched from above as the staffer hosed down the pool furniture surrounding the edge of the pool. As he did this a number of small quail went scurrying from under the lounge chairs away from the water spray. The staffer then reached down and picked up a small pail and took several handfuls of white chlorine chips and sprinkled them into the water as he walked the length of the pool.

Bill continued, "This will be tough to explain to the review board. The more I think about this, the more I think we have a real problem. We'll have two resources on the ground and the FBI will have one too. It's critical this operation stay black John, and I'm afraid if we fail to get a handle on this in the next few weeks, it could escalate and we'll have a lot of explaining to do. If it goes *wet*, and it could easily go that way because our risk of exposure is even greater now with more assets on the ground, a number of us might be looking for new jobs."

'Wet' was a term used in the agency meaning that other much more clandestine and sinister teams could be brought in to resolve the problem. 'Wet' meant literally to liquidate. That was rare, but it had happened once recently on a case in New Orleans involving John's predecessor which resulted in the suspicious death of a turned agent and banishment of the ops administrator. That is how John came to have his position, hired in as a replacement.

John replied, "I just can't believe it will ever get that far, and if it does, how can we be held accountable?"

Bill responded, "John, this is not just our problem, it's an agency-wide problem now. I think you better set up another face-to-face meeting with our friend."

"Bill, we just dropped Jason in there; I think we should leave him there, at least to give him a chance to make some progress before dragging him back here for a meeting. He's only been there two days!"

"John, I'm not talking about Jason Kraft!" Bill yelled into the phone. "I want you to set up a meet with Patrick Bobka from the research team. He's going to tell us what's going on and where he stands. We've heard it all before but this time I'm putting the pressure on. We're in this mess because this thing was their idea and they can't control their guy. What's his name again, their scientist; the man responsible for this strain?"

"Marco. Marco Pinto. What a stupid idea it was to leverage a civilian's expertise for that project. The whole idea is crazy. What were they thinking?" John asked, rhetorically.

"I don't know, but it's an agency problem now. This can't get out John. We'll get skewered in the press if the strain hits the street and it ever becomes known we funded the whole thing. I suppose it makes perfect sense to pull in the FBI at this point. I just hope the FBI isn't involved now to initiate the wet team. That's been done before. What a fricking mess!"

Bill heard his wife calling through the closed slider, "Bill, who are you talking to? Come back to bed. It's too early to get up!"

"John, I've got to go. Please set up the meeting. I'll conference in from here. Remember I'm three hours behind you. Text me the meeting schedule. Leave the agenda open."

Bill yelled back to his wife, "Just a minute dear." Then he went back to John, "Thanks John. Talk to you soon." John said goodbye and Bill pressed the 'OFF' button to hang up.

"Oh my God," he said to himself. As he looked down, two additional hotel staffers had arrived and were rolling white towels into 3-foot by 6-inch rolls and placing them onto the lounge chairs surrounding the pool. Today *was* going to be a great day he thought. No chance of that now as he opened the slider.

Just before he left the balcony, he glanced down to see a large black and white magpie fly down and scoop up a tiny lizard lying on the bricks. He turned, walked back into the room and closed the slider.

Chapter 22

I watched Silvia weave through the crowded hotel restaurant, until she stopped at my table. “Would you like another glass of wine Mr. Kraft?”

“No Silvia, I’m waiting for someone; maybe I’ll have another when she arrives. But you can do me a favor.”

“Sure what can I do for you?” she asked.

“You can call me Jason. ‘Mr. Kraft’ sounds so old. I don’t want to be old, so Jason works better.”

Silvia smiled, “Sure Jason, from now on, no more ‘Mr. Kraft’. They tell us to do that with customers if we know their last names, I mean to use the prefix. But I’ll break the rules on request and call you Jason from now on. What does your party look like? I’ll make sure she finds you.”

“Thanks Silvia. I’m waiting for a petite Hispanic woman named Alondra who has a striking resemblance to the actress Naya Rivera. You can’t miss her.”

“I’m sorry, I don’t know that actress.”

“Oh, well, look for a great looking, deeply tanned woman with long black hair; it may be in a ponytail.”

“Okay, I’ll keep an eye out and send her right over.”

I took another sip from my almost empty glass of Syrah. I

still had time; Alondra's note said she would meet me in the restaurant at 6:30 for dinner. I had twenty minutes to think about the past few days' events and to plan my conversation with her.

John had also texted me. I was sure he wanted to tell me about Alondra and I would have some fun with this one; it was highly unusual for agents to be injected into an ongoing case without communicating first with agents already there. The fact this was an unplanned event (to the DEA) and that the FBI was bigfooting the case meant an escalation of some sort had occurred at high levels. I got that, but why?

I was also having trouble understanding the motives for inserting a woman into the case. I couldn't fathom how they expected to fit Alondra into the scam. This would be a revealing discussion with her and I hoped under the circumstances of our rekindled relationship, we would trust each other enough not to hold anything back. I decided a direct approach was best and I was going to level with her about everything I'd discovered in the past few days. I was hoping she would tell me what was going on in FBI world, and what their true motives were for her involvement.

The FBI had ways of finding things out, but I was sure they had no previous knowledge of the true nature of my relationship with Alondra. We'd been very careful and that couldn't change. The agencies frowned on inter- and intra-agency affairs and I could think of more than one incident in the past that led to the termination of one or more employees. If it did come to that, a case for wrongful termination could never stick against the agencies because employees sign strict employment contracts and these kinds of activities with fellow agents are clearly forbidden.

The potential of getting caught was a factor in our previous breakup. I was hoping we could overcome that fear and continue our relationship. We seem to have picked up where we left off and that was fine with me; my feelings for her were never stronger. It would mean we'd have to be careful and it was important to be seen only as platonic business partners.

I was sure Alondra had spent at least part of her day scouting the area for an alternate hotel as her luggage was gone. We hadn't discussed it, but it was obvious she wouldn't be staying at the Marriott. That left her with a large chunk of time to do other things and I had no clue what those things were, except for the morning briefing she told me about.

I still had fifteen minutes to kill before Alondra arrived, so I took some time to reflect on events after Kevin dropped me off at the experiment station.

Marco and his associate Becky took me on a quick 15-minute tour of the facility. I saw nothing to indicate any strain work was going on there; just a lot of lab equipment for soil analysis and a small library stocked with pamphlets on gardening, fertilization and pest control.

Marco and I then drove back together in his car and we spent the rest of the day in the #5 seed house cutting seed pods from the tops of the tobacco plants. It was a simple yet laborious process of going from strain to strain on the footstools and cutting the small green and brown ripened pods from the tops of the plants.

I was especially tired tonight, having climbed and dismounted that footstool what seemed like a thousand times.

Marco worked alongside me working the next row over and we worked our way down from one end of the house to the other, up and down the rows, gathering the ripe pods and being careful to separate them by strain number into small stackable Tupperware containers. The plastic lids were labeled with the strain numbers and had small holes punched in them so the pods could breathe and continue to ripen. It took all day to pull only the ripened pods and fill all 47 containers from the strains.

I had noticed the #13 strain had no container; it was missing and I was in the position to naturally ask him about it without him attaching any significance to the question. He said his father was a superstitious person and it was common in his family to avoid the usage of the #13 whenever possible. On a plane he would never take a seat in row #13, or in a hotel he couldn't stay on the 13th floor, or in a room with a '13' in the room number. So he had naturally skipped the #13 strain. I knew there was a reference to the #13 strain written into the XXXX folder; the question was where to go from here and how to ask him about it without garnering suspicion. Then again, was this the special strain? I latched on to this numerical anomaly early on and it may be nothing at all. I needed to follow up with Kevin in the morning and get the field name listing. The 'BL' field designation might help shed some light.

It wasn't long before Silvia the waitress appeared at my table, interrupting my reverie of the day's events.

"Mr. Kraft, I mean Jason, your party is here but she wanted a more private table, so I seated her in the booth around the corner. Follow me, I'll take you there."

"Excellent," I replied.

Leaving my now empty wine glass on the table, I followed Silvia across the room and around the corner into a back section of the restaurant I had not seen before. There was a line of booths across the wall and in the last booth tucked into the corner I saw Alondra. She was wearing a loose fitting light blue sweater and jeans. She was smiling as we approached. Alondra had already ordered wine for herself and a full glass for me, too. Silvia put two menus on the table. I thanked her and she walked away.

I went over to Alondra and kissed her on the cheek before taking my seat across from her in the booth. I was familiar with her perfume and it reminded me of the night before. She was smiling; her long black hair was parted on the side and pulled back. She was radiant.

"So you like this table better?" I asked.

"Yes, I hope you're okay with it. I saw you in the middle of the room and I thought it would be better for us in a more private setting."

"You thought right. So what did you do today?"

"I should be asking you that. You have a three-day head start on me. I had the morning briefing with the coordinator, and that lasted about 30 minutes, then I was free to do what I needed to do. Get some new clothes; sneakers, a new jacket and some other things, and to find a new hotel."

"So where are you staying?"

"Up the street at the Hilton. I asked them for a discount for a week's stay. They offered me 10 percent. We settled on 15."

I wondered where her gun was. I'd been used to seeing her in pantsuits and jackets and her gun was always concealed under the left side of her jacket in a body holster. Today she was wearing a light blue sweater and no gun. So I asked her about it.

"I see you left your gun behind."

"Actually I didn't." She reached down and pulled up her jeans on her right leg to reveal a small concealed gun strapped to the inside of her leg just above the ankle. It was silver and looked like a miniature colt 45.

"I call her Betsy or Betz for short. She's tiny, but she can be a handful if you get her mad." She smiled broadly as she said it.

I reached out my hand and she gave me hers. I was in love with her smile, her accent and her sense of humor. A flood of memories were coming back to me as we sat across from each other in the booth holding hands. I'd been with her for less than three minutes and I felt a warmth coming over me I hoped would last forever. I shouldn't be thinking this way so soon, but I couldn't help it. I knew I was in love with her; being here like this was confirmation.

She said, "Maybe we should talk a little business; I think this is private enough here if we're careful and we keep our voices down, but first let's drink a toast." She held up her wine glass prompting me to do the same.

"To TobaccoNet, let us discover its true meaning."

As we clinked glasses I chuckled and said, "Now that was corny. My turn now."

She smiled back. I held my glass even higher and said, "Here's to us, good people are scarce."

"Bravo!" She replied as we clinked the glasses once more and we both sipped the wine.

Silvia had been standing just out of view, with a water pitcher. When we were finished with the toasts, she came over and asked, "Are you ready to order?"

I responded, "No Silvia, sorry, we haven't even looked at the menus yet. Do you mind coming back in a few minutes?"

"Not at all Jason, take your time." She walked away.

"Ah, I see you're on a first-name basis already! She's cute too." I could see Alondra was joking and having fun with it.

"Not as cute as you are and she's known my first name for about 10 minutes. Let's change the topic and let me ask you some questions. Number one, did you enjoy our rendezvous last night and number two, what in heaven's name are you doing here?"

"Well, the first question is easy. Yes, I very much enjoyed our 'rendezvous' to use your term. I apologize if you think I came on to you a bit strong last night, but sometimes you have to take matters into your own hands."

She was smiling again and proud of her witty double entendre.

"The second question is not so easy to answer." She moved closer to me by extending herself over the table and continued in a hushed voice.

"Jason, some of what I'm about to tell you is highly

classified and should not be discussed with your case handlers. If what I'm about to say gets back to them, it may put you in an awkward position. I was able to convince my review team that I know you well from our work in the past and that I would easily fit in here to help you solve this case.

"I know what I'm telling you today may ultimately be difficult for you Jason and I'm sorry about that. I hope you'll understand and won't think any less of me when this is all known to you.

"Truth is the FBI is very unhappy with the way DEA is handling the case. They want me to work closely with you to make sure you really understand what's going on. Both agencies consider you a top agent and you probably would have figured it out on your own given enough time, but the stakes are too high and they want to move the timetable up. That's why I'm here."

"Jesus Alondra! You've said a lot, but you really didn't say anything. Now you've got my curiosity peaked."

I was even more shocked than my reaction revealed to her in my response. Just five minutes ago, I was hoping we would work together as a team and continue our relationship but I was not prepared at all for Alondra's tenor. She and the FBI were intruding into my case as the alpha dog and that was not sitting well with me. She appeared to be saying I should trust her and the FBI, and not the DEA. In my experience, the two agencies had always worked together; this was very different. I was inclined to trust her, but I needed more information first.

She continued, "Before I say more, I want to ask you a few questions."

I figured I had no choice. This was her show now. “Okay, shoot,” I said.

“Can you remember anything odd about the case background presentation? The presentation about shade tobacco given by the RoJac architect team? I just had that presentation last week, by the way.”

“Yes, something has been bothering me about that. The Admin was not leveling with RoJac on some of the key facts in the case. They swapped in some phony elements and never mentioned they were after a special strain of tobacco. They said it was plain marijuana they found in the cigar factory.”

“Exactly. Now didn’t you think that was odd?” she asked.

“I did, but they explained it away saying the fewer people who knew about it the better because the issue was so sensitive.”

“That’s all a true statement, this whole thing is very sensitive. That’s what they said to me as well. Anything else bother you?”

I thought about telling her about John lying to me about his whereabouts when I texted him last Friday. He didn’t exactly lie, but he didn’t tell me the truth. I decided not to throw him under the bus just yet. I wanted to hold back and try to figure this one out on my own.

“No, I guess not. Did I miss something?”

“Maybe, not sure. But I want you to think back to the discovery session you had and the timing. Do you remember when that was? Not too long ago right?”

"That's right. About three or four weeks ago. So what?"

"Do you remember when the man in Puerto Rico was arrested? What date that was?"

"Yes," I said. "I think it was sometime in January of this year. Right, I remember now, it was January. So what's unusual about it? The tobacco harvested in the fall here is processed the next winter in Puerto Rico. I see nothing wrong with the timing."

"No, that's not the issue. The issue is there's a three to four-month lag between the time of the incident in Puerto Rico and the architects' session. Why so long? Why did we wait for three months before they ran the workup and pulled you in?

"I don't know. It's a mystery to me, but to be honest, I hadn't thought about it before, but you're right. It is odd; they shouldn't have waited so long to pull me in."

"Why they waited so long is a mystery to me too, but we'll work on that later. I have more to tell you first. I pushed a little harder with some close friends I have in the FBI on the inside. I found out the real reason they're keeping such a short leash on this. It might explain why RoJac was kept out of the loop."

"I'm all ears," I said.

"This whole thing is a DEA plan gone bad from the start. I don't know all the details, but a research group in the DEA was experimenting with marijuana strains. They weren't getting very far so they called in some UCLA partners for consultations. One connection led to another and eventually this guy Marco Pinto at Treadwell, who is well known in the conference circuit, was tapped by the UCLA team to provide expertise on plant DNA recombination. The goal was to see if it was possible to concoct a strain of tobacco exhibiting properties of marijuana. The project was called the 'TarLight' project."

"Wait, time out. Why would the DEA ever want to be involved with a crazy scheme like that? Designing a strain of potent tobacco?"

"I don't know, but the research crowd has always been known to be on the cutting edge. These are crazy times, especially with the states popping up here and there with the legalization of marijuana. I can see the government stepping into this business and licensing the growers, etc. Big tax revenue opportunities here. Someone probably had the wondrous idea potent shade tobacco leaves could be a natural wrapper for marijuana cigarettes down the road."

I was dumbfounded. Alondra was silent too, but only for a few seconds. She started up again.

"There's more. The UCLA team has been reporting to DEA Research all along they've made no progress with the strain. The word is that Marco Pinto insists he's had no luck with it; he doesn't think it's possible to cross a tobacco plant with a marijuana plant. That would be like crossing a cat with a dog.

"You and I are here now because the incident in Puerto Rico is strong evidence the strain does exist."

I asked, "Why not just confront Marco? Ask him point blank about the strain."

"We could, but Marco has no idea his efforts are being

funded by the DEA; he thinks he's working with UCLA-NIH grant money. He's probably an honest guy and he's innocent of any real crime. If we make waves we run the risk of blowing this wide open to the press. Plus, the DEA still wants the strain. Before they confront Marco directly and risk wholesale discovery, they decided to send you in, covertly."

"So obviously he's created the strain and he's keeping it for himself. This puts Marco in a very bad position doesn't it?" I asked. "I mean this thing has backfired on the DEA in a big way. Marco doesn't know it, but he's playing with fire and he might get burned."

"Yes, that could happen and I hope it doesn't; but I think we are headed down that road," she said.

"So the real reason you're here is to do an assessment. I know the FBI isn't as squeaky clean as everyone thinks they are. What do you think the chances are Marco has crossed that line?" I asked.

"I don't know, but it's a definite possibility; the line's close. They want my assessment in a week. I'd hate to see something happen to Marco or anyone if it's not warranted."

Silvia appeared from around the corner and asked, "Can I take your order now?"

"Yeah, another glass of wine for both of us," I said. "I think we need a few minutes more to look over the menu."

"Sure, " she replied and left.

I looked at Alondra across the booth and asked, "Are you

hungry?"

"Famished," she replied. "Let's eat, then you can tell me all about what you learned the past three days on the case. Upstairs in your room."

"That's a great idea. I was thinking the same thing."

Chapter 23

John Trane and Patrick Bobka had been silent for the past ten minutes. The ride from the Sky Harbor airport to the Fairmont Princess Resort in Scottsdale, Arizona, was a 25-minute drive and John had spent the better part of a five-hour plane ride from D.C. to Phoenix not discussing the TobaccoNet case; John felt it was not appropriate for him to debate any aspect of the case without Bill. Patrick understood the urgency but still had some difficulty seeing the need to travel all the way to Scottsdale just to meet in person with Bill Sweeney who was on vacation there. John had proposed the face-to-face meeting as a better alternative to a video conference call. Meetings of this kind were better in person due to the sensitive nature of the topic. Private sidebar off-the-record discussions were always more effective than the electronic variety.

Bill was waiting for them now in a secluded spot in front of the lagoon on the south side of the resort. He had paid a bellhop to keep an eye out for John's rented BMW X3. For a small tip, the bellhop would use a golf cart to drive the two from the hotel entrance to the lagoon for the private meeting. The meeting was to last no more than half an hour followed by a dinner reservation at a five-star Mexican restaurant on the property called La Hacienda.

John pulled into the resort at 6:05 p.m., just a few minutes late. The connection was made in less than a minute and John and Patrick found themselves scooting along in a green and yellow John Deere golf cart on a brick pathway toward the designated meeting spot at the lagoon. Neither John nor Patrick had ever been to the resort. They were amazed at the surroundings they found themselves in.

“I can't believe how incredible this place is,” Patrick said.

“I agree,” John replied. “It is an exotic place. I’ve never seen so many palm trees, birds, and so much lush vegetation in one spot, in the middle of the desert no less.”

If circumstances were different it would be even more beautiful for Patrick Bobka. At 37 years of age and an imposing figure at 6’ 4” tall, Patrick was the youngest director at the DEA. As director of DEA Field Research, he had oversight knowledge of the original program called ‘TarLight’ to create the strain of tobacco that had marijuana-like properties. What he didn’t understand was how the potent strain had surfaced on the street almost a year later. TarLight was partially funded through a UCLA research grant which was a common practice, to assign legitimate funding sources to covert projects. Funding this way enabled the DEA to more easily inject needed expertise into the projects. The research team had hired a renowned tobacco geneticist named Marco Pinto into the failing project as a last resort. They had funded the hydroponic garden in his basement with the hopes he would be successful where they were not. As far as Patrick knew, the project had died over a year ago when Marco had become convinced it was not possible to engineer a tobacco strain with marijuana properties. The fact the strain was alive and had surfaced was a complete surprise to Patrick.

They rounded the next bend and Bill Sweeney came into view sitting alone at a square granite table with flaming rocks in the center. The sun was going down and a chill would soon descend upon the resort. The chill was countered by the warmth from the gas flames emanating from the center of the table.

Ten feet from the edge of the blue-green lagoon, a six-spout fountain was shooting water twenty feet into the air. Past the lagoon was a beautiful lush green golf course framed in the distant background by a mountain range. The lagoon itself was surrounded by palm trees, desert cacti and incredible flowering plants of vibrant reds, yellows, and greens. A cadre of crow-like black birds was squawking loudly in and around the palm trees. It truly was a pristine spot.

The bellhop pulled up to Bill and stopped, letting John and Patrick off in front of the flaming table before speeding away. Bill had picked a very private setting for the meeting; not a soul was in sight.

Bill went directly up to Patrick first and shook his hand.

"Gentlemen thanks for coming all this way. I really appreciate you coming here so we can have our meeting in person."

Bill made no move to shake John's hand so John quickly reached out to Bill and they shook.

Bill was wearing a casual blue denim shirt and light colored khakis. John and Patrick were more formally dressed in dark pants and white shirts.

"I think it would be nice if we all took a walk around the lagoon. Let's go this way," Bill said, as he pointed in the direction of the brick path surrounding the lagoon. Bill was in the center with John on his left and Patrick on his right. There were very few other guests on the path at this time of day. It was also Wednesday, traditionally a slow day for the resort, two days ahead of the weekend crowd.

They were empty handed as they started their walk around with the lagoon on their left. They were told ahead of time not to bring any documents, briefcases, notepads or recording devices to the session. This was to be a verbal exchange only with no possibility of compromise.

Bill started up, "I asked you both to come this morning so we could meet in person to try to get a handle on this case."

Bill had an authoritative way of walking and talking John quickly remembered. He was slightly ahead of them and gesticulated with his hands as if the person he was orating to was directly in front of him and up in the air about five feet.

He continued pompously, "I think the gravity of the situation warrants the expense of bringing you here for one night. Thank you for you willingness to come without complaint. I hope after our talk and dinner tonight you'll have an opportunity to relax and enjoy the resort before heading back tomorrow."

They were both quiet, but John and Patrick were thinking the same thing, they had absolutely no choice but to submit to Bill's request. To do otherwise was the closest thing to political and professional suicide. John looked over to Patrick and their eyes met in recognition. Bill continued his oration.

"Let me try to recap where we are now. We're at a crossroad, a dangerous one, one of our own making. In our relentless fervor to stay ahead of the curve, the research team concocted reasoning and will, and attempted to create a strain of tobacco holding potent properties. Forgive me for any inaccuracy regarding the description here; I'm not a scientific person, nor do I pretend to be.

"Look at that!"

The group stopped walking as Bill pointed across the lagoon at the opposite bank. Standing very still in the water near the edge was a large Blue Heron. It was standing erect like a statue. The bird was on the opposite side of the lagoon, but they were walking toward it and would soon be upon it, as the path they were on circled the lagoon and closely followed the water's edge. The bird was standing so still it didn't look real.

Bill continued walking and John and Patrick followed. "Sorry for the interruption. The display of nature here amazes me.

"Where was I? Oh yes, our research friends were busy. So here we are today faced with a real problem. The horse is out of the barn so to speak and we need to rein it in. How do we do that? Well, we do what we do best in covert ops. We send in our best and brightest agent to figure it out. But this time is different. We normally give our agents all the necessary information and tools they need to do the job. A complete understanding of the case and all the details. Not this time. In fact, we have multiple agents on the case working independently. Okay, that may not be so uncommon; I'll give you that one.

"Need to know gentlemen, need to know. Not even our best agents in the field need to know what we know so we can protect our dirty little secret."

Bill stopped again and the two followers stopped along with him. They had walked around the end of the lagoon and were coming up on the Blue Heron, much closer now. The bird was motionless, standing very still in the water about fifteen feet from them. Bill turned to speak to Patrick directly.

"From a distance, I thought that bird was plastic the first time I saw it. It stands so still it looks lifeless. If you look closely at its yellow eyes, you can see it blink every twenty seconds or so."

Sure enough, as they stood there watching, the bird, standing in a frozen pose, blinked.

"I think it stands perfectly still like that so the fish it's hunting won't see it move. I'd expect if we keep watching it, we'd see it dart down and grab a small fish."

They continued walking, past the Blue Heron. Bill started up again, "So the landscape has changed now. We're not in this alone anymore. The FBI has a bug up their ass and they're called to action. Why, you might ask? Is this little secret of ours so damaging it has to be escalated to that level?

"You know John, I talked to Nick Parsons this morning. He told me he lobbied to stop their intervention. He was overruled. I asked him why. Know what he said? He said the case was now a matter of national security. Sounds like Nixon and Watergate doesn't it? I told him that was poppycock. We hired this Marco guy. Talk to him, confront him, arrest him, pay him off or buy him out, whatever. Parsons says he might be telling the truth and he could be innocent. The fact this special tobacco surfaced took everybody by surprise. Marco Pinto also has a large Italian family and has two brothers who are attorneys. He's a solid member of the scientific community, yada, yada. If they arrest him there will be a major stink; we could be connected and then we're skewered. They just want the whole thing to go away and feel the covert approach is the best approach. The question is, how much time do we have?"

They had walked almost completely around the lagoon and were almost back to the starting point, at the fire table. Bill pointed to the bird still standing rigid on the far side now.

"He's still there. He hasn't moved an inch.

"So, our conversation isn't really a conversation is it? I've been doing all the talking. Why don't we hear from Patrick? Patrick, can you tell us anything we don't already know? Why don't you start with what our motivations were that started this whole thing? I'm most interested in hearing that."

They had completed a full circle and were back at the fire table. It had cooled down considerably as the sun was setting behind the mountain range in the distance filling the western sky with a bright orange glow. Dusk was approaching. The warmth spreading from the open flame in the center of the table felt good.

Before Patrick could answer Bill's question, Bill said, "Please sit down, both of you. I haven't been a very good host. I'll find someone to take our drink orders."

With that Bill headed in toward the bar fifty yards away that was nestled between the South Pool and the main building of the resort.

They would be alone now for a minute or two while Bill

went to find a server. Patrick looked over to John and said, "That wasn't so bad. I thought it would be much worse."

They sat at the table in couch-like wicker chairs. The flames in the table were getting brighter as the sunlight began to fade behind the mountains to the west. A few large black birds had settled into a small tree about twenty feet away. The birds were squawking loudly hoping someone would feed them.

The two men sat and watched the Blue Heron standing like a statue on the far side of the lagoon.

Patrick started up before Bill came back, "Something tells me it's not over and we haven't seen the worst. I agreed to come here John because you promised me Bill doesn't shoot the messenger. I hope you're right. The TarLight program was not my idea. I was responsible for oversight, yes, but we closed that program more than a year ago and we have nothing to show for it except a ballooned taxpayer expenditure. It was a stupid idea from the onset.

"You still have to convince me your find is a result of our program."

They could see Bill headed their way now, followed by a young waitress in a short blue skirt. She was wearing a green blouse and carrying a small tray.

As Bill approached he said, "This is Cindy. Gentlemen, what would you like?"

John and Patrick both ordered Guinness, and Bill ordered his favorite, a ginger-pear martini.

All three men watched her turn and walk back to the bar.

Bill took his seat, positioned so he had the best view of the lagoon. As he sat he noticed the bird still frozen in place on the opposite shore. They could all feel the heat radiating from the yellow gas flames in the center of the table.

"So Patrick, let's start at the beginning. I'd like to know if you are aware of the motivation behind the TarLight project in the first place. Why don't you tell us so we'll have a complete picture?"

Patrick responded, "First, let me say I appreciate the opportunity to be here tonight to meet in this desert oasis. I have to admit I was reluctant at first to travel all this way for a meeting we could have had on the phone. But now that I'm here, we can have our meeting in person and there are always advantages to consulting this way.

"Before I answer your question Bill, I have a few comments to make.

"No one has convinced me yet your 'strain' found in Puerto Rico is, in fact, the result of the TarLight program. We never had a result in that project so how can you be so sure your strain is the TarLight strain? We have nothing to compare against. I remind you TarLight was closed down over a year ago without even the slightest hint of impropriety.

"From the onset, we had an indication positive results would be a stretch. In fact, pulling in Marco Pinto was more or less a last resort; the review board had already made their decision for closure but the PM appealed and he won the reopen on the basis we could tap into a civilian who was a tobacco genius. We took a big gamble, set up his hydroponics at his request. The project never had a chance from the beginning and he knew it. He used us. He used our setup to improve the shade tobacco on the farm where he worked. TarLight never got off the ground.

"As far as our motivation for TarLight, it's simple. Marijuana is quickly becoming legal across the country. It's legal for medicinal purposes in 25 states now and recreationally in five states. We're okay with that. In fact, we see marijuana as a huge opportunity for federal and state tax revenues. But marijuana has a problem. When you smoke it, it has five to ten times the tar residue compared to tobacco. We were attempting to mitigate that burgeoning health issue with the TarLight project. We were endeavoring to make marijuana more like tobacco. We were forward thinking. Can you blame us?

"So you tell me, what makes you so sure Pinto is responsible, and your special tobacco is from TarLight?"

Bill had been listening intently but staring into the flames on the table. He glanced up to see the Blue Heron standing across the lagoon before answering.

"Patrick, let me state the obvious for you. There is overwhelming circumstantial evidence the tobacco in question came from Treadwell. That can't be disputed. We did a careful analysis; to be more accurate, the FBI did the follow up at the facility in Puerto Rico. The tobacco there traces back to the co-op where 96 percent of the material sources from that farm.

"It must just be a wonderful coincidence then, that your guy Marco just happened to be close by, directed by your team to produce a similar result. You really can't be serious you still don't believe he's not responsible."

Patrick replied, "I'm just saying until you show me some real evidence that, one, the strain exists, and two, Marco Pinto is responsible, I still don't think he had anything to do with it."

The waitress arrived with a full tray of drinks. She positioned each drink on the table one by one on small square napkins before turning to walk back toward the bar. All three watched her go, which was difficult for Bill as he was facing the lagoon and had to turn almost completely around in his chair to see her.

Patrick took a long pull on his Guinness and then continued, "But that's what your team is there to find out. Right? So why haven't you been successful?"

John answered the question, which were the first words uttered from him since they arrived. "Our guy has made excellent progress in just three days; he's the best we have. Give him a few more days and we'll have the evidence and the strain, we're sure of it."

"That may be John, but you've had another agent, that woman in there for almost two months now. What progress has she made? The FBI is in our hair now, not because your best agent's had only three days on the case, but because you've been there for two months with no results!"

John shot a glance to Bill before answering, "We were so sure in the beginning, and we still are. It didn't pan out with our first agent. We're confident we're on the fast track now."

Patrick replied, "Well I'm still not convinced it's a Marco problem and I won't be until you can show me some real evidence. As far as the FBI goes, let them jump in all they want; we could use their help in my opinion. This thinking some in the agency have shared with me about the pending 'escalation' is really overdone. It will never come to that."

Bill responded, "Patrick, with all due respect, you are wrong on all counts. That Marco Pinto is involved is plain as day and the FBI is taking this very seriously. If that strain makes it to the street and we were responsible, you can't imagine the shit storm that will hit us. That, my friend, is driving us all, including the FBI, to the edge on this case."

They all sipped on their drinks and Bill checked his watch. It was 6:40 which meant they were ten minutes late for the dinner reservation.

Their attention began to focus on a hotel maintenance crew member who was driving a golf cart on a path on the opposite side of the lagoon. He was wearing a straw hat and wore a black mustache. As he approached the Blue Heron across from them he stopped. He quickly got out and walked over to the bird at the water's edge, reached down and picked it up. He then walked back to the cart, placing the fake bird on its side into the back of the cart, jumped in and continued on down the path.

"I don't believe it!" Bill blurted out.

"Yeah," Patrick said. "Things aren't always what they seem to be, are they?"

Chapter 24

I looked at my watch on the nightstand; it was 10:45 p.m. Alondra was always into taking a shower after sex and it didn't bother her she had to put on the same clothes afterward. She had just gone into the bathroom and I could hear the water running in the shower. I took this opportunity to call John. It was after the designated time for me to call and standard protocol was for me to wait to the top of the next hour, but I wanted to get the call in before Alondra came out. I jumped out of bed and slipped my underwear and jeans on and grabbed my iPhone.

I texted the secure code and the call number came right back. I selected the call number and John answered the call immediately.

"Jason, you're late but thanks for calling. I need to bring you up to speed on the case. There are some significant new developments you should be aware of."

I decided I would not tell John about meeting up with Alondra. Nor would I tell him I knew about the DEA involvement with Marco. I wanted to see if he would tell me first.

"Sure John, what news do you have?"

"Remember the FBI agent you worked with a while back on that hospital case, I think the name of the case was *Nursery1*?"

"I do. You mean the cute Hispanic woman; she has an odd name."

"That's right, her name is Alondra Espinoza. Well, the news is the FBI has joined the case and they've assigned her as their agent. You might be running into her."

"That's interesting, and a bit unusual don't you think? I can assume this all comes as a surprise to you too or you would have told me when we talked on Monday. Can you tell me anything more, like why the FBI wants in on this case so soon? I've been here for all of three days John."

"I know Jason. You know how sensitive this case is. I heard the FBI has been on the fence for a while. They just pulled the trigger and decided to send their agent in. I just found out this morning. I know nothing more than that, and it really doesn't matter; we're just going to have to deal with it."

Here was John's opportunity to level with me about the real reason the FBI entered the case. I was hoping he would come clean and admit the research team at DEA had screwed up, involving Marco to create the strain. I was also pissed I was not in the know and I had to hear the truth from Alondra. I knew all about the information approval levels within the agency, but so far in my career here, I hadn't been on the receiving end of information holdback and had not experienced or suffered from those rules. But this case was different because I was right in the middle of it. Being left out was taking its toll on me.

I heard the shower stop running and I knew Alondra would be out soon. I wanted to push John on the issue, without telling him I knew. I had a few minutes left so I asked him a pointed question.

"John, is there anything you're not telling me about the case and why the FBI has such an interest all of a sudden?"

There was silence on the line for about three seconds, then he answered.

"Jason, I know the FBI was initially involved due to the interstate aspects; the potential for a Puerto Rico drug connection with a U.S. supplier was their main reason for involvement from the onset. The nature of this problem, if not contained has overwhelming consequences for the country. The FBI, as we are, is worried this strain might hit the street and if it does we are all in serious trouble. That's all I can tell you."

John's wording was telling. It was 'all he could tell me' because even though I was the key agent in the case, he wasn't authorized to tell me the real story. The DEA had screwed up royally; they were responsible for creating a nightmare strain of tobacco with potent marijuana properties. The FBI was here to take over and remediate in any way possible which could mean liquidation of a civilian. It sounded bizarre and the stuff movies were made of but the truth was the government was duly capable of such things, had implemented similar operations in the past and would be wholly proficient in future actions given the right circumstances and provocation.

The shower had stopped running for a while now and Alondra would be coming out of the bathroom any minute. I wanted to ask John about Alondra's role and hear his answer before she came out.

"John, okay, that makes a lot of sense. Thanks for this. Do you know what this woman's role will be in the case? What should I expect?"

"That's a good question. We're not sure. RoJac is looking into her background and will work up some material for you. We'll send it along in secure email as soon as possible, but it will be at least a few days. In the meantime, if you by chance run into her, please try to cooperate with her fully. As you know, the FBI won't take direction from us so you're going to have to work it out on your end. Our hopes remain high here Jason. We're confident you can determine the whereabouts of the strain and we can nip this thing in the bud before it's too late.

"If you hear from this Alondra woman, please work with her and not against her, and let me know right away."

"Okay John, if I hear from her I'll let you know," I said.

"Good Jason. I know I can count on you."

The bathroom door swung open and Alondra came out wearing only a towel. She saw me on the phone and she pantomimed a question with her face and hands mouthing the words "who is that?" I pulled the phone away from my mouth and mouthed back "John, D E A." She got it and turned around and went back into the bathroom. I decided not to tell John anything more about the case; I wanted to debrief with Alondra first. I was also burning mad John didn't trust me fully.

"I gotta run John, room service is knocking on the door. I decided to eat in tonight."

"Okay Jason. Good luck and hope to be hearing from you soon. I'll take a status from you next time unless you have some critical information to share now."

"Nope, all set John," I said.

With that, he clicked off. I put down my phone and yelled to Alondra, "I'm off now, you can come out."

Alondra came out dressed in the same light blue sweater and jeans she was wearing at dinner. Her hair was dry and pulled back and she looked great. She made me smile; I felt like grabbing her and starting all over again. She sat down in the chair across from me where I was sitting on the couch.

"Who was that on the phone?" she asked.

"That was John Trane the asshole, I mean my case handler. He's something else. I gave him an opportunity to come clean on the case, but he held back. True company man, 'need to know' and all that. I'm not telling him I know about the DEA's involvement with Marco. My trust factor with him continues to decline. There are some other things bothering me too but let's not get into that now."

"That's okay, you can tell me more about John whenever you're ready, but put your shirt on and let's talk about your activities on the case." She grabbed my shirt from the arm of the chair and threw it at me.

"Okay, but I have a better idea. Instead of me putting my shirt on, why don't you take yours off?"

"Nope, you had your chance. Now we're talking business with shirts on."

We were both smiling; I was only kidding and she knew it. I pulled on my shirt and without hesitation I began to tell her all about Treadwell farm: Peter the foreman, my initial conversations with Cody in the yard, Marco and his seed house, watering the plants with Julio, the special strain coding, the pink trays and the XXXX folder in the file cabinet with the reference to the #13 strain.

She was fascinated I'd learned so much in a short three days.

I also filled her in on my conversation with Kevin earlier in the day in the truck, about the hydroponic greenhouse in Marco's basement, and the rumored girlfriend whom I'd met that day at the experiment station. That prompted her to question me further.

"Kevin told you about Marco's basement where he grows tobacco and marijuana and he's never been there himself?" she asked.

"That's what he said. I didn't ask him how he knew. But I think it may have been his friend Cody who worked closely with Marco last year. And there may have been others too as Kevin implied in conversation he had more than one source."

"I think you need to ask him about that right away. Or ask Cody. Marco may be crossing tobacco with marijuana right in his basement. I wonder if he's brought others into this with him. Do you ever get a chance to talk to Kevin or Cody during the day?"

"I did today, but I can't count on it. Peter tells us what to do every morning. I don't know what I'm doing tomorrow. You know it seems to me we have enough info now to blow the whistle on Marco. Why not just send the Heavy Team into Marco's house and wrap this case up with a nice neat bow."

'Heavy Team' was a DEA expression which meant the SWAT-like crew with the body armor and M16s.

She replied, “We’re not ready yet. We don’t have the strain and Marco may not be all that cooperative if we bust him in his basement. Washington is convinced he has the strain and he’s keeping it for himself or selling it to a third party. We’re on hold for another week, until I give my assessment. We’re close Jason, but we’re not there yet. Have you told anyone else at the DEA about the basement greenhouse?”

“Nope, not yet. I found out this morning. You’re the first to know, but I’ll bet the research team knows all about that,” I said.

“Well, maybe not. I wouldn’t tell anyone just yet. When’s your next status?”

“Today is Wednesday, so my next status is Saturday.”

“Perfect. That might give us enough time to get us even closer.”

“That brings me to my next question, that being, what are you doing tomorrow? And how do you see yourself fitting in here? You must have some ideas about that.”

“I have some ideas, but what do *you* think Mattie?” she asked.

“You’re not supposed to call me that, remember?”

“I couldn’t resist,” she said. “And what’s the expression, if the shoe fits, wear it?”

Mattie was my nickname in high school and college, a reference to Matthew McConaughey. I never openly condoned it, but I went along with it because I did look like him.

I had been thinking about how Alondra could fit into the case earlier when I was cutting seed pods on the step stool. I had a possibility in mind and now was a good time to introduce it to her.

"I have an idea too," I said. "The migrant farm workers here, most of whom are Hispanic from Puerto Rico, need an advocate to help them improve the working conditions, and living conditions, and all of the above. I'm talking about unions. I know you have a social conscience. You could really help them I think. It would also get you closer to some key individuals who work here which might in itself, shed light on the case."

"You really think they need unions?"

"Yes, I do. Kevin went on and on this morning about some pretty ugly personnel incidents that really make the case for more oversight; there isn't one bit of that here. The owners are completely responsible for the goings-on in farms like this and I know they could use some 21st-century upgrading. Don't you think it's a bit odd that here we are in Connecticut, the richest state in the union, with the average per capita income approaching $65,000, and we're still operating with migrant non-union help making minimum wage? This place is a throwback to the 1930's. I think you could step in and really make a difference. This farm could be the place where unions make an entrée into tobacco farming in the Connecticut River valley as a whole. It really is perfect for it; the atmosphere is ripe and the owner's never here."

"You know you are playing me don't you? You know I would jump at the chance to help to improve the lives and working conditions of my sisters and brothers from Puerto Rico in an instant, but how can I work this case and do that at the same time?"

"Alondra, think about it. There are guys working here on the farm who've had involvement with Marco. This one guy Julio even may have been working with him in his basement last year. I can introduce you to him in the morning maybe, and you can take it from there. I know he'd jump at the chance to speak Spanish with you, especially with you, so please be careful. I don't know these guys very well, but I think Julio is an honest person and probably is the one you should be dealing with. I think the bosses have been showing him preferential treatment and he could be the most potent source for us, especially if you can get him talking to you in his mother tongue. He does speak English, but not very well."

Alondra continued to listen, but her body language told me she was still skeptical.

"Keep talking," she said.

I continued my sell job, "So you'll need some union material to give them as part of your cover. You can get whatever you need I'm sure, off the internet. You'll need to go shopping for a color printer. You'll need to print brochures and other union material you can give to them. There's a Staples store near here and they have several small printers under 150 dollars. I would also look to the internet, maybe the State of Connecticut site, for information on agricultural agencies and the like. They may have some material you can read up on to give you current background on any recent developments in unionization and farm labor laws, etc. There must also be sites about shade tobacco farming in Connecticut. I know you saw the RoJac presentation but any additional facts you can glean to help you relate to the men in conversation would be good. Are you convinced yet?"

"Yeah, I think this might work. I'd want to see their working conditions and hear their grievances first hand. Then I can build good arguments for how unions would help them. I think I'd be better off if I don't link directly to the unions at the first meeting. Let me build some trust first on my own with them. This should be easily done; I normally don't have any trouble striking up favorable conversations with Puerto Rican men. Of course, I would never admit that to you," she said with a devilish smile.

"You think this guy Julio is the best shot at getting at Marco?" she asked.

"Yes, as far as I know, Marco trusts him and they worked together in the seed house last year; at least he implied they did. I think he's sympathetic to unions and is the best person to deal with. The other men respect his youth and position on the farm. I think Julio is it. The more you can build trust with him the faster you'll get to discuss Marco and maybe this will lead us closer to the strain."

"I hope you realize I may need to communicate with him away from the workplace. I mean after hours. Can you handle that?"

I knew she was referring to the last case we worked together on, *Nursery1*. She was scamming as a nurse's aide targeting a Mexican cartel kingpin who was a patient in the hospital. I was scamming as a maintenance person washing floors and I saw them making out one night behind the curtain in the room. This was before I became involved with her. I was wondering if her activities would go in the same direction with Julio. I hoped not, but Alondra was her own person and I knew better than to question her on it. I wasn't interested in scaring her away with petty jealousies, but I did wonder how far she would go and how I would react to it. I could feel my feelings deepening for her and at some point, her behaviors in a scam would cross a line for me. I wasn't too sure now where the line was, but I felt it inching closer and closer.

"Jason, are you okay?" she asked interrupting my thoughts.

"Yeah. I'm fine. I was just thinking. So why don't you meet me in the yard tomorrow morning, right down the hill from here on the left in front of all the trucks and tractors? You'll see a whole crowd of people gathered there. I'll try to introduce you to Julio. You can talk to him briefly and set the stage for something later. You can have most of the day tomorrow to get the printer and get some documentation ready."

"Okay. I'll do it. That takes care of me. What are you doing tomorrow?" she asked.

"I'm not sure but I know the key to this problem is Marco and I need to focus on him. Cody knows something I'm sure of it. I'll try to get to him and get him talking. I'm supposed to be getting a list of field names from him. I will hit him up in the morning."

"Hey, it's late and I'm tired. I have a better idea for tomorrow morning. Do you want to meet me there for breakfast, at my hotel?"

"You're on. What time?"

"Meet me in the lobby, say 6:30? No better yet, come to my room at 6:00 and help me wake up. Room 517. Knock twice so I'll know it's you."

As she made her way to the door I stopped her and spun her around, giving her a passionate kiss. Then I asked, "Who else would it be?"

She broke away with a sexy smile, opened the door and turned around, backed out of the now open door and said, "You never know. See you in the morning Jason. Don't be late."

The door slammed shut and she was gone.

Chapter 25

My watch said 5:55 a.m. I was five minutes early for my rendezvous with Alondra. It was raining this morning and I parked as close as I could, but that still translated to running through the rain for about 100 yards and I was chilled and damp standing in the hallway in front of her door.

I gave the door two quick knocks as I always had. We started that early in our relationship and doing it now again felt good like we hadn't taken more than a year off from our affair. A strong desire was gripping me this morning; the lustful anticipation of sex with her. It was an intense feeling surrounding me as if it were in the air whenever I was near her or in her presence. I knew I loved her and thoughts about holding her and making love to her began to overwhelm me.

After a few seconds, the door opened inward as I pushed through it and I found Alondra standing in the entryway naked. As I opened the door, I saw her first from the reflection in the mirrored closet wall. I could see her long black hair partially covering her perfectly shaped breasts. The entryway was lit but the room was still dark as the shades were drawn and the room lights were out. I came in and closed the door and we embraced. She whispered good morning and we kissed each other passionately. I took off my damp jacket and threw it on the chair. She took my hand and turned and led me to the bed.

"Let me help you undress," she said and started

unbuttoning my shirt. “Wait,” I said. “My sneakers.” I untied them and slipped them off, then my shirt and undershirt and unbuckled my belt. I turned back to her and she carefully unzipped my fly, unbuttoned my jeans and gently pulled them down. I stepped out of them and stood there in front of her next to the bed in my underwear.

As we embraced again and kissed, she reached around and took hold of my underwear from the front and asked, “Can I take these off now?”

“Of course you can.”

In response, she pulled them down and they were off and we embraced again, both of us naked this time. I was really hot and I assumed she was too as she pulled me down onto the bed.

We cuddled closely lying next to each other and Alondra put her head on my chest and we talked. We were mostly catching up and she started asking me questions about my background.

"Jason I never knew much about your past. Why didn’t you tell me you went to Harvard Business School?"

"How did you discover that little fact?”

“I saw the RoJac presentation and at the end they ran through your profile. I know all about you now.”

“Oh great,” I said.

“What was Harvard like?”

"To be honest with you, it was most challenging. They locked us in a small apartment with five other super egos and made us read and discuss over a hundred case studies. Carried on like this in classes for three months."

"Did you learn anything?"

"I did. I learned a ton of stuff about how to make money and be greedy in corporate America. It was really not my cup of tea, and not something I want to sign up for. Kind of wish I'd never gone.

"It's not that I didn't enjoy it. I did. But the emphasis of that course was strongly focused on maximizing corporate profits any way possible. I knew right away that wasn't for me.

"I don't want to sound like a communist or anything, but I have a theory. It's like the Peter Principal, but it applies to corporate America. Ever hear of that principal?"

"No, I don't think so. What's that?"

"The Peter Principle says an individual will rise to the level of their incompetence in an organization and then they stop and won't go any further. That same theory applies to corporations. Corporations need to keep reinventing themselves to stay current and on the cutting edge. If they don't they'll stop growing, lose their customer base and eventually die. Customers are constantly looking for the latest new thing; corporations need to change to accommodate new markets and new approaches to survive. It's the reinvention phase that's so painful. People often lose their jobs during this phase and that's hard to take. I suppose it's necessary, but I'll never get used to it."

"Didn't you use what you learned at Harvard in your job at the bank?"

"So they told you about my former career?"

"Yes, they did. I bet I know more about you now than you do."

"Probably true. To answer your question, yes I did use what I learned at my job in the bank. Unfortunately the role I had there magnified my understanding and reinforced my disdain for corporate America and its quest for profits at any cost."

"Can you tell me about it?"

We had never discussed my background before. Alondra was obviously more interested now having seen my profile in the RoJac presentation.

"Sure, I can tell you about it. I was responsible for mergers and acquisitions. That's where big banks swallow up the small banks. They do this to expand and increase market share. Regulatory agencies police these takeovers, but this has been mostly a rubber stamp. Once a big bank sets its sights on a small bank, the small bank is toast."

"What do you mean they're toast?"

"A number of things are set into motion. Mostly backroom operation consolidations, layoffs and usually some branch closings. Customers are hit hard too. In many cases, local services are replaced with the big bank's equivalent services which can be far from an even replacement. Gone are the small bank's personal touches. Lending policies are usually drastically changed. Lending autonomy is basically gone and most decisions once made by a local committee known to customers are now the responsibility of some faraway corporate underwriting team.

"Want more? Or are you good?"

"Is that why you left banking?"

"That and for other reasons."

I wasn't sure I wanted to get into all the reasons why I left. There were some things I wasn't ready for Alondra to learn just yet. I had trouble understanding it all myself.

"Jason, I'd really like to know why you left. You had a great career going. What happened?"

"Nothing happened. I just made a decision I wasn't going to go down the easy path."

"The easy path? What do you mean by that?"

"It was too easy. The management team had advance notice of mergers and acquisitions and even following strict rules to prevent blatant insider trading it was too easy to legally make money. The insider trading laws we have today are a joke. I had a real conflict watching coworkers make a ton of money in the stock market as we laid off hundreds of people. I did it for more than a year. I really couldn't live with myself. That's why I left."

"I can understand that Jason. I think I'm just like you. I wouldn't have stayed there long either."

She looked up at me and we kissed.

"I know," I said. "This was years ago and I didn't know you

then, but I often think about what you'd have done. I joined the DEA for a complete change of scenery and because I wanted to do some good. What I do now is about as far away from big business as I can get.

“I know you, like me, have a social conscience and that’s why I think it would be a great thing if you were to jump into the union thing here as a means to help us get a handle on this case. What do you think?”

“I think it might work. But I don't think you should be the one to introduce me as a union rep to your friends. If I meet strong resistance, my association with you may make it difficult for you.”

“You're right. I was thinking the same thing. So how are we going to introduce you to them?”

“Why don't I just show up where they stay at their camp and introduce myself? I can bring brochures and try to seek out this Julio person.”

“That may work if Carlos, the men's boss doesn't throw you out first. Both Julio and Kevin mentioned Carlos is like the controller around here, and he hates unions.”

“I can handle him. Like this.”

As she said that she smiled playfully, reached down, took hold and started massaging my manhood.

“If you do that I'm sure he'll let you stay,” I said. “And if you keep that up I'll be late for work.”

“Okay. I'll stop. I'll need an address for where the men are staying. You can text it to me or give it to me when we meet for lunch.”

"Meet for lunch?"

"Yeah, today at the Marriott. Why not? It's raining. I thought farmers don't work in the rain."

"I think they still work in the greenhouses. I'll have to text you on that one."

Alondra left the bed and said, "I'm taking a shower."

It was 6:25 on the clock when she got up, and I watched her walk to the bathroom. We had made passionate love twice in the darkened room.

As I lay in the bed I could hear the shower running and see a sliver of light on the edge of the closed window curtain. I wondered how I'd gotten into this mess with the case. It had started off in the right direction, but it was tracking a bit off course now. It was probably on the wrong heading from the beginning; I just didn't know it. If John had been honest about Marco's relationship with the DEA from the onset, I could have acted more quickly, or taken a different approach with Marco. Their call for a cover up must be coming right from the top and I credited Alondra for cluing me in on what was really going on. Thank God we were close and she'd been the one selected to 'evaluate' the situation and she'd been up front with me on it.

But something was still troubling me; was she telling me everything? In the past, she always put her job first ahead of our relationship. That was the main reason we parted last time. She was too involved with her work. As our relationship had deepened, I caught on to her reluctance and to protect myself I stepped in to help end it, but that was more face-saving on my part. The real story was she was the one who couldn't compartmentalize and separate her work from her personal life. So it appeared to be a mutual parting, but she was the driver for it. The fact that she was putting 'us' ahead of her assignment this time was different for me and something I had some difficulty accepting without reservation. I wanted her badly; she was so vibrant, so sexually and emotionally stimulating; I wanted to believe we could make it and have a future together. But I was having doubt. Alondra had entered my scam and my life again and it was not a natural thing for us to mix the two. I did love her and was satisfied, for now at least that we could be together and there was a good chance that our relationship would grow stronger and would last this time. I just hoped she was being honest with me and I wasn't just a piece of her case she needed to manage with yet another agenda. I had no evidence of that, but I needed more time with her to dissolve those reservations.

I heard the shower stop running. I quickly jumped up and dressed, pulled on my sneakers and grabbed my damp jacket from the chair.

I went to the bathroom door and called out to her, "I'm leaving. I'll be late to work if I stay any longer."

"Okay," she called back through the bathroom door. "Be that way."

The door opened and she came out naked again. Her hair was wet. I reached down and kissed her passionately. Then we hugged tightly.

"I love you, Jason Kraft," she said.

"And I love you too Alondra Espinoza. Good luck with your union errands today. I'll see you tonight."

"Yes, but you'll see me for lunch too, remember?"

"Right. How can I forget? No promises; not sure I can get away. I'll text you."

I kissed her once more then broke away, opened the hallway door and exited her room. I stood outside her door for about 30 seconds gathering my thoughts. I was hungry and realized I wasn't getting breakfast today, or I'd be late. Being late to the yard was worse than being hungry. Due to the rain, it might be a short workday anyway and it was likely I could break away for lunch. I could go without breakfast for one day. With those thoughts in my head, I left her doorway, found the elevator and punched the button for the first floor.

I looked at my watch and it was 6:55 a.m. It was raining hard as I made my way down Night Valley Road to the Treadwell yard in my Prius. I was excited I might be seeing Alondra both for lunch and dinner; perhaps too excited. I needed to get my head back into the case and find a solution for the Marco problem but all I could think about was Alondra and what I was feeling. I was filled with a deep passion and I wanted to be with her.

I forced my thoughts back to the case. I was hopeful we could find a solution soon and we could avoid an escalation, whatever that meant. It was not a good sign Bill and John were keeping me out of the loop about the DEA's involvement with Marco; or was it? They obviously had a very tight rein on this information and wanted to keep it from me at all cost, possibly for my protection in case of a *wet* escalation. The best outcome I could hope for was to find the strain and close down the case quickly.

That might just be Marco's only way out, too.

Chapter 26

7:00 a.m. at the experiment station meant Becky Sadler would have the lab almost to herself before most of the others arrived. She looked up from the counter and quickly surveyed the lab room to make sure she was alone. She had just finished the final steps in preparation of the test solution for the mass spectrometer run. She was supposed to be testing for pesticide residue in a batch of store-bought basil plants suspected of causing a severe allergic reaction in a two-year-old. This was a routine test and she'd already run it once that morning. She'd prepared a new test solution for a second run, but this one was different; it was prepared from a small sample of the THC tobacco originally confiscated from the man in Puerto Rico. She didn't have much of the sample left, but she didn't need much; the equipment was state-of-the-art and very sensitive.

She would need to run two samples. The first one was of the solvent by itself; the second one was with the solvent mixed with the sample. As the solvents were different from the previous test, she would need a new solvent run. The end result would be a chart showing only the chemical components from the sample with the solvent subtracted out of the picture. She was after a clean profile of the strain on a graph with the peak locations on the chart indicating a strong concentration of THC. She would then be able to compare the special strain's THC concentration to a run she'd done earlier in the week using plain marijuana.

It was important she do this alone as there were others working in the lab on Thursday mornings and they could easily recognize she was not running the standard pesticide test. The solvents were different and the printed chemical profile was unusual if anyone was prompted to look at it. She was watching specifically for her lab partner Cheryl Kingman, who she could hear now making coffee in the breakroom.

She had spent a reasonable amount of time in the lab for the pesticide test and she was worried Cheryl would be coming in soon, wanting to start her day and take her turn with the sampling. To prevent Cheryl from getting too close and to counter any suspicion, Becky had conjured up a red herring of sorts. The experiment station had just purchased a new Kofie-Cup 2.0 coffee brewing machine but the staff was unhappy with it because they couldn't use the small plastic coffee filter cup used to manually load ground coffee into the machine. As the K-Cups were expensive, the lab crew always used the manual filter cup.

Kofie-Cup, in their marketing wisdom, had devised a mechanism to ensure only authorized Kofie-Cup K-Cups could be used in the new 2.0 machine. There was some kind of electronic code built into the top ring of the K-Cup. If you tried to use the manual filter cup, the machine wouldn't work. Becky's idea was to use a sharp box cutter and cut the top ring of a K-Cup completely off and then tape the ring to the top of the filter cup. She had already done it at her condo and it worked perfectly; the new electronic ring fooled the machine into thinking it was using a real K-Cup.

Cutting the hard plastic ring from the top was difficult and it took a razor sharp knife, a strong hand, and full concentration for at least four minutes. Her plan was to keep the partially cut ring and the box cutter handy in case someone came into the lab. As a diversion, she would switch to cutting the ring if anyone entered while she was running the strain test.

Her planning paid off for just as her test was completing and the chart was printing, Cheryl walked into the lab from the adjoining breakroom. She had a coffee cup in her hand and immediately noticed Becky was doing something with a box cutter and a K-Cup.

“What are you doing?” she asked.

“Oh, I’m fixing the Kofie-Cup machine so it can use the manual filter cups,” Becky said. “I think if we can cut the top off a normal K-Cup, then we can tape it to the filter cup and we can reuse it in the new machine.”

“What a great idea Becky!”

“One second more and I’ll have it. Here.” Becky handed Cheryl the small plastic ring she’d just cut from the K-Cup. “Try taping this to the top of the filter cup. I think that should work.”

“I’ll make you a cup of coffee if it does.”

With the small white ring in hand, Cheryl turned and walked back quickly into the breakroom.

Becky pulled the printed chart out of the machine and walked over to her briefcase on the desk on the opposite wall. She opened the case and pulled out the chart of the plain marijuana she had run earlier in the week. Holding the two charts, she compared them and could easily see the two THC peaks in the exact same place on the charts. The strain's peak was about a third higher, indicating a more potent THC content.

She smiled and said to herself, "This is exactly what I need."

She dropped both charts into her briefcase and quickly turned back to the lab counter to scan for traces of anything she may have left behind. She poured out the vial of solvent into the sink and rinsed it thoroughly. Then she went back to the desk and reached into her lab-coat pocket withdrawing the small glass bottle of light brown strain sample. She placed that in the briefcase too, shut and locked the case by rolling the combination lock away from the 0 0 0 combination. She made a mental note to change the combination; basically anyone who had the same briefcase knew the combination because it came that way from the store.

She heard Cheryl yell "It worked!" from the breakroom.

"I thought it would." Becky yelled back across the room, "Where's my coffee?"

Right away, Cheryl came out with a steaming cup of coffee.

"Becky, you're a genius!"

"Hardly. Just thought about it a bit, that's all. Shame on Kofie-Cup for engineering a revenue stream by licensing the coffee manufacturers into selling only their certified coffee, with a magnetic strip embedded into the K-Cups. I bet if consumers knew beforehand they couldn't use the manual filter cups, they wouldn't buy the new machine."

"Hey Becky, what's this?" Cheryl was holding a chart print of the solvent used to run the special strain. Becky had left the report on top of the machine.

A blast of adrenalin shot into her stomach and her heart began racing. She knew Cheryl would recognize this chart as something she hadn't seen before. She had to think quickly.

"That's a new solvent I've been experimenting with. It's supposed to be better than what we're using now for pesticide analysis on some vegetables and herbs."

"Becky, you look a little flushed. Are you feeling okay?"

"I'm fine. Becky said. I feel a hot flash coming on. I've had some signs of early menopause. I'll be okay. Thanks for asking."

"Hope you're feeling better.

"This run was this morning," Cheryl said looking at the date stamped on the top of the report. "Did you have any luck with it?"

"Not yet. I have yet to run the sample. I just ran the solvent. I'll run it later today. When I get the results I'll let you know."

"Great. Hey, thanks again for your help with the coffee machine." Cheryl handed Becky the mug and the scan and turned and walked back into the breakroom.

Becky folded the scan and stuffed it into her lab coat pocket.

"No problem, glad I could help," she called out.

Becky saw her box cutter, blade open, on the counter. She grabbed it, slid the blade into the handle and pocketed it.

"That was a close one," she said to herself. "Almost blew it. So close. Have to keep it together." She felt a calm sweep over her and she relaxed. She picked up her briefcase and held it tightly. She almost had what she needed to take her plan to the next level. She felt her luck was changing; she just had to be patient and work out one more issue.

Marco had just entered the lab and snuck up behind her.

"Morning Becky!" said Marco, right behind her.

Becky jumped and turned, "Marco, you startled me."

"Good, I was trying to. You look great today."

She smiled, "So do you. Good morning." She leaned up and gave him a quick hello kiss on the cheek. At this point she didn't care who saw them together showing affection, the word was out they were dating.

"I was just thinking about you," she said.

"You were? What were you thinking?"

"Oh, the usual. Let's have lunch at the Marriott again today," she said.

"Okay, we can do that. 12:30?"

"That works. I'll meet you there. I need to run an errand this morning so I'm leaving now, but I'll meet you back at the hotel."

"Busy lady. You're walking out on me so soon? It's 7:15 in the morning. I just got here."

"I know. Sorry, duty calls. I guess I'm leaving in the rain. I heard on the radio this morning we're getting one to two inches."

"Yes, it's raining hard now. Better take an umbrella. We need the rain. Planting starts next week."

"See you later, at lunch," she said as she grabbed her coat off the desk chair and ran out of the lab.

Marco moved over to the window and saw her Subaru in the parking lot. The rain was coming down hard now and he saw Becky run to the car and jump in with her briefcase. The tail lights came on and Becky pulled out and drove out of the lot taking a right onto the main road. He watched her go until the tail lights were out of sight.

"That is a special woman," he said to himself. He was also thinking the time had come to tell her more. Their relationship was special and she was going to play a big role in his future; he was sure of it. The timing was right. Maybe he would tell her this weekend.

Chapter 27

The short drive from Alondra's hotel to the Treadwell yard was punctuated by the sound of heavy rain pelting the roof of the Prius and the cadence of the windshield wipers on high speed. I turned into the yard at 6:57 a.m. to see only Peter's tan pickup in the center of the yard. No one else was around. It continued to rain hard and visibility was down to almost zero.

I pulled up on the wet matted grass opposite the truck's driver-side window and as I did, I noticed his window coming down about two inches. I could see Peter sitting in the truck in yellow rain gear. It was chilly; about 50 degrees and pouring, so I rolled my window down just enough to keep the cold and rain from gushing into the car. We exchanged greetings.

"Good morning!" I said, loudly enough so he could hear me over the sound of the rain. "Nice day for a picnic don't you think?"

"That's for sure!" Peter responded smiling, almost yelling because of the rain. "Do you want the day off? Okay by me if you do. If you want to work that's okay too. Kevin and Cody are in tomato house #1 with Bob doing some bed work. You can join them if you want. Marco may want you too but I'm not sure about that and he comes in later anyway. You can switch over to the seed house when he gets here. Just keep an eye out for him."

“I’ll do that. Can I park up near the houses?” I asked, pointing toward the greenhouses and still yelling.

“Sure go ahead. I’ll stop in later. I’m going to sit here awhile in case anyone else shows up. You can drive right up and go in. I know you haven’t met Bob yet. Get Kevin to introduce you.”

“Okay thanks.”

What luck. I wanted to talk with Cody about the field names. I’d have my chance today.

I rolled up my window and drove off the grass onto the muddy path up to greenhouse #1 which I just learned was a tomato house. There were three other cars parked along the front side and I had to double-park next to the first car in line, a BMW 330i. I quickly dashed to the door and entered into the plastic covered house.

It was warm inside and I recognized a strong floral scent as I stood just inside the door on the gravel floor. I could hear the rain loudly assaulting the plastic roof. What I saw in front as I looked into the house was surprising. Spread out before me on both sides were thousands of green foot-high potted plants set out on 4 by 8-foot plastic grid tables held up by what looked to be waist-high aluminum saw horses. There were pathways to walk down the sides of the rows of tables.

I expected to see tomato plants, but these plants were not any tomato variety I had ever seen before. In fact, they were not tomatoes at all but some kind of exotic house plant variety all looking the same but different at the same time. Each plant had colorful sprigs, surrounded with green and red leaves. Some were striped, some multicolored and others had multiple odd shaped and elongated shoots sprouting from their centers.

As I looked down toward the back of the house I noticed a distinct change about a third of the way down. The plastic grid tables gave way to floor-based earthen beds. Sprouting from the beds were five-foot tall tomato plants surrounding a square green lattice wire mesh. I could see Cody and Kevin and another man walking toward me from the far end of the house. I could also confirm these were the tomato plants as most plants were covered in small green tomatoes already.

Cody looked as I saw him the first time in the yard. Naturally handsome, clean shaven and in superb shape, I was sure he would be the life of the party, remembering what a great personality he carried with his good looks.

Kevin looked scruffier like he'd been up all night.

The man I didn't recognize had to be Bob. It took them almost a full minute to make their way from the back end of the house to the front where I was standing. Bob introduced himself as he approached.

"Hi, I'm Bob Kingman. I manage the tomato operation here on the farm," he said as he stuck out his hand and we shook vigorously. He had a vice grip.

"You must be Jason Kraft. You met my wife Cheryl at the experiment station yesterday. She told me all about you. I have to admit she was right. You do look just like that actor. What's his name?"

"Matthew McConaughey," I said.

"That's right. Hey guys, he looks like him right?" Bob asked as he pointed my way and looked over to Kevin and Cody who had moved up closer. They both nodded in agreement.

Bob was in his mid-thirties and solidly built. Bob had one distinguishing factor you could not miss: he was completely bald. I could see he had hair on the sides and top of his head but had made a choice to shave it all off. He had a great tan on his face and head, obviously a result of many days spent in the greenhouse. He was also in excellent physical shape; he had the build of a weightlifter. He looked like someone who could hold his own in a fight.

"How long have you been here Jason? I mean at the farm," Bob asked. The rain had let up some and was not as loud on the plastic roof.

"This is my first week. Been spending some time with Marco in the seed house and in the other houses watering the plants. Haven't done a whole lot yet."

"You here for the summer?"

"Yup. I teach history at one of the local schools, or I hope to. Have some promising applications in at three schools. I expect offer letters any day now."

"Well welcome aboard. Glad to have you. As Harry says, this is one big family where we all live together every day for half our waking hours, working together for the common goal to bring the best product to our customers. Sounds corny doesn't it? but he's right. Without the customer, we might as well pack it in and go home."

Kevin spoke up, "Bob, tell him who Harry is."

"Oh, right. Harry is Harold Treadwell, the owner. We call him Harry. He comes in here at least twice a month to look over the tomatoes and the bromeliads. Tomatoes were his passion before the bromeliads came in last year. These things are somewhat of a pain." He motioned and pointed to the thousands of plants on the tables before them.

"There are 7,000 bromeliads here. Each one wholesales up to 30 dollars depending on the size and color. That my friend is the definition of a cash crop. I wouldn't care so much except as the manager of this little operation I get a percentage of the sale price on everything here. That includes the tomatoes. The deal I made with Harry is the best one for him and me. If I succeed in raising the best crop, we all make money. We all win."

"So that's what these are, bromeliads," I said.

"That's right. Let's take a tour. Guys, no worries, you can come too."

Bob spent the next ten minutes discussing the care and feeding of the exotic bromeliad plants. He was growing ten different variations, but it looked like more. Some varieties were grouped together, others were clearly mixed. The colors and varieties seemed to blend together. The plants were all roughly the same size, lined up on the tables in six-inch plastic pots. These were strange looking mysterious plants. I could easily believe they would garner top wholesale prices as they were so unusual.

As we walked toward the tomato section, which I could see was about three-quarters of the floor space in the huge house, Bob's intensity changed. I sensed he had a real passion for tomatoes.

We were walking now between rows of bedded plants all tied to square green wire lattices anchored into the raised beds of black earth. I could see the black plastic irrigation system running the length of the bed. The plants were all at the same height, about five feet tall, and were poised to grow to the height of the lattice, another three feet. Not one weed was to be found in any of the beds, an indication this vegetation was very well cared for. The plants were lush and full of small tomatoes already. The tops of each plant were covered with small yellow flowers which I assumed would wilt and shed following pollination. I recalled each flower represented a new tomato. I could tell someone had taken the time to groom the beds to remove any decaying flowers or leaves as the soil on the surface of the beds was spotless. There was also a pungent odor emanating from the plants.

Bob halted the three of us about 20 feet into the tomato section. The rain had almost stopped and could hardly be heard now on the roof.

He began his memorized oration with emotion, like he was the lead in a play.

"The best tomatoes come from the right soil, water, fertilizer, pollination, climate, pest and disease control and care. Notice how consistent the fruit is. The size and the shape are important. Each plant is tied carefully to the lattice to support the weight of the tomatoes. When it comes time to harvest the ripe fruit, we'll tag and track the weight picked from each plant. There are slight variations in the strains you see here and we are constantly trying to improve the yields. It's not uncommon for some plants to yield 25 to 30 pounds of tomatoes. That's an exceptional return. We have an organic line too, in house #2 next door.

Those yields are less, but we get a premium price for that fruit.

"Here the tomato is king. Our goal is constant, stress-free growth. Plants, like people, get stressed. When that happens, yields are lower. What you see here are stress-free, happy plants. Can you feel them? They're listening to us now."

I looked at Cody and Kevin standing behind Bob. They were trying hard not to laugh. Bob turned to notice them.

"So you think it's a weird thing to say, right? Let me tell you a true story. It happened about eight weeks ago. Cody and Kevin, listen up. This will be news to you both.

"This past winter was horrendous as you know. We had two weeks of below zero weather in February and tons of snow. We also had low oil prices, so Harry gets the idea to compare natural gas heat with oil heat as a hedge against high prices. They bring in new furnaces into house #1 that burn either fuel. We have natural gas already, but we don't have oil here so they drop off a thousand-gallon oil tank between houses #1 and #2. They dropped it right on top of two feet of snow that hadn't melted yet between the two houses.

"Harry wanted to start burning oil so we switched to oil just as we were preparing the beds. It's late March now so we had a small ten-man crew in here to plant the seedlings. We planted like crazy and finished the job in one day. It was warm during the day inside the house but still cold at night and we still had snow under the tank."

Bob paused to make sure we were all listening. No problem with that. We were.

"The next day about 3:30 in the morning I was awakened out of a deep sleep with the strong feeling something was wrong. I can't explain to you how I knew this, but I feared the tomatoes we planted that day were in trouble and were crying out to me. I pictured the plants and the furnace there and the snow and the tank and then it hit me. The snow had melted unevenly under the tank so the tank was not level on the ground. One end was about two feet higher than the other end. I noticed it the day before. What I hadn't noticed was the oil lines to the furnaces were attached to the high end of the tank. I measured the oil the day before from the center of the tank and we had plenty of oil. But now the oil line must have been high and dry as the far end of the tank slipped further down into the snow. All the oil had pooled in the wrong end of the tank.

"It took me less than ten minutes to dress and race out to the house. I was right, both furnaces were out and the house temp had plunged to just below freezing. I called the oil guys and they came out right away to add more oil to the tank.

"We lost about a quarter of the plants that day. No big deal, we had more seedlings in the #2 house which was still running on gas, and we just planted them again. But I tell you the truth. Those plants woke me up that morning, screaming for me to help them. I'm a sound sleeper as my wife Cheryl will tell you and nothing wakes me up. They did that morning.

"Yes, plants have souls. I was skeptical once but not anymore. So if you think I'm a looney tune, go ahead and think that. Since that day I've decided to give all my green friends here the benefit of the doubt, do the best job I can and treat them with the respect they deserve."

I looked over at Cody and Kevin. Their eyes were locked onto Bob and they were reverent without a hint of doubt or betrayal. Bob broke the moment's silence.

"We better get some work done before Peter comes in and sees we've been standing around for the past ten minutes. Cody and Jason, why don't you work up there turning the bromeliads and Kevin and I will move to the back of the house and do some pollinating."

Cody protested, "Bob, why do I always get stuck with the crap jobs and Kevin gets off easy?"

"Cody, that's not a hard job. Don't be a wuss. Today's a good day to do that, nice and cool in here and without the sun, it'll be that way all morning. You know the drill so have at it. Start from the south end and work together across the tables from one another, working toward the north."

As I turned I saw a tiny white fly landing on a small green tomato.

"Bob, what's that?"

"What's what?" he asked.

"That small white bug. I just saw it fly and land on the tomato."

"That's a whitefly. They're usually bad much later, but they're here earlier this year. We've got to fumigate to kill them; add it to the list of things to do around here. Cody, I want you to fumigate this house again, tomorrow maybe. There's never a dull moment in tomato land."

Cody motioned for me to follow him back to the front of the house where the bromeliads were. He walked to the southwest corner of the house with me following behind.

"What are we doing today with these plants?" I asked.

He looked at me then looked back at the plants. "We're standing in the south end of the house. Do you see how the plants are bent slightly in that direction?" and he pointed to the front of the house which was due south.

"The sun traverses the southern sky. The plants are always reaching for the sun in that direction. Our job is to turn them 180 degrees so their lean is pointed toward the north. We do this because the plants are worth more if they're straight. It is a pain in the ass job because we have to lean way in over the table to turn them. Don't be alarmed if you get wet. Water pools in the center of these plants. That's normal."

Cody started turning the plants around, one by one working in a small two-foot square section on the table in front of him. Soon he had turned all the close plants and had to reach in, far into the center to get the rest. I was on the other side of the 4 by 8 table and if we worked from both sides of the table mirroring each other, we could fix all the plants.

Cody was faster than I was so he quickly got ahead of me. I worked harder to keep up because I wanted to stay directly across from him at each table so we could converse. If I went too fast, water would slosh everywhere from the centers of the plants. It took only fifteen minutes to become acclimated to the operation so we were working smoothly at the same speed. I felt now was as good a time as any to start the conversation. I was interested in how he would react to my questions.

"Hey Cody, did Kevin mention to you something about a list of field names? When I asked him about it, he said you had a complete list."

"Yeah, he did. I have it on my phone. I took a picture of a list Marco had when I worked with him last year. I was meaning to send it to you. I need your phone number, and I'll text it to you."

Cody reached into his pocket and pulled out his iPhone. As he was bringing it up from his pocket, the phone slipped out of his hand and fell into the plants in front of him.

"Damn it!" he said loudly. He reached down and quickly scooped up the iPhone, now dripping wet. The phone had fallen squarely into the middle of a large bromeliad with a pool of water in its center. He immediately attempted to dry the phone with his shirt and then tried feverishly to activate it by swiping it, but it was too late. He held his phone up to show me a bright white screen void of icons.

"Isn't that special," he said. "Guess you have to wait for me to send you the list. I needed a new phone anyway. This is an old iPhone 4. They say sometimes you can recover it by putting it in a bag of rice overnight. I might try that."

"Sorry Cody. If I hadn't asked you, you'd still have a working phone."

I couldn't believe it. Another delay of this critical info. Then again, even if I found the 'BL' strain location, there was no guarantee this would be the strain, but it was something I was clinging to, basically because it was all I had.

The timetable for results had compressed and landscape had changed now that Alondra was on board and she confirmed Marco was involved. It was finally sinking in I may have wasted three days and it was time to hit the reset button and start from scratch, this time focusing with more intensity on Marco, as I would have done had the case handlers been honest with me from the beginning. But I wasn't ready to throw away everything I had just yet. I had a hunch if I followed my instincts we'd be okay. I'd only invested three days in the case and I was programmed to keep trying to figure it out so I would do just that.

"Jason? Jason, are you okay?" Cody asked, trying to get my attention. "Please don't worry about the phone; it wasn't your fault. I dropped it you didn't."

"I'm fine Cody. You just caught me deep in thought. I'm really sorry about your phone." We both went back to turning plants.

"What did you want to know about the field names? Maybe I can help you anyway. I remember most if not all the names."

"Oh, it's a simple thing. We were logging strains in the seed house from a sheet Marco had, you know, using the location marking codes to indicate where the strains are planted. I just saw some abbreviations and wanted to know the names of the fields. I'm always curious about everything, that's all.

"TH was one."

"TH stands for the THINK lot," Cody responded.

"How about BB?"

"That's an easy one. BB stands for BIG BEN."

"Where do these names come from anyway?" I asked.

"Who knows?" replied Cody. "These fields have been around for a long time. I'll bet Kevin knows. Not much he doesn't know about this place."

"I have one more for you and then I'll stop."

"Shoot," said Cody who was busy turning plants.

I looked up from across the table at Cody, to make sure I'd see his reaction. Then I said, "BL."

Cody immediately stopped what he was doing and looked up and stared right back at me. Our eyes met frozen on each other for two long seconds that felt more like twenty. The color drained from his face. He looked down and continued to turn plants but much more deliberately now. I had clearly hit a nerve.

"I don't recall a BL. I think you mean BI. That would be BISON lot," he said.

"Right, that must be it. Hey, thanks for your help."

"No problem," he said. "When I get home later I'll send you the list from my email using my laptop. What's your email address?"

I gave it to him and thanked him.

He was really into turning his plants now and was pulling away from me at a constant rate. I let him go ahead without commenting. He was reacting to our exchange I was sure of it. He was about forty feet ahead of me by the time he reached the tomato section. There were three sets of tables on each side of the house, so by the time I would reach where Cody was on my side of the tables, we would have completed only a sixth of the bromeliads.

When he reached the end of his side, he surprised me by crossing over and continued working on my side working back toward me. We met in the middle and finished the first set of tables twenty feet from the tomato end. Cody had done at least 30 percent more work than I had.

I checked my watch and it said 8:55. It had taken almost an hour and a half to turn a sixth of the bromeliads. This meant we wouldn't finish until sometime after lunch. I was supposed to have lunch with Alondra today back at my hotel so before we started a new row of tables, I wanted to ask Bob about working a half day.

The rain had started up and we could hear it again on the roof.

"Cody, I think I'm taking a half day today; meeting someone for lunch. Do you think that'll be a problem?"

"No way. As a matter of fact, I'm taking off in a few minutes myself. I figure I'll use the time to get a new phone; get that out of the way. The fact it's raining usually makes for a short day anyway. Peter usually gives us the day off when it's raining. Not the case for the men, though. They usually work in the rain. Sucks for them. Listen, I'll find Bob and tell him I'm leaving now. I'll mention that you'll be here till noon. Okay?"

"That works. Thanks, I appreciate it."

Cody nodded and made his way toward the back of the house into the tomato side to find Bob. I went to the front of the house and began turning plants on the second table set. After about ten minutes, Cody reappeared and waved calling out, "All Set. I let Bob know you're working till noon. See you tomorrow."

He walked quickly past me and out of the house.

I stopped and listened to his car start and heard him drive away. I also looked down to the tomato end of the house, but I couldn't see Bob or Kevin. Steady light rain was playing on the plastic roof.

I spent the rest of the morning turning plants alone. Marco never showed up so for the next three hours I turned about 3,000 plants myself.

I had hours of time to think. I wasn't sure Cody really was just buying a new phone or if my question about the BL location had spooked him enough so he felt he couldn't deal with me. He had clearly reacted differently with my mention of it. I had triggered something; the question was, what was his involvement with the BL strain and Marco and how do I follow up on it? I always thought Cody might be important as he worked closely with Marco last year and indications from Kevin were Marco trusted him enough to show him his basement garden. So there was a good chance Cody knew something; maybe he knew a lot. I wanted to question him but if I appeared too anxious I would definitely scare him away.

Then again, I wasn't in the position to let this play out over time. Normally I would take my time and build trust and try to work the case from the inside out. I clearly didn't have that luxury now, not with Alondra involved as the FBI's oversight operative preparing her 'evaluation'.

The good news was her activities were not totally out of my

control. I had to be honest with myself; the union proposal was partially my attempt to keep her focused and away from my core activities. That was an easy sell because that challenge appealed strongly to her sense of social justice. As her union involvement grew, I hoped there was enough interaction with the case elements to keep her satisfied as a participant. This needed light guidance from me only. If I steered her with too heavy a hand, she would suspect I might be manipulating her. I probably was to some extent, but due to the time compression we were faced with, it didn't matter. I had the strong feeling we were about to make critical progress soon and this case would all be over in a matter of a few days. Then again, I'd been wrong before.

At 11:50 I texted Alondra and told her I would see her at 12:30 in the restaurant at the hotel. She responded right back with a smiley face which was her way of saying she'd meet me there. I was hoping she'd made progress with her union errands.

Just before noon, Bob and Kevin came walking up from the tomato section toward the front of the house. I had just finished a whole section and was prepared to start another until I saw them coming, obviously stopping for lunch. Bob came over to me followed by Kevin.

"Nice work today Jason. Sorry you had to work without a partner this morning. Cody was worried about his phone so he asked for the rest of the day off. I understand you're done for the day too."

"Yeah. Got some things to do this afternoon. Seeing someone for lunch. Hope that doesn't present a problem for you."

"No, that's quite all right. No worries here.

"Hey, there is one thing you may be interested in. We're having a going away party for a close friend of mine tonight after work, around 7:00. We'll all be gathering at a bar in Simsbury about ten miles from here. A place called McLadden's. Great Irish bar; good food too. You're welcome to join us. Guy we're celebrating with is Wes Ackerson. He used to work here in the summers, but he's leaving to go to Moscow to teach. I think Peter may have hired you in to replace him. You'll get to meet him. Great guy, we're really going to miss him. We'll all be standing around drinking and telling stories. Hope you can come; it's bound to be a good time."

'I'd love to be there. You can count on it."

"Okay great. See you there. Hey, have a great afternoon. I hope you won't be seeing bromeliad plants in your dreams but don't be surprised if you do."

"That happened to me after spending the day watering plant trays in the #4 house on Tuesday. I woke up dreaming about green and white trays, thousands of them."

"I bet," he said as he made his way out of the house.

I followed him out with Kevin behind me. The rain had basically stopped, but there were huge puddles on the gravel path. We all got into our cars, but I had to leave first as I had blocked Bob's 330i in.

As I started the car I wondered what the afternoon and evening would bring. I had enough time to take a quick shower before seeing Alondra for lunch. I was excited to be seeing her and after lunch we could plan her entry into the camp to begin her union activities. Then the gathering at the bar in Simsbury. I could GPS over to the restaurant so I wasn't worried about finding it. Should I bring Alondra along tonight? We'd have to see about that. Today was already a good day for the case; Cody was probably involved with Marco. He should be at the bar tonight at the party in all likelihood. I bet I could get him to open up to my good friend Mr. Tanqueray.

Chapter 28

Becky Sadler passed easily through the security line with her briefcase at Bradley International Airport's A terminal. She understood the necessity of the protocol but as she sat on the bench adjusting her shoes, she cursed Osama Bin Laden for masterminding 9/11 and causing the death of more than 3,000 innocent civilians. The security precautions as a prelude to every flight were a salient reminder of that fateful day. We all had to suffer from now on; it would never go away.

She had purchased a round-trip ticket to Las Vegas, but she wouldn't be using it; not today anyway. Southwest Airline tickets were good for a year and changes were free so she'd use it eventually to fly somewhere. Today was not about traveling. It was about meeting a traveler who was arriving here in Hartford. She had chosen a circuitous route to the airport and stopped at a Starbucks for coffee before parking just to make sure she wasn't followed.

Her private meeting was to take place at 10:30 a.m. in the Black Bear Saloon restaurant at the terminal and inside the security gate. She would find a secluded table in the back and her party would have no trouble finding her wearing a peach colored blouse and dark glasses. She had her hair up in a bun so she was almost unrecognizable to anyone who might know her. She knew something about spycraft and was putting it to good use today.

She was hopeful she'd be leaving this all behind, with

Marco, but she was prepared to be without him. She had saved enough money on her own to make changes in her life, but she had always held herself back. This would be different. She was so close to real money now. Life changing money. She could go anywhere and start over. She could say goodbye to John and the DEA and the constant lie she lived day after day. It was not who she was. She wanted out, to be free, to be her own person.

She debated with herself how much she loved and wanted to be with Marco. Was her relationship with him real? Were her feelings part of the scam and did she concoct them to fulfill her dreams? She didn't know anymore because her life had become such a lie she couldn't distinguish reality from the con she was playing.

Selling the strain was her way out. She had reservations at first, but now she was sure, sure Marco had the strain and he would see it her way. She would tell him about her plan once the deal was secure. She was taking a risk Marco would reject her plan and then reject her, but if the deal was good enough she was sure he would come around. She knew he wanted her. She knew he would do anything to keep them together. They would be together and she would grow to really love him. This was her break, their shot at happiness to live like a queen and king for the rest of their lives. She had to take the chance.

Becky found the bar about halfway into the gate. She quickly walked into the back and found a private table. She looked at her watch and it was 10:25 which meant she had five minutes before Randolph Haussmann would walk in and take a seat across from her. She was meeting Marco for lunch at 12:30 at the Marriott so her meeting could only last an hour; that should be enough for the quick exchange. She could always call Marco if the meeting went over. The waiter arrived and Becky ordered a mimosa this time, breaking from her traditional neat scotch due to the early morning hour.

Randolph Haussmann was a project manager for the European American Tobacco Company. His company had agreed to this meeting to procure samples of the strain and spectrometer reports that identified the THC content, in exchange for 5,000 dollars cash. The report Becky carried with her was meaningless; she knew they would be doing their own rigorous sample testing. If the sample proved out, Becky would provide enough seed for 500 acres of plants. The price was to be negotiated, but it would approach seven figures. The sale was also to be completely off the books.

European American Tobacco was based in Vienna, Austria and it was known to be an aggressive company, bordering on reckless. They were the fifth largest tobacco company in the world and as such, they were rich with cash. They had their hands into many different things, one of which was to stay on the cutting edge in the arena of marijuana cigarette production. They knew marijuana would soon become even more important than tobacco; they considered it the cash crop of the future in the United States. As the states were falling one by one into recreational usage, the need for marijuana cigarettes was about to explode. They wanted to be there as the number one player when that happened.

Several calls placed to the corporate headquarters had paid off for Becky and this meeting was arranged in less than two days' time. They were intrigued by what Becky had offered and felt the small expenditure for a plane ride and the 5,000 dollar compensation was well worth it. If this panned out, it would mean millions in cost savings.

The company had been searching for a marijuana source that was more like tobacco. This was important because of the huge investment required to retool the cigarette manufacturing assembly lines to accommodate marijuana. Marijuana in its cured form was inherently very different than tobacco. If they found a tobacco-like substitute they could save millions on the retooling effort.

Becky scanned the restaurant and looked at her watch again. It was 10:33. She noticed a tall man with a leather portfolio coming toward her. He stopped and stood at her table looking down at her for three seconds before saying anything.

"You must be attorney Feinman," he said in a distinctive Austrian accent as he bent down and reached out his hand for Becky to shake. She reached up and shook it firmly.

Becky knew enough not to reveal her real name. She would be Gretchen Feinman - Attorney, for this transaction, representing a client selling the product. She even printed phony business cards from her PC with her name and title, and a phone number linked to a burner phone she'd purchased three days before.

"And you must be Randolph. Glad to meet you. I hope you had a good flight. Please sit down. And please call me by my first name. It's Gretchen."

"Thank you," and he took a seat at the table.

Haussmann was a tall man in his fifties with a large gray mustache and light gray hair. He wore a Harris Tweed suit jacket and carried a brown leather case. His face, hair and mustache reminded her of the man on the cards of the monopoly game. Becky noticed the strong smell of stale tobacco in his presence. He was clearly a smoker.

"It was a good flight. I'm based in D.C. and the flight is an easy one, only 90 minutes. I was hopeful the rain this morning wouldn't delay my arrival, and it didn't. I normally have no reason to come to Hartford, but I love New York City and Boston, and Hartford is just in the middle. I always wanted to come here to see the sights, but not this time. I have a return flight back to Virginia in three hours so I trust we can do this quickly."

Becky nodded in agreement as the waiter appeared, placing the mimosa down on the table in front of her.

"Can I get you a drink?" he asked looking at Randolph.

"Of course. It's a bit early but she's having one, so why not? I'll have an Irish coffee. I could use a coffee and the whiskey couldn't hurt."

The waiter jotted down the order on his pad, turned and walked back toward the bar.

"I want to say I'm fully aware of the need for us to use hush tones here as a preventive to others around us who might be listening in to our conversation. It is not in my firm's interest our arrangement or even the topic be known to others."

He continued in a low quiet voice, "So Gretchen, let me take the lead and tell you we are intrigued by your proposal. Let's get down to it. May I see the sample?"

"Yes, I have it here." Becky reached down, dialed in the

combination and opened her briefcase. She took out the small glass sample bottle and the mass spectrometer report. She handed the sample over first, then the report.

“This is it? This sample is quite small,” he said as he held the bottle up to the light.

“And this is a cured sample,” he said. “We must see an uncured sample, a live green product of sufficient size.”

“I know you asked for that, but I made it very clear to my contact in your company, the sample my client is prepared to give you today was cured and very small. I assured them after your analysis proves this sample to be the real thing, he’ll comply with your request for a green specimen.”

Randolph looked nervously around the restaurant first to make sure no one was listening then he stared intently at Becky. “Why not give it to us now up front? That will help us make our determination sooner. Doing it your way essentially forces us to double the work effort and do our analysis twice.”

Becky replied, “My client wants to do it this way, cured sample first. That is our stipulation.” She shifted nervously in her chair. “Why is this an issue now? My contact assured me this wouldn’t be a problem.”

The waiter then appeared and dropped off Randolph’s Irish coffee. “Would that be all?” he asked.

Becky dismissed him sharply, “Yes that will be all.” He turned quickly and walked back toward the bar.

“I’m sorry I upset you Gretchen. I was instructed to ask you about that specific point in case there was a possibility your client had changed his mind on it. Please don't take offense."

Becky took a long sip on her mimosa. Randolph sipped his coffee.

Randolph continued, "Now, I have the initial payment, as you requested, in 20's, 5,000 dollars. Please understand, in the event the sample turns out not to be what you say it is, this sum will be refunded back to us.

"When we have analyzed this sample and we have recorded a positive result, your client will provide a second larger green leaf sample, uncured. We'll send another courier here to pick that up; it will not be me. Understood?"

"Yes, of course," Becky responded. "But the second sample will not be a green living sample. It will be green, but it will be quite dead. You know as well as I do, green living plant leaves can be used to root complete plants. So my client will make sure the next sample remains a sample and not something more."

"As you wish, as long as there is sufficient quantity for us to make a solid determination."

"You'll have more than enough sample for that," Becky said.

Becky was starting to feel uneasy promising things she could not guarantee. She had no choice but to push on and continue to ignore those feelings.

"Good," continued Randolph. "That brings me to our final topic, compensation. We will agree to your terms of deposit into a numbered account in a Swiss bank. We normally don't do business this way and this protocol is rather unusual and not something my company does routinely," he lied. "The stakes are high enough in this case where we can bend the rules to accommodate your client. We also realize we are not the only buyer in town, so we'll try to be agreeable when we can.

"What I'm not prepared to do today is offer you a final price. That will be dependent upon the quality of the product, how potent it is and how close the leaf sample resembles tobacco. We can have another discussion after we examine the second sample.

"We have not discussed compensation really at all except for your ball-park requirements. There is a new aspect you'll need to take to your client and get approval on. That's the compensation schedule."

"The schedule? This is a single payment deal. There is no schedule."

"My company needs to plant the seeds and grow some plants to make sure what they're buying is a legitimate product. What we are proposing is initial compensation of one-half the agreed upon sale price, followed by monthly payments for six additional months to compensate for the remaining half. The monthly compensation is contingent upon a viable planting, growth cycle and analysis result for the product."

"That sounds fair to me, and we have no reservations you will be pleased with the product, but I must bring this wrinkle to my client and get his approval as you mentioned before. The only question I have is what your definition of '*a viable planting, growth cycle and analysis result for the product'* translates to? What exactly do you mean by this?"

"You catch me at a disadvantage; I was not privy to all the conditions or to this definition. The one example I do remember when we talked, was someone raised the possibility of stunted growth plants. For example, what if the purchased seed turns out to produce low yield plants that are only two feet high? Issues of that type were our main concern."

"I have no concern for this type of issue; I think you will find this product to look and feel like normal tobacco. I will bring your proposal to my client," Becky shot back.

"I was hoping you would say that," said Randolph confidently. Randolph was sure the deal was legitimate now that Gretchen had not even tried to negotiate against the half payment holdback. She obviously was confident her client was selling a legitimate product and was not worried about losing half the payment.

Randolph sipped his coffee again. It was cool enough now so he took a big gulp. Becky followed suit and drank the rest of her mimosa.

Becky looked at her watch. It was 10:50; she had plenty of time to meet Marco for lunch at 12:30. The meeting was now over and Randolph placed the sample bottle and the report in his portfolio. He then extracted a large manila envelope and slid it across the table to Becky. She took the envelope, opened the top flap just enough to see a ream of bills, then reached down and secured it in her briefcase. She then pulled out a fake business card she had printed the night before.

Becky looked up at Randolph and touched his hand with hers. "Thank you Randolph. Here's my card. Please don't hesitate to call me as soon as you hear something. Don't worry about the tab. I'll get it. Enjoy the rest of your short stay in southern New England."

"Thank you Gretchen. I'll be calling you as soon as possible. It might even be later today, provided I can get this sample to the right people. Give my regards to your client. Take care."

He stood up and made his way out of the restaurant and out toward the ground transportation. Becky watched him go. She looked up and saw the waiter walking over.

"Should I bring the check?" he asked.

"You can bring me another mimosa please."

"You got it," he said, turned and left.

I guess I do, don't I? ... she thought to herself.

Chapter 29

Alondra parked in the first curbside parking spot she could find near the State Bureau Check Cashing Company on Park Street in Hartford. She was pleased to find a parking spot close to the storefront; the rain was coming down hard again.

The company name was deceiving; this was a private concern and had no affiliation with the State of Connecticut which was a good thing. The last thing she wanted was contact with a state agency. She suspected a formal name was chosen by the owner to add credibility.

She couldn't stay parked there long for two reasons: one, she was meeting Jason for lunch at 12:30 at the Marriott and two, she was worried someone might break into her small SUV and steal the printer in the back. The dilapidated neighborhood she had driven into was telling her the latter was a real possibility.

She had finished her purchase errands at Staples in West Hartford and used the rolling pull-cover in the back of the Rav4 to hide the color printer, ink and other paper supplies she'd bought. At least these things were not in plain sight.

This morning Alondra was masquerading as a reporter for the *Puerto Rico News*, an online publication specializing in all things and people from Puerto Rico. She had called ahead and talked to the check store owner and manager Wendell Hansen. He was interested in giving her an interview, as long as his name and company were mentioned and he could proofread the article before it went to print.

Her article was to be about how the migrant Puerto Rican Shade Tobacco workers worked hard all week long and then ran to cash their checks every Friday. She was hopeful she could get the manager of the store talking and telling stories about how the men who frequented the establishment carried on and spent their money. She would then move the questions to the union topic, learning all she could and possibly even getting names of individuals that might be willing to help her.

She opened her car door pushing out the small umbrella she purchased at Staples. The wind was picking up and she almost lost the umbrella as she opened it and a gust came along, nearly pulling it out of her hands. She struggled a bit, slammed the door and locked the car with the fob, then made her way quickly to the store entrance about 30 feet away. She looked at herself in the door's glass reflection before she went in. Her hair was tied back; she was wearing blue jeans and a white sweater and was purposefully not wearing much makeup. She carried her large green leather Michael Kors bag.

A sign on the door said '*No Personal Checks, Company or Bank Checks Only*'. Another smaller sign below said, '*No Eating or Drinking inside the Store*'.

She went in and was immediately waved over across the room by a man standing behind the well-worn counter. He was a scruffy thin man in his sixties with long gray hair and a ponytail. He also had an unkempt gray and black beard that was at least ten inches long. She walked up to him and had his full attention as the office was empty. Behind the counter on a long work desk, she could see three computer screens, a printer and several piles of opened envelopes. Not much else. Behind him on the wall was an array of framed pictures. They looked like magazine covers; some were small scenes and others were portraits.

As she approached the counter, he said to her right away in a pronounced southern drawl, "How can I help you, darling?"

She placed her bag on the counter and responded, "You must be Wendell Hansen."

"That's right. *Lo que trae una hermosa dama como usted a mi establecimiento*?"

"Oh, you flatter me, Mr. Hansen. But if it's all the same to you, let's talk in English. The majority of my readers are English speaking and my article will be written for them, in their language. If the editors decide to translate my piece to Spanish, they'll do so after the initial publication."

"Oh, I see. So you're the newspaper woman and you're here to gather info from me about the farm workers cashing their checks."

Alondra responded with a broad and friendly smile which was, by all measures, captivating. She reached out her hand to shake Wendell's, giving it a strong business-like shake.

"Let me formally introduce myself. My name is Alondra Espinoza and I am a journalist and I work for an online publication called *Puerto Rico News.* Thank you for agreeing to meet with me and answer some questions relating to my next story, which maybe I didn't mention, will be on the front page of next Saturday's online version. As we agreed on the phone, I'll be sure to get your email address and will send the link to you along with the pre-print copy of the article. I will also be taking some pictures of you at work in your store if that's acceptable to you."

"Acceptable? Why I wouldn't have it any other way. I'd be happy to grace the cover of your magazine, or article or whatever you call it, with my mug."

"Good. Do you mind if we start the interview now?"

"Absolutely. You don't mind standing across the counter?" he asked.

"No, not at all."

"Then shoot little lady. What do you want to know?"

Alondra pulled a pen and a small notepad from her bag and began to take notes.

"Mr. Hansen, can you tell me how your business works? I mean, if I had a check to cash today, could I just show up and you'd cash my check?"

"Well yes and no. First things first. You'd need to be registered in our system. Name, address, date of birth, employer, you know all that stuff. We don't cash personal checks; we only cash company or bank checks, and the majority of checks we cash today are payroll checks.

"We need to make sure your company is a valid company and we've processed checks from them before. First time company checks are accepted too, but we charge extra the first time so we can buy special insurance each time we add a new company. It's a risk for us, so we manage that risk and charge the customer for it. Business 101. Basic stuff.

"Once you're registered and your company's on file, you can come in anytime and we'll cash your check right away."

"What's in it for you? How do you make money doing this?"

"Simple answer. We charge a fee, a percent of the check amount for the service. This is regulated by the state; in Connecticut, it's two percent."

"That seems hardly worth the trouble."

"Oh, you'd be surprised. It adds up quickly. Last Friday we cashed 500,000 dollars' worth of checks. Two percent of that is 10,000 dollars, in one day. Not bad, wouldn't you say? Uh, please don't print that; make that one off-the-record.

"We do the most business in Hartford. There are other places around where you can get your checks cashed, but they're small potatoes compared to us. That's why you're here, right? To talk with the best?"

"That's right, that's why we chose your company for the article Mr. Hansen. But I'm surprised so many people are still getting payroll checks and not using direct deposit."

"Sweetie, the folks coming in here to cash their checks, most of them don't have checking accounts. We're talking about the migrants mostly. Most of these folks are going hand-to-mouth each week. And that's good for us. If they were more well off and had checking accounts with direct deposit, they wouldn't be here right?" He hesitated, "Don't print that either."

"Can you tell me if the tobacco farm workers are in that group? I mean on Fridays?"

"Oh yeah. I'd say at least 30 percent of the check volume is related to tobacco. Between the farms and the co-op, it's at least that. These are small farms mostly, but big farms come in here too."

"And these migrants, as you call them, the tobacco farm workers, what would you say is the most common nationality?"

"Let's see, we've got Jamaicans, Mexican, some Caucasian, but I'd have to say mostly Puerto Rican. Yeah, the Puerto Rican Hispanic community is easily the largest group in the farm circuit. You're Puerto Rican aren't you darling?"

Alondra ignored Wendell's question and asked, "Any one farm in particular?"

"Hmmm, hard for me to answer that without looking at some reports. Hold on, let me find them."

Wendell turned around to the large desk, opened a drawer, reached in and began leafing through a pile of reports. Not finding what he was looking for, he walked over to an adjacent desk and opened a second drawer and pulled out another file of reports.

Above Wendell on the wall Alondra noticed a large framed portrait in the center of the other portraits. It was a picture of a red-haired woman holding a sandwich, a lunch box that said 'ROSIE' and a large rivet gun in her lap with an American flag waving in the background. She wore blue overalls and goggles. Her feet rested on a tattered book labeled 'Mein Kampf'.

Wendell turned back around to face Alondra. "Here's a report showing the check volume for last week. It lists the payer and the volume. The biggest farm I see here is Treadwell Enterprises Inc. That's right, Treadwell's the biggest. These guys are in here every week like clockwork, starting in April and lasting all summer into November. They stop here with a big green bus out front every Friday."

"A bus? What kind of bus?"

"A large school bus, but it's painted green. Says 'Treadwell Farm' on the side of it."

"Do you know any of these guys personally?"

"Well not to spend time with any of them, but some have been coming here for years and I get to know them personally, yes. Some talk to me, we have some light conversations. Most don't bother, they just come in here and cash their checks."

"Do you know what they spend their money on?"

"That's a good question. Here are a few things you can count on. One is that crowd comes in here, gets a fistful of money and they go right next door to the package store."

"What kind of packages?"

"Oh, sorry, 'package store' is the local term for a liquor store. They call it a package store because at one time there were laws on the books saying you had to cover up the booze and couldn't walk out with it unless it was in a paper bag. Anyway, they buy booze next door and lots of it. The bus driver waits for them too. I suppose it's not much different than an executive coming home to his mini-mansion and opening a bottle of wine after a stressful week."

Wendell paused and looked up at the ceiling, talking to himself, “Hmmm, I guess that’s real different isn’t it? Well, kind of the same thing.”

He continued, “Sometimes we’ll do a check split. That’s when they cash a check and for a small fee, we’ll cut them another check made payable to a third party, usually to support their family down in Puerto Rico. These guys only take a small amount in cash back. Treadwell has a few men doing that each week; it’s pretty common, but I wouldn’t say it’s the norm.”

Alondra scribbled some notes in her pad. Then she asked, “How much is the average check? Can you tell me that?”

“Let me think. Hmmm, I’d say between three and four hundred, give or take a hundred. Hard to make ends meet on those wages. And they get nothing else to boot. No health care, no retirement, no employment guarantee, no nothing. Then again there are some part-timers working second jobs and they make less, and there are a few, I think only one at Treadwell who does really well. As a matter of fact, he stopped coming into the store because maybe he finally got a checking account and must be direct deposit, or he doesn’t work there anymore. Not sure. I try not to be nosey, none of my business. He drives the Treadwell bus most Fridays or he used to anyway.”

“Do you remember how much his checks were? I’m just curious.”

“Yeah, I do. Carlos’s checks were almost 1,000 per week. An unusually large amount, that’s why I remember it, he must have been a big boss there or something.

“Please don’t print that. Maybe I shouldn’t have told you

some of this; personal information and all."

"Not to worry Mr. Hansen, I won't print it."

Alondra's thoughts flashed back to a conversation she'd had with Jason about Carlos being anti-union. She suspected one of his responsibilities was to keep unions away. It appeared he was being very well paid for that.

"This is all very interesting. Can you tell me anything else about payday?"

"It gets pretty busy in here with lines out the door some days. On Fridays we have more help, three extra staff to help with the overflow. We stay open until seven on those days and I usually don't get out of here until eight."

"I apologize in advance for asking this question, but you know readers, they want all the dirt. What was the most disturbing memory you've had in your career here?"

Wendell brought his hand up to his chin and stroked his long beard, "Hmmm, let me see. Oh, I know. It's a Treadwell story too. You'll like this. It was a hot Saturday afternoon. The guys got their checks on Saturday that week due to some payroll screw-up. Or maybe that's what they tell the men in order to get 'em to work on Saturdays; it happens from time to time. Anyway, that day, Carlos wasn't driving the bus, it was one of the college kids. The men liked this kid, I remember they were very fond of him. They used to try to give him beer from the package store; he always refused it. I never knew his real name, but they had a nickname for him; yes I remember now, it was 'Cisco Kid'.

"Anyway, that day was a tough day for Cisco. He was parked in front, sitting in the driver's seat in the bus waiting for the men to finish cashing their checks. Out of the blue, some idiot comes right up to him and shoots him through the open driver's side window using a sling shot and a paper clip. Hits him right in the neck with it. He comes staggering into the store with this paperclip sticking out of his neck. We called 911 and they came with an ambulance. One of the men, I can't remember his name, but I know they're good friends; oh wait, I think it was Julio, went to the hospital with him; he rode in the ambulance. Cisco was back driving the bus the next week. But what a scary thing. That's my most disturbing story. It's the kind of stuff happening around here, especially in this neighborhood. Disturbing enough for you?"

"I guess that's disturbing, but it wasn't serious, right? I suppose it could have been worse. What I find really disturbing is there is still a backwardness surrounding this whole sector of people working on the farms here. What hope do they have life will improve for them?"

"Oh now don't go getting all upset about our class society that's here today and has been here for a hundred years. It will be here tomorrow too, don't think it won't. I make a really good living from the migrants and I expect to keep doing it. The way I look at it, whenever someone's benefitting there's someone else struggling and I intend to stay on the benefitting side. I sell a seasonal service they need and I won't be lifting a finger to make any changes that jeopardize my gravy train. That you can count on. And don't you get any of those hi-fluting ideas about educating folks to give 'em bank accounts and auto deposits. If they wizen up and do that, that'll be another nail in my coffin. I might as well close up shop."

Alondra responded, switching to his first name, "I'm really

sorry you feel that way, Wendell. I thought an enlightened person like you would want to see progress. You know, higher wages and less poverty. Maybe the tobacco industry here in Connecticut is ready for unions. It looks to me the farm workers here could use a hand up."

"I suppose it will happen someday, but I hope it ain't soon. Unions bring credit unions and payroll deposit systems. I'll need to find something else to do once it goes that way. I hardly think Treadwell has that on the horizon. They're stuck in the past and have no rudder to turn the boat into the future. Soon as someone tries to steer it that way, they get thrown overboard. Good thing too, for me I mean."

"How do you know that?" Alondra asked.

"Oh, I keep my ear to the ground and I'm a good listener. I hear what's going on. Men talk; some of them do anyway."

Alondra stuck her neck out with the next question, "I'd like to talk to some of the Treadwell workers, to get their perspective on things, you know the work, their daily lives, their pay and cashing their checks in your store each week and maybe sending some money home to their loved ones in Puerto Rico; what it means to them. How it all fits together. Is there someone you could recommend who might agree to speak with me about it? You know, as a follow-up to the main topic about you and your operation here."

Wendell didn't look pleased the spotlight was being potentially diverted from the main event, but he didn't want to create waves and displease Alondra. He was thrilled someone was actually paying attention to him and taking this much interest in what he did. He felt he owed her something.

"I can give you a name of someone who fits that bill, yes. He might even be willing to talk to you about unions. I think he might even feel the way you do."

Alondra positioned her pen on her pad to take down the name.

"His name is Julio Rodriguez. I think he's pro-future and has some better ideas about going places. He's one of the ones sending money home to his family each week. If you talk with him, he'll give you a more modern perspective and he'll definitely give you an earful about unions. I think he lives in Treadwell's labor camp in the summers; he has in past years I know. It's the only place he can afford, as most of his weekly check is mailed to his wife in Puerto Rico."

"Thank you Wendell. I really appreciate you taking the time to speak with me this morning."

"No problem. Do you have any more questions?"

Alondra looked up and pointed over Wendell's shoulder to the portrait of the red-haired woman with the sandwich on the wall behind him. "Yes, one more question. That is a beautiful portrait. Who is she?"

Wendell responded proudly, "That is Norman Rockwell's most famous painting; *Rosie the Riveter*. It was printed on the cover of the Saturday Evening Post magazine in 1943. It is a symbol of the resolve of the American women to aid in the war effort to defeat Hitler. It's my favorite portrait. That's why it's over the center counter and is larger than all the rest of his covers you see here. Beautiful don't you think?"

"Yes, I do. It's beautiful, such a powerful image. It's so

inspirational."

Wendell watched Alondra stare at the picture of Rosie over the counter for a full thirty seconds before she stuffed her pad into her bag.

Then she said, "I'll send you an email of the article for your approval before it goes to print. Oh, I almost forgot, the picture."

She reached back into her bag and took out her iPhone.

"Wendell, please move back under the picture of Rosie and I will get a nice shot of you at the counter."

He stepped back against the wall and slightly to his left so he was directly under the framed portrait.

"Okay, smile," she said, as she purposely zoomed in on Rockwell's *Rosie* portrait and left Wendell below, completely out of the shot.

"Got it!" she exclaimed. "Thanks again Wendell, I'll be in touch," she said as she made her way out the door.

Wendell watched her go and couldn't help thinking she'd made a really quick exit. Had he forgotten to tell her something? He really wanted to talk about the article she was writing and he'd lost that chance. Damn, she didn't have his email address and he didn't have her card. No worries, he was sure she would call him back.

Chapter 30

The hatchway door to Marco's basement was positioned near the back of the house on the wood's side. Adjacent to the woods there, one hundred and forty yards in to the north, was a residential street and a cul-de-sac without houses. The 2008 recession left this section undeveloped and abandoned.

It was a simple matter to park in the cul-de-sac and walk through the woods on the now well-worn path into Marco's small back yard and then to the hatchway. The door was not the usual metal door found on most hatchways, it was a heavy wooden door, lying almost flat on the ground. It had no lock, but it was so heavy it required all of one person's strength to lift it up against the post and hook it with the metal eye hook so it would stay open.

Once the outer wooden door was open, there was another locked door at the bottom of the stairs. The inside door never presented a problem because anyone using this entrance had a key to it. Such was the case today.

The rain had stopped, but it had rained so hard in the morning, the fields were too wet to work in and Peter had given the whole crew the afternoon off. It was safe to be there now because the word was out Marco was busy in the seed house preparing for Harold's visit later that day.

The house had an excellent security system, but early on the security trip on the inside cellar door had been shunted, as had the motion detector in that section of the basement. A hidden bypass switch had also been installed behind some insulation in the ceiling to turn off all the motion detectors in the basement. These mechanisms had been in place for more than a year.

Today's mission was routine. A request was made to collect buds and leaves from a specific marijuana bed, being careful not to leave traces of the removal. This was easy; the target section was lush enough so nothing would be missed. The plan was to obtain enough highly potent weed for the after-party following the dinner at McLadden's. It was Wes's party; he was well liked and he loved weed, so the whole team was anxious to accommodate his request.

The intruder, inside the basement and standing on a step stool, reached up into the insulation between the rafters and switched off the motion detectors. He stepped down opening the inside door to the basehouse and was met with the fragrant and moist smell of greenhouse plants. He stepped in and closed the door.

The grow lights were on and fans were running, circulating the air in large plastic hole-laden tubes running the length of the house. The tobacco plants in front of the door were huge, pushing flowers all the way to the top into the grow lights. It was like a tobacco jungle, complete with the gurgling cadence of the hydroponics. All that was missing were the bird noises.

He looked around toward the front and noticed the workstation near the door with the large monitor showing the driveway on the south side of the house. He also saw the camera pods attached at regular ten-foot intervals on the ceiling. He was familiar enough with the security features to know an alarm would sound if anyone tried to approach the house using the driveway. Fortunately, no such measures were in place in the back of the house.

He turned away from the front section and made his way into the back section on the right side where the marijuana was growing. Reaching into his jean pocket he withdrew a large plastic zip-lock bag. He opened it and took out a small yellow post-it note. There was a number written on the note. The number corresponded to the number of the strain he was to collect. Buds and leaves, but definitely the buds if he couldn't take leaves without it being noticed. He focused on the numbers written on the red tags hanging from the plants. He quickly found the number 9 strain. There were six large plants with this strain number. He was surprised how massive these plants were; not only were they tall but they were bushy. He reached into the middle of the growth and stripped off several large buds from the internal sections of the plant. He then did the same for the leaves, taking care not to drop any of them into the water-filled beds. It probably wouldn't have mattered; leaves were falling into the water all the time, but he was careful anyway.

As soon as the zip-lock bag was full, his job would be done. He judged the bag was reasonably full, but he could afford to add one more large bud. That was the priority over leaves so he reached up into the middle and took hold of the last bud, but didn't snap it off because doing so would leave a noticeable bare spot on the plant. There were other buds he could take but not from this side of the bed; he would have to walk around to the other side to reach them. As the beds lacked crossover points, he needed to walk all the way to the end of the bed and then over and walk back up the other side to where the number 9 strain was.

As he made his way down around the end of the bed, he marveled at all the different strains of marijuana. Some were tall and thin, others fat and bushy. Some had very short leaves and huge buds, others were all leaves and very small buds. Additional grow lighting had been set cleverly into the center of the plants so the light would penetrate from all angles. All were healthy and had red tags prominently displayed.

As he started up the other side, he noticed a small section of tobacco plants with purple tags. Initially, two things struck him as odd. One, why were tobacco plants growing in the marijuana section? And two, he'd never seen a purple tag used for any labeling here in the basehouse or the seed house back at the farm.

There were three plants here like this and he could tell by the spacing a forth plant had been removed. All three had thick two-inch stalks and large wide leaves, and you could see where a few of the bottom leaves had been picked off the stalks, but there were still more than 15 leaves left on each plant. The leaves were slightly different than normal tobacco leaves; the straight smooth edges gave way to tiny saw-tooth edges. The flowers at the top were also different; they weren't the classic light yellow trumpets, they were light green. The characteristic seed pods were absent; they had already been stripped off. He eyed the purple tags hanging from the plants; he could see the number 13 written on them and that was different too. Marco would never use a number 13 for anything.

As he made his way past the section, he looked back and spied a purple tag on the concrete floor just sticking out from under the recessed section of the bed. Someone had dropped it or this was probably the tag belonging to the fourth plant.

He reached down, picked it up and pocketed it. He would show the team and ask them about it back at the farm.

He quickly found the number 9 strain, reached up and pulled down a large bud from the interior section he knew wouldn't be missed. He added it to the bag, sealed it and carried it to the workstation.

There was one more thing to do before he left. He had to erase the recorded video of his visit today and set the record timer to give himself ample time to leave the basehouse without being recorded. He sat down at the monitor and used the mouse to call up the video software. He canceled the record mode first. The software was very sophisticated; each one of the 16 cameras on the ceiling was recorded separately and could be displayed on the screen all at once in a 16 picture grid. He rolled the timer back to just before his entrance and marked the starting point for the deletion. He fast-forwarded through the playback of himself pulling the buds and leaves of the number 9 strain. He continued to watch himself move through the house, into view from screen to screen on the grid in fast-motion; he looked like Charlie Chaplin walking around the end of the bed, studying the number 13 tobacco plants, pulling the final bud and at last sitting himself down at the workstation. He marked the deletion endpoint to the last picture before the recording was stopped. Confirming the deletion, he set the recording timer to begin in two minutes, more than enough time to exit the basehouse where all the cameras were. He closed the video software and the screen returned to the shot of the driveway in front of the garage doors.

Had he been paying attention to the driveway scene, he would have noticed a Subaru parked there, in front of the garage doors.

He stood up and repositioned the chair exactly as it had been. Putting his hand on the knob, he looked back into the greenery, listening to the fans and the gurgling hydroponics. Did he leave anything? He had his zip-lock bag. All set.

He opened the door and exited quickly into the hatchway section of the basement. Closing the door carefully he turned around and came face to face with a woman he knew he'd seen before but couldn't fully place. He was so startled by her he let out a yell and dropped the bag.

"What are you doing here?" Becky demanded.

"I, I... I'm just getting weed for the party," he stuttered in his thick Spanish accent as he reached down and picked up the full zip-lock.

"Does Marco know you're here?" she asked, hoping he'd say no. If he said yes, she had a problem; she'd have to explain to Marco why *she* was there.

"Ah, no he doesn't," he hesitated. "We wanted to surprise him with the weed for the party." He lied, but it sounded plausible.

"What's your name?" Becky asked, softening a bit this time.

"Julio, Julio Rodriguez. Please don't tell Marco. You'll ruin the surprise." Julio suddenly realized the woman standing in front of him must be Becky, Marco's rumored girlfriend. He'd seen her around, but he'd never been introduced.

"So you're Julio? Marco talks about you a lot. He tells me

you do excellent work."

"Thanks. You're Becky, right?"

"Yes I am, nice to meet you," as she reached out and shook his hand.

"I won't tell Marco I saw you so you can keep your surprise. It'll be our little secret, just between us."

"Thanks Becky. I didn't hear the driveway alarm. Did you drive here?"

"Yes I did; I'm parked out front. Marco mentioned the control's batteries need replacing. The driveway alarm isn't working now. I see you came in through the hatchway," she said as she pointed to the partially open inside door across the room. Light was pouring in on the stairs from the open hatchway door.

"Yes, I better leave now. This weed needs to be cured first."

Becky noticed he was fidgeting with the zip-lock bag full of buds and leaves. "You better get going."

"Okay, thanks Becky," he said as he walked to the door, turned the button on the knob to lock it and closed it behind as he bounded up the stairs. He unhooked the heavy outside door and let it down gently onto the frame.

All he could think about during his walk through the woods back to his car was the trouble he was in if Becky told Marco he was in the basehouse stealing pot. He might be good for the party, but what about after that? He had to tell the team he'd been caught. What could he say? It wasn't his fault; the alarm batteries were dead. If he'd only been faster and hadn't taken extra time to take the last bud and examine the purple-tag tobacco, he'd have been long gone before Becky arrived. What was she doing there anyway? It didn't matter.

Maybe he should tell Marco first, admit to him Becky found him in the basement and he had the key and used it once and a while for himself, to take pot. He knew Marco liked him and trusted him; he'd only seen Marco really mad once and that was with Peter. It just might work. His mother always told him to be honest; it was something he always tried to do. Bob and the others might not like it, but they're not the ones who were caught. He just couldn't lose his job; his wife and children in Puerto Rico depended on his checks every week. He was in a real mess.

He started his car, but before driving off, he stuffed the full zip-lock bag into another paper bag lying on the passenger seat. He then stuffed it under his own seat, so it was completely out of sight.

As he drove around the cul-de-sac, he thought about the party. He knew he'd have to smoke some weed tonight, enough to build the courage to tell Marco everything. Then he got the idea to talk to Kevin. Yeah, Kevin would know. That made him feel better. Kevin always knew what to do.

Chapter 31

Delta's Sky Lounge at the Phoenix Sky Harbor airport was approaching seedy. It had started off as a luxury perk for first class passengers but over the years with so many travelers upgrading to first class, the volume of people using the lounge had taken its toll. The leather chairs were worn out and cracked and the carpet was in need of replacement.

John and Patrick found two empty seats in the first row in front of the windowed wall. They had a view of the tarmac where the planes were parked.

The two didn't have much to say to each other in the car on the way back to the airport. Notwithstanding their hangovers, there was somewhat of a Mexican stand-off taking place on the issue of Marco's culpability for creating the potent strain. Patrick firmly believed Marco was not responsible while circumstantial evidence said otherwise. They decided to agree to disagree on this point, with the proof resting with the efforts and results of the DEA agents in the field.

The previous evening's meal at La Hacienda set John back almost 300 dollars. The DEA has strict rules regarding meal expenses logged outside the beltway, so John took it upon himself to use his personal AMEX to pay the bill. It wouldn't have been so bad, but the meal ended with a drink-off of sorts with a wide variety of tequila flights.

John won the contest, but he was paying for it now with a

college-age tequila hangover. Bill and Patrick were smart enough to let John win. They were only moderately in pain.

Their plane was right outside the window; an Airbus 320 bound for Washington and scheduled to depart in one hour at 10:00 a.m. They had about 30 minutes to kill before boarding. Patrick was reading his Nook.

John stood up from his chair, looked at his watch and reached into his pocket for his phone.

"Patrick, I have to make a call. I'll be back in 20 minutes."

"Sure," Patrick said looking up from his book. "We're boarding in 30 minutes. Don't get lost," he said and went back to his read.

John continued to walk in front of the first row next to the window on his way out of the lounge into to the main concourse. He walked by the entry desk which was manned by two Delta staff, a man and a woman. Exiting the lounge he checked again to make sure he had his boarding pass; without it, he couldn't get back into the lounge.

Exiting through the double doors, he joined the throng of travelers walking in both directions, to and from the gates.

John found a more private spot to call from along the wall in a bank of pay phones. Ironically, they were abandoned these days as everyone had cell phones. John punched in the link number, received the secure tone, then dialed Becky's code. It rang four times before Becky picked up.

"Becky, John."

"I know it's you, I can tell by the secure ID."

"Sorry to bother you; I know this call is off-schedule. There've been some new developments in the case and I need you to know about them. Are you secure?" John looked around himself to make sure no one was listening.

Becky could hear the PA system in the background telling passengers not to leave their luggage unattended. It was the standard airport ATSB message she'd heard a hundred times since 911.

"Yes, I'm alone and secure. What's going on? Are you in an airport?"

"Yes I am. That's not important. Just so you'll know, I'll be in the air for most of the day and I wanted to get this message to you ASAP. I should have called you yesterday, but this traveling has made it difficult."

"All right. What info do you have for me?"

Becky was surprised her phone was working in Marco's basement. She only had one bar, but the clarity was good. She had no trouble hearing John over the gurgling sound of the hydroponics.

"You need to know the FBI is bigfooting our case. They have agents on the ground, or will have soon; I'm not sure about the timing."

"Why John? This is our case. What right do they have to butt in?"

"It's complicated; I'll explain more to you later. Ever since they used an agent in Puerto Rico to interview the cigar company they've been involved; you know, interstate jurisdiction, and so on. They're even more involved now. I just wanted you to know ASAP so you're not in the dark."

"I appreciate that John. How many agents are we talking about?"

"I'm not sure, but I think they're starting with one. They may already be on board. Their agent's name is Alondra Espinoza. She's worked with Jason in the past."

Becky was silent as she digested the surprising news the FBI had entered the case. She had to move quickly now.

"That's all I have Becky; just a heads up. Keep an eye out for her and watch yourself. You haven't seen any indication of her involvement yet, I'm assuming?"

"No John, I'm watchful, nothing like that.

"Status quo here. We're no closer than we were last time we talked. If anything changes I'll be in touch. I'll cooperate fully with the FBI if I need to, of course."

Becky was standing right in front of, and examining the #13 strain as she talked with John. She was sure this was the real thing; tobacco-like plants growing right in the middle of the marijuana section. The saw-tooth edges on the leaves were one telltale sign these plants were a combination of tobacco and marijuana.

"Okay Becky, we're counting on you. Good luck, and take care."

"Thanks John. Have a good flight. I'll talk to you on the regular schedule on Saturday."

"Right," he said, hanging up.

After placing her phone in her sweatshirt pocket, she produced a small plastic zip-lock bag she kept tucked away in her jeans. She reached up as high as she could around the back of one of the lush plants and plucked off a small 10-inch leaf from the thick stalk. No one would miss one small leaf taken from that high up from the back side of the plant.

She folded the leaf carefully, placing it into the plastic bag. She needed to dry it thoroughly with a hair dryer before presenting it. Even if Randolph called tonight, she had at least the afternoon to prepare the sample before another courier would come to pick it up.

Looking up into the grow lights she could see Marco had clipped off the seed pods as they were conspicuously absent from the tops of the plants; she could see the clean cut snipped ends where they should have been. If she had even the slightest notion Marco could be left out of her plan, that was no longer possible. The seed was everything; without it, she had nothing. She was resigned to bring him in now, and that's how it should be.

She also knew she was running out of time if FBI agents were assigned to the case. She couldn't procrastinate any longer. She would tell him tonight after the party, after the long awaited romance they would share back at his house. Tonight she would finally give in to him. He had to go along with her plan after that. He loved her and would do anything to keep her in his life, for the future they would share together, she was sure of it. Just a few more hours and it would be done.

Tonight was the night she would give it all to get it all.

Chapter 32

I was pleased my workday was ending early, but I was rushing now, running late for my lunch meeting with Alondra at 12:30 downstairs in the restaurant. I texted her to tell her I'd be fifteen minutes late. I hated being tardy, and today it wasn't my fault; it took longer to leave the yard. A monstrous new John Deere tractor attached to a huge cucumber harvester had been delivered this morning and they parked it haphazardly, blocking the gravel path to the greenhouses. Normally it wouldn't have been a problem, but because of the heavy rains, the grass on either side of the gravel path turned to mud and we couldn't drive around the equipment without getting hopelessly stuck.

So we all waited in our cars until someone showed up to move the giant tractor. That someone turned out to be Everett O'Malley, the manager of the pickle operation. Everett was really upset the delivery was made in the rain and his new equipment was getting a shower. They had strict instructions not to deliver in these conditions, but they did it anyway. Everett was more than upset; he was livid. After listening to his rant, we made some quick introductions and I asked questions about the new machinery. I was rushing to leave so we made promises to see each other and talk later that evening at the party at McLadden's. I was thrilled yet another facet of the farm was revealing itself.

As I was dressing after a shower, stuffing my damp legs into fresh jeans, I reflected on my time with Marco. I needed to work closely with him from now on, now we knew he was intimately involved. Damn John and Bill for keeping me in the dark about the research team's involvement. Marco was keeping the strain somewhere and undoubtedly possessed seed and had grown enough of it to get it into the production stream. Cured product had made it all the way through the co-op and down into the Puerto Rican manufacturing plant. How much cured product was there? How much seed did he have? If I could win his confidence I might be able to get him to open up and talk about his work. I learned from the little time I'd spent with him he had an enormous ego and he just might be waiting for someone to recognize his genius. I hoped to be in that position, but if I couldn't spend work-time with him in the seed house, I'd never have those conversations. I needed to work on Peter to make a case to spend more time with Marco. Taking half the day off today wasn't getting me any closer to the goal.

As I rode the elevator down to the restaurant level, my watch said it was 12:44. I would check the bar first looking for the beautiful long black hair known to catch eyes from most men. I saw her sitting at the corner of the bar, positioned so she could see other patrons coming in from the main entrance. She hadn't seen my approach from the elevators.

"Well good morning a second time," I said as I took the seat beside her at the bar. "Nice to see you here. Did you finish your errands and get what we need at Staples?"

"Yes, I did. I've been busy on my own with something else too. I visited a check cashing company in Hartford. Have some interesting information for you. I'll fill you in later. I was hoping you'd want to take the afternoon off, especially due to the rain. We can use the time this afternoon to create the union material. Did you have any trouble getting away?"

"Check cashing company? That's sounds intriguing.

"I had no trouble leaving early. You know I should be spending my time with Marco and not you. It's not that he's cuter," I said and paused to get her reaction; she ignored me, except for a smile. "But we're never getting to the bottom of this case unless I can spend more time with him. I think I can get him to open up, but that takes face time, something that's hard to come by, especially when Peter assigns me to do other things. He's been giving me the option to work with him if he comes in and needs my help, but Marco was AWOL this morning again and he never showed. He must be working at the experiment station all the more often to be with his lady friend."

"Oh you mean the woman Becky you met yesterday at the experiment station?" responded Alondra.

"That's right. I think he's spending all his time with her."

Something started to bother me, but I wasn't sure what it was. It was a thought creeping in and I couldn't put a handle on it. Before I could resolve it, my attention was diverted to a couple walking into the restaurant holding hands. It was Marco and Becky being led by the host to a table.

"Don't look now, but Marco and Becky just walked in here and are being seated for lunch in a booth behind the partition. They must really like each other if they're holding hands in public at their age."

"Are you sure?"

"Positively sure," I said. "Do you want to crash their lunch? I mean we could go over and I could introduce you. Maybe they would invite us to sit at their table with them."

"I'm not sure that's a great idea. How will you introduce me?"

"Hmmm, let's see... I'll say you're my cousin from Venezuela who just arrived at JFK, and you're traveling through Hartford on your way to Boston to visit your parents."

"Wow, you came up with that one fast. Sounds just different enough it might work."

"So you're ready?"

"Lead the way, Cousin Jason."

We slipped off our chairs at the bar and made our way across the room behind the partition to see Marco and Becky sitting at a booth. I went right up to Marco extending my hand to shake his.

"Marco! Great to see you here. Nice day to take a break from the rain. Hello Becky. Nice to see you again so soon."

"Hi Jason," Marco responded warmly. "I see you're keeping better company these days. Who's your friend?"

"This is my cousin Alondra Espinoza, she's from Venezuela. She just arrived this morning at JFK and she stopped on her way to Boston. We're all very proud of her; she's a professional model, very successful and very well-known there."

"Oh stop Jason!" exclaimed Alondra. "You're embarrassing me. Please don't exaggerate."

"Nice to meet you Alondra; nothing wrong with a little familial pride. You're quite beautiful and I can see you're in the right profession," said Marco as he looked over to Becky, who was clearly not happy with the conversation and that Marco had taken interest in Alondra. I couldn't help smiling about it.

Marco asked, "Why don't the two of you join us for lunch. Jason, you remember Becky from the experiment station. Alondra, this is Becky Sadler. We work together on various agricultural projects; to be honest, we're dating."

"Very nice to meet you Alondra," said Becky as she reached out and shook Alondra's hand. She did not look pleased we crashed her lunch date.

They were sitting across from each other so they both scooted into the booth so we could sit next to them. I took the lead and sat next to Becky leaving Alondra no choice but to sit next to Marco. That procured a look from Alondra, but I was hoping she'd understand the strategy. I didn't exactly know what that strategy was, but I was hoping it would come to me soon.

I looked around the table and to break the ice I said, "Thank you Marco and Becky, for inviting us to sit with you."

"Our pleasure Jason, isn't it Becky?"

"Oh yes, of course," said Becky.

Then she turned toward Alondra, "So Alondra, what a pretty name. You're from Venezuela. Your English is perfect. How long have you been in this country?"

"I was born there and came to the states when I was six years old," replied Alondra in a thicker accent than I'd heard before.

"My father was transferred to Pittsburg and worked there for years before being transferred back. I went to high school and University in Caracas, studying English, and I teach English there, in addition to modeling. My parents moved back to the states and live outside of Boston now. I visit them at least twice a year."

I was impressed how easily this fabricated life history rolled off her tongue. They both bought it.

Becky, staring at Alondra asked, "How nice. And you and Jason are cousins; you must be close."

"We are close," I said. "We've always been close and it hasn't been easy to stay in touch over the years, but we try to see each other whenever we can."

"Where's that waiter?" Marco asked. "Let's see if we can get him over here to take our drink order."

Marco stuck his hand in the air and started waving it. One of the waiters saw it, came right over and stood next to the booth.

"Do you like red wine?" Marco asked looking over to both Alondra and me. We both nodded in agreement.

"I know you want red too Becky, so that makes it unanimous. Let's get some good Cabernet. We'll each have two glasses right? So let's make it two, two bottles of the good Cabernet."

"Yes sir," said the waiter who turned and walked away.

Seeing Marco here today initially gave me a thought of going back to work with him after lunch. Little chance of that now if we're downing a half bottle each of Cabernet. On the plus side, this much wine will loosen tongues.

"Jason, how long have you been at Treadwell?" Marco asked.

"This is my first week. So that makes it three and a half days? Not very long. I was hoping to get a chance to work more with you Marco. I find what you're doing fascinating."

"I think there's a strong possibility we can work more closely."

I noticed Alondra across from me watching Becky.

Marco continued, "Peter promised me I had you as much as I needed for the first few weeks. I've been tied up with work at the experiment station the past few days, but I need to spend more time at Treadwell now that planting starts next week. Would you be interested in working with Kevin and me planting the strains?"

Two waiters arrived at the booth, one with four wine glasses and menus, the other with the two bottles of wine. One bottle was quickly opened and four glasses were poured. I waited for the waiters to leave before answering.

"Absolutely, I would like to help you with that."

"Well let's make it happen then. Let's drink a toast," said Marco. "Here's to a successful growing season at Treadwell Farm."

We all clinked our glasses and sipped the wine. I noticed Marco downed half his glass. The wine was good, but not that good. I wanted to get Marco talking about his work, but I had to start slowly so not to appear too interested.

"Marco, Kevin tells me you're on a quest to develop some super tobacco strains to improve yields by ten percent." Alondra stared at me, raising her eyebrows with a look that said 'not yet'. I ignored her.

"That's true Jason. I've made progress toward that goal and this year I'm confident we'll reach it."

Marco took a long pull on the remainder of the wine in his glass. We'd been seated for less than four minutes and his glass was emptied. I began to think Marco might have a problem which we could capitalize on. He then poured the remainder of the bottle into his glass and drank from it again.

"I love this Cabernet. It's a good one, don't you think Becky?"

"Yes, it's very good. We have a bottle every time we come in here. I think it's a good idea if we all looked at our menus. The food is really good here too," Becky said.

We all spent a few minutes looking over the menu until I broke the silence.

"So Marco, what kind of a cash crop is shade tobacco? I mean, how profitable is it really? Seems to me there's a ton of labor and equipment necessary to grow it. I've only been here for a few days, but I can see it's expensive to grow."

"Oh it can be very profitable. Of course the stars have to

align just right."

"What do you mean 'the stars have to align'?"

Marco hesitated and spoke directly to Alondra, "I don't want to bore our women with farm talk. Maybe we can focus on another topic more to their liking."

Alondra responded using her thick accent, "Marco, I'm very interested to hear your opinion about tobacco. I've always been curious about the nets and the barns and how it all works. Please, continue and tell us more."

Marco looked over and smiled at Alondra who smiled back at him; she was playing right along with me.

I was beginning to feel sorry for Becky; Marco was clearly attracted to Alondra, as most men are. He was also insensitive to Becky's recognition of his sudden interest in Alondra and his mild flirtation. I felt some tension in the air from Becky's body language; she was being ignored, had competition and wasn't used to this. If I could get Marco focused on the farm topic and away from Alondra, problem solved.

"You asked me what I meant about the stars aligning. What I mean by that is you could never make any money growing shade tobacco if you had to start from scratch. There are too many hurdles; too much infrastructure needs to be in place. The land, the sheds, the greenhouses, the labor. So, as long as you were born with it and had it in your family, had all the assets and were doing it year after year, for years in the past, only then you can make real money growing shade tobacco. Your 'stars' have to be aligned.

"Of course the market has to be there too. You can grow

anything in the fertile Connecticut River valley, right? But if there's no market, you can't sell it. So the market for expensive luxury tobacco, premium cigar wrappers, is a critical component. We get top dollar for the best tobacco; no holes, large pliant leaves with good color and good aroma. Up to 100 dollars per pound for the highest grade leaf.

"My job is to improve the weight and size of the leaves by ten percent. I can do that, I know I can. In some of the test trials, I'm seeing 15 to 20 percent improvement."

As he said that, he waived over our waiter and asked him to open the second bottle of wine. His glass was empty and I noticed Becky had hardly touched hers. The waiter opened the second bottle and poured a third glass for Marco, which he promptly started in on. We also made sandwich selections for lunch and the menus were collected.

Left alone again, I thought now was a good time to nudge the conversation toward marijuana. He was loosening up after his second glass of wine. I looked across to Alondra and winked at her. She nodded imperceptibly back.

"Marco, I'm interested in your opinion about something. What are the chances marijuana could be a major crop here in the valley?"

He raised his eyebrows and smiled at the question.

"I think it's a definite possibility. But you have to solve the security problem first."

"Sorry, what do you mean by the security problem?"

"You may not know this but today almost all marijuana

grown commercially is grown indoors. Many growers are using multi-tiered warehouse space, requiring artificial lighting and irrigation at each level. If the plants are locked indoors, there is little likelihood for theft.

"And yes, marijuana would be an order of magnitude more profitable than tobacco. If you think shade tobacco is expensive at 100 dollars a pound, try buying marijuana in Colorado today for 250 dollars an ounce, or 4,000 dollars a pound! Growers won't get that much at the wholesale level; that price is riddled with taxes and fees to the state and federal governments, but you get the idea there could be substantially more profit in this than not.

"To grow marijuana in open fields could be easily done, provided the proper barriers were in place to isolate and protect the plants from intruders. I can envision tall chain-link fencing with barbed wire on top might do the trick. Another hurdle will be the state legislatures; some states have laws preventing the cultivation of open field marijuana."

I continued to poke at the topic. "Harvesting operations would be massively different, I mean between shade tobacco and marijuana, wouldn't they?"

"Yes, and there lies the challenge." Marco continued, "No one has attempted to grow marijuana on the same scale as tobacco. If anyone was even close to growing it this way, marijuana would have to be very different and it should be different too, for the benefit of public health."

"I don't follow you," I said. I was on a roll and this conversation was going exactly where it needed to go. I watched Alondra listening intently to Marco, and he was speaking mostly to her now. Becky stared at Marco, expressionless. Marco's third glass of wine was almost finished and Becky still hadn't touched hers.

Marco continued, "Today marijuana is a specialty crop in the few states where recreational marijuana is legal, and in some 25 other states allowing medical marijuana. Most of those growers are small and what I would call 'boutique' growers, meaning they focus on the buds, the potency, and color, not the volume; the whole thing is so new they're just content to hold on to a sliver of the pie. They're not thinking about the future and where marijuana should be going."

"What were you starting to say about the public health?" I asked.

"I'm getting to that. As a society, we're learning our way. First things first. We'll legalize marijuana and bring it mainstream. It will take time though. What do we say to all the men and women still in prison who were convicted of marijuana crimes? Do we set them free? Sorry, you're in jail because you saw the future and wanted it now. Oh well, timing is everything, right? That's one of the really big hurdles in front of us."

Marco finished the last bit of wine in his glass.

"Another hurdle is this question: does anyone care marijuana, as we know it today, poses a major health risk that's much worse than cigarettes? Marijuana smoke has ten times the tar compared to cigarette smoke."

We were all completely focused on Marco now. I had an opportunity, an open door to a place we wanted to go, so I stepped in.

"Marco, if that's the case, why not develop a strain of

marijuana that's more like tobacco?"

"Ah, there's a step in the right direction Jason. But that might not get you where you need to go; Marijuana is still marijuana and tar producing components will be the same. Why not take a different, more novel approach to the problem. Why not develop a strain of tobacco that's more like marijuana?"

Alondra looked across at me and raised her eyebrows slightly, which I took to be my queue to keep going.

"Have you ever attempted to do that? Do you even think it's possible?" I asked.

Marco, with an odd smile on his face, paused and reached over, took the wine bottle and poured himself another glass of wine.

Becky protested, "Marco, I've been counting and that's your fourth glass. Are you sure you want that? You definitely don't need it; I think you've had too much already."

Marco took another sip of wine and continued, his smile gone now.

"Let's just say this could be done, hypothetically. With the right funding and environment, it would be an interesting challenge. The outcome is not guaranteed, of course, but with a little luck, one might be successful and manage to create a new super-hybrid species of tobacco plant holding the best characteristics of both tobacco and marijuana."

Marco was talking more emphatically and louder now, as the wine was taking hold.

"That being said, if, and I do say 'IF' we did produce this

tobacco hybrid, would it really be a good thing for the planet? I don't think so. Think about the consequences and what it would mean if people could walk around smoking a cigarette and the authorities couldn't easily tell the difference between tobacco and marijuana. So yes, it might be possible, but is that something we should introduce into the world?"

Before I could say another word, we heard a phone ringing at the table. Marco pulled an iPhone from his shirt pocket and looked at the screen.

"I'm sorry Alondra, but I have to take this call. Will you all excuse me?"

"Sure," Alondra said as she stood up from the booth to let Marco out. He left the booth and quickly walked out toward the exit, the phone to his head.

Alondra sat back down as I stole a glance at Becky sitting next to me. She looked back at me nervously and looked away.

In less than a minute, Marco was back to the table.

"Jason and Alondra, I'm sorry, but I need to cut our lunch short.

"Becky, Harold called from the airport. He made an earlier connection in Denver and he arrived at Bradley an hour ahead of schedule. We agreed to meet him at the airport so we need to leave now."

"Marco, I'll drive," said Becky.

I stood up to let Becky out.

"So this is Harold Treadwell you're picking up?" I asked.

Marco replied, "Yes, he's flying in from Sonoma to attend a going-away party tonight for Wes Ackerson. He's the teacher you replaced actually. Harold is very fond of him. I hope you'll be there. It's at an Irish restaurant in Simsbury. A place called McLadden's."

"I'll be there," I said, as Becky reached back into the booth to grab her handbag.

"Good. Alondra, I hope you can join us tonight too."

"I'll be there too Marco."

"Great. See you both there. Sorry we have to go. Let's go Becky, you're driving."

He threw the keys to Becky and they walked out together, as we both sat back down in the booth.

Chapter 33

I decided I liked the furniture in Alondra's hotel room more than mine. I always thought the Marriott hotel was a better hotel than the Hilton, but side by side, the Hilton had the best stuff, no doubt. We had discovered the land for this hotel was also previously owned by Treadwell, but it was built after the Marriott. The hotels were literally a stone's throw away from each other so there was a stiff competition for business. The Hilton wanted a leg up on the Marriott, hence the higher-end furniture.

The TV was on, but the sound was muted all afternoon while we rehashed our lunch with Marco and Alondra briefed me on her visit to a Hartford check cashing company. I gave her a breakdown of my conversation with Cody earlier in the greenhouse, including his reaction when I brought up the 'BL' field name. We closed out the afternoon creating and printing the union brochures using some free software we found on the internet.

Marco's ethical position regarding the potent strain hitting the street was surprising. He clearly stated his position in global terms: it wouldn't be a good thing for the planet if said strain were to be widely released. Was he being honest, or were his comments for our consumption, to throw us off the track? He all but admitted to creating the strain but stopped short. We both agreed our next steps were to confront him directly on the topic and to do so in a way he would feel free to respond truthfully and not feel threatened. The question was how and when to do that.

The brochures didn't turn out too bad; Alondra had done her research and found enough union-oriented feeder material on the internet so the main effort was copy and paste. The paper was photo quality semi-gloss so the final result looked really professional. The brochures were printed on both sides and they folded nicely into a six-sided pamphlet. We also had an FAQ section printed in both English and Spanish. The content described the pros of union membership in both languages, and it was all true, especially in work environments as lean and unsophisticated as tobacco farming where unions weren't established yet.

Her business cards were printed on cream-colored card stock and hand cut with a paper cutter. They turned out great too.

I picked up one of the cards and studied it in the light of the window; it said: *Alondra Espinoza, Equal Rights Attorney - Union Expert.* Underneath was the Spanish version: *Alondra Espinoza, Igualdad de Derechos Fiscal - Unión Experto.*

It really was hard to believe in this day and age, common sense benefits and protections we take for granted in almost every other industry had yet to take hold. Benefits for the workers here were non-existent. Why was this industry left behind? Hard to believe Connecticut was the richest state in the nation, yet there was this dirty little secret everyone closes an eye to. Nobody cared enough I guess, or maybe everybody was in it for themselves. Surely it wasn't a new industry; it's been around for a century and there's been enough time for corrections, but it hasn't happened.

When you thought about the workforce I supposed it made sense. Migrant workers, many non-educated and non-English speaking carry no clout and never get established with a voice for change. School children as a summer labor source are in the same position. Farm owners, many of whom had real wealth and loads of political capital, were using the same captive labor source for years and no one with any influence had reason or desire to change the status quo.

There is also the concerted effort from within to squash any forward thinking. Guys like Carlos, the men's boss, were well paid to post those "KEEP OUT" signs and block any attempt to organize.

The more I thought about it the more I understood and aligned with Alondra's point of view. I had come around to embrace her passion. We were still working the TobaccoNet case, but now there seemed to be another urgency driving us.

I shouldn't have let her go to the men's camp alone, but she insisted. She felt having me along would put them all on guard and I had to agree with her on that point. We also both thought it was best I not be involved in the union topic; if word got out I was openly in support of it and we were connected, my employment here could be jeopardized.

Her mission was to go there specifically to seek Julio out. I knew Julio was a forward thinking individual who might be sympathetic to her cause. We both believed he was her best shot at finding someone on the inside who could help her organize. Ironically, it was a bit of a Catch-22 for her. She was in there to establish worker's rights and protections so men like Julio couldn't just be fired without cause, yet Julio's involvement in union activities, if it blossomed, could eventually lead to his employment termination.

Her main obstacle was the men's boss, Carlos. It was he who could give her real trouble. She was savvy and could handle herself. In extreme cases, she had 'Betsy', her tiny pistol in the ankle holster she could use if she had to. She promised she wouldn't be long and she'd be back in less than an hour. I looked at my watch; it was 5:30, which meant she'd been gone for 20 minutes.

I turned and gazed out the window and watched the cars streaming down the hill on Night Valley Road. The rain had stopped and the roads were dry now. I saw the lush green rolling hills of the Connecticut River valley. I could see some of the white cheesecloth nets in the distance and tried to imagine the men and the kids working in the hot fields. Somewhere out there a special tobacco strain would be planted and it was my job, our job to find it. But it wasn't our only mission anymore.

Guided by her GPS, Alondra pulled into the camp yard and took a parking place next to a silver Honda Civic. She eyed the car's low profile, fat racing tires, and altered exhaust. She was familiar with these modifications on Honda Civics; her brother in Puerto Rico had done similar things to his car.

With the car still running, she looked around the grass parking lot and immediately felt her Rav4 stood out as the newest, most normal car there. Most of the other cars were older and beat up looking. Many were station wagons, rusting, dented and in need of body work and paint they would never have. It was tough owning a car making minimum wage. And there weren't many of them; she counted only nine other cars.

The camp was old too; in disrepair. It was very much like the pictures of the camp building she'd seen in Jackie's presentation. Some of the second story dormered windows were broken and the place looked seedy, in need of paint with a rundown appearance. Definitely not a place one would be proud to live in.

She turned off the ignition and noticed two long wooden picnic tables placed ten feet outside the main entrance in the middle of the grassy front yard, 50 yards away. No one was sitting in any of the benches or lawn chairs surrounding the tables. She noted the time was 5:35; a bit too early perhaps for the evening meal if a normal workday ended at 5:00. Then again, it had rained today and she remembered the crews may have been given the day off, so they might be eating earlier than usual.

Just then a chef wearing a white smock and a tall white chef's hat walked out the front door toward the picnic tables carrying a large steaming bowl of pasta. Another man followed him with a tall stack of plates and silverware. They were setting the tables now, placing plates and silverware all around the two tables.

Alondra reached over to the passenger seat and took her portfolio of brochures. She assumed the chef was familiar with everyone living here so he was the best person to ask.

Alondra checked her makeup in the mirror. She exited the Rav4 and made sure to shut the door loudly enough for them to hear her. She was wearing tight black pants and a loose-fitting red blouse. Her hair was down, but she had draped it all on the right side so her face was more exposed.

Once they looked her way, experience told her she would have no trouble keeping their attention. If her sexual magnetism could ever be measured, it would be off the charts; she was well aware of this phenomenon. Using it to her advantage only when she chose to, it had served her well in life.

The noise from the door shutting did its trick as the chef and his helper immediately focused on Alondra coming toward them. When she was close enough, Alondra began the exchange, entirely in Spanish.

"Veo que está a punto de cenar?"

"Yes we are. Normally we eat later but the men worked only half a day today due to the rain. They'll be out in a few minutes. The rain stopped hours ago and with the sun out now the benches are dried enough to sit on," answered the chef. The helper was frozen, staring at Alondra.

"Can I help you? Are you lost?" he asked.

"No, I'm looking for someone. This is the Treadwell farm camp, right?"

"Yes it is. Who are you looking for? Maybe I can help you. But I have to tell you there's a strict no-solicitation policy here and if you're selling something, I'm supposed to ask you to leave," he smiled.

"I have nothing to sell; I only wish to speak with someone. Maybe you know the person I'm looking for, his name is Julio, Julio Rodriguez."

The chef looked over to his helper and barked, "Get Julio."

He responded with, "Julio's not here. He left earlier and he hasn't come back. I know because just before lunch Peter came to do the roll call for this morning's hours and they said Julio left to do an errand."

The chef looked back to Alondra and shrugged with a hand gesture which looked like an apology and said, "I'm sorry, but Julio isn't here right now. We expect him back shortly, he never misses dinner. Who can I say was looking for him?"

They all turned and watched as an older black mustang rumbled into the yard and parked next to the Rav4.

"There's Julio now," said the helper.

"Wonderful, I guess I'll get to speak with him after all. Thanks."

Alondra smiled at the two men and turned and walked quickly back to the cars where Julio was now climbing out of his car. They both watched her go.

"That Julio is a lucky guy," the helper said quietly to the chef.

"Maybe. Maybe not," replied the chef, still watching Alondra at a distance as she walked right up to Julio to greet him.

Julio reached out and shook her outstretched hand. Standing next to the cars, they were out of earshot from the others and Alondra wanted to keep it that way, so she started right in.

"Hello Julio, my name is Alondra Espinoza," she said in Spanish. "I'm so glad to meet you. I hope we can stay right here for our discussion; I want to keep it private, just between us for now."

Julio was still in a state of shock and recovery from his earlier encounter with Becky and what it would mean. He hadn't had a chance to see Kevin alone when he stopped at the greenhouses to drop off the weed for the party. Bob was there and asked him how it went, but he didn't have the courage to tell him he'd been caught. He wanted to talk to Kevin first, but he couldn't with Bob there. He'd have to wait to see him at the party.

Julio had no idea who Alondra was. He momentarily stared at her, wondering why this beautiful dark-haired Puerto Rican woman in red and black wanted to speak with him. Alondra interpreted Julio's silence as confusion, but before she could continue, he bluntly asked, "What do you want?"

"I'd like to talk with you about an important topic."

"What topic is that? And why do you want to speak to *me* about it? If you're selling something I have no money so you're wasting your time."

Julio was having trouble. She was so beautiful he had to look away from her and not imagine anything further, as loyalty to his wife was one of the most important things in his life. Just being in this woman's presence and looking at her was exciting him as a man and that was wrong. He was getting a nagging notion maybe this was a trap of some kind and he should stay away.

He continued, "I'm not sure I should be talking with you. How do you know my name?"

Alondra replied, "I got your name from someone who wanted his name kept out of it, but he assured me you might be interested in what I have to say. Here's my card."

She pulled out her business card and handed it to Julio. He looked at it and smiled.

“Ah, so that’s what this is about. You’re a union person. Here please take this back. I can’t have this here.”

She took her card back and slipped it back into her portfolio.

“Well actually, I’m not a union person, I don’t belong to a union per se, but I’m definitely pro-union and I’d like to see them established here in the valley in the shade tobacco business.”

Julio looked back toward the front door of the camp where the picnic tables were. He could see both the chef and his helper had gone back inside. It was critical the discussion they were having not be heard by anyone else. He relaxed now somewhat because they were alone. He had some familiarity with the union issue, but he didn’t feel right discussing it openly, knowing how Carlos felt about it. He also had no reason to trust this woman; she was a total stranger.

Alondra sensed his reluctance and she tried again to put him at ease.

“Julio, please don’t feel frightened to talk with me about this. I know from good sources you are one of the best and most respected workers here, and you’ve been here for many years and you can see the possibilities for change. Unions are good, especially for large farming operations like this where workers rights need to be heard. The time is right for this, you know that’s true. If you can embrace this, and lead the way I know the others will follow. We can improve the working conditions, establish real benefits, protections and more pay for you and the others. I know people on the outside who will help us get started. Will you help us?"

Julio looked up to see several of his coworkers coming out of the camp, making their way across the lawn toward them; one was Antonio, his bunkmate. They were close friends and obviously the chef had said something. He had about forty seconds before they'd be there.

"I can't talk to you right now, they're coming." Alondra turned around and saw the small group of men walking toward them about 100 feet away.

Julio continued, "I don't know if I can help. I know you're right and we need unions here. I don't know you and you seem nice, but I have my own problems right now. I don't know how much longer I'll be working here.

"Do you have a pen?" he asked.

Taken by surprise by Julio's comment, Alondra reached into her portfolio and quickly gave Julio a pen.

He reached into his pocket and pulled out the purple tag, turned it over to the blank side and scribbled something on it.

"Here's my cell number. There's a party tonight, until 9:30 or 10:00 so better to call tomorrow. I'll talk to you if I can, in private. If you call at 10:00 it's better; we have a 15-minute break every morning."

Alondra took the tag and pen and slipped them both back into the portfolio.

The men were almost there. Alondra had made contact and started the ball rolling and that was all she hoped to accomplish in her first meeting.

She reached out to shake Julio's hand and said, "Thank you Julio. I'll be in touch with you very soon."

Julio turned to face his friends as Alondra moved to the Rav4. She climbed in and shut the door. She couldn't hear them now, but she saw Julio pointing briefly back toward her and shrugging. Julio's back was to her and she could see the other men trying to look past Julio in her direction. She started the car, backed out of the spot and made her way out of the yard on the grassy entrance road.

Driving back to the hotel, she wondered how many other men besides Julio would be going to the party tonight. She needed to pull him aside and talk to him again to ask him what he meant about not working at Treadwell much longer. Her connection to Jason would be out in the open too; maybe that would work in their favor as he would see he wasn't alone with Jason's support.

She wondered how long she had before the case would end, one way or the other. She had so much more to accomplish; she wasn't ready for it to end just yet. So much was beginning to hang on a very thin thread. She had to be careful the thread didn't snap.

Chapter 34

I gave the waiter my last five dollar bill as a tip when he brought the bottle of Chardonnay up to the room. He opened the bottle and left it chilling in the ice bucket next to two new wine glasses on the desk.

It was 6:30 and Alondra would be back soon from her errand at the camp. I went over and poured myself a glass of wine. Social events were not my strong suit so I had no trouble starting early with a glass or two before the party. I'd changed my clothes and was wearing khakis and a long-sleeve blue and white striped shirt. Party attire.

I didn't have to wait long. I heard her room key unlocking the door and she entered the room, with the door closing behind her.

"I see you started without me," she said.

"No worries, I have one for you too. That was fast. How did it go?" I said as I poured her glass and made my way across the room handing her the glass and giving her an affectionate hug and kiss.

"Not bad, I found Julio at the camp. You were right; the place isn't a great place to live, but I didn't go inside. I saw him when he was pulling in, in the parking lot. I gave him my card, but he wouldn't take it. We chatted for a few minutes, but we couldn't talk for long without a group of men hearing us. They came out and interrupted our conversation. I did get his phone number and I can call him tomorrow morning at 10:00 a.m., during his morning break. I think we might have a chance with him."

"That's right, I remember he said he had a phone, but he couldn't call Puerto Rico with his plan. He borrows Carlos's phone to call home. We may have trouble selling union to him if he shows too much loyalty to Carlos."

I moved to the couch and sat down, still holding my wine. Alondra sat sideways in the chair at the desk, facing me.

"He gave me his phone number without me asking for it. That's a good sign. I'll add it to my contacts."

Alondra reached into her portfolio and withdrew the purple tag with the phone number written on it. She placed it on the desk and proceeded to enter Julio's number into her phone as a contact.

"There, all set. I'll call him in the morning. But we'll see him tonight too at the party, so you'll need to help me talk to him. Once he sees us together he'll know we feel the same way about unions."

"Why is that?" I said, smiling. "I don't have to carry the same torch as my cousin."

I got up from the couch with my wine, walked over to the large window and looked out at the lush greenery. The view of the valley from the fifth floor didn't disappoint. The rain had stopped several hours ago and the sun was poking through the clouds. It was 6:40 and we had about an hour of light left. The small side window was open and I could feel the chilled air pouring in. No more rain, but the chill was going strong. Tonight would be a cold night in the greenhouses, a respite from the hot weather of the past few days. The heat was good for the seedlings and they'd grown faster because of it. I overheard Kevin saying they might move the planting schedule up a day or two, especially since Treadwell was in town. The rain was the problem now; the fields might be too wet. I wondered what I'd be doing tomorrow; possibly working with Marco and Kevin planting some strains.

"We have a 15-minute drive to McLadden's in Simsbury. I Googled it. We'd better leave soon. Fashionably late is only a plus in the movies."

I turned from the window and walked over to Alondra still sitting at the desk.

I looked down at her as I said, "I'm assuming you're dressed and going as is. Red and black suits you. Are you taking Betz along?"

Before she could answer I saw the small purple tag lying on the desk with the phone number written on it. I picked it up and noticed a piece of green-stained string still tied to the tag. I turned the tag over and saw the #13 written on the back in heavy black ink.

"Where did you get this?"

"Julio gave it to me. He wrote his phone number on it. Why, what's wrong?"

"Alondra, sweetheart, do you know what this is? This isn't just one of the strain tags. It is *THE* strain tag. I've seen red tags and some yellow and orange tags but never purple tags, and this tag belongs to the #13 strain. This means the #13 strain exists and Julio knows where it is."

"We can ask him about it tonight."

"No, we can do better than that.

"Alondra, we're close now, I can feel it. This tag must have come from the seed house. If Julio had this tag, the strain has to be there. This could be the beginning of what we need to close the case. Let's go now, before the party."

"Go where? To the greenhouses? What if someone's there?"

"Everyone will be at the party. We'll be all alone. The door might be locked, though; we'll need to enter from the back if it is." As I said that I was hoping Peter hadn't put the new locks on the back doors.

"Are you sure?"

"Yes, I'm sure. Come on, let's go."

"What do we say if we're caught?"

"I'll say I wanted to show my cousin the seeding operation, so she'd have more background to be engaged with conversation at the party. Simple as that."

"Okay, I'm coming." She stood up and grabbed her jacket. "We can go to the party from there."

"Alondra, when we find the strain, we're not going to the party."

"I was hoping you wouldn't say that."

Chapter 35

As foreman, Peter Roscoe rarely did anything alone. He always had someone with him. That was either one of the men, or one or more of the inner circle, usually Kevin, Cody or sometimes Julio. One, two or all three would ride with him in the pickup, one in the back and two in the front. Riding with Peter was considered a definite benefit because often times all he wanted was companionship and there wasn't any work involved. He just wanted you in the truck with him. You'd drive from field to field, shed to shed, checking on things, or dragging water barrels around so the crews could take a water break. It was how he managed, MBRA – manage by riding around. It also meant you'd be plucked from a field's work crew to get a respite from the heat or where real physical labor was going on. Occasionally Peter would stop at Wendy's or McDonald's to treat his guests to a meal.

Some days Kevin and Cody would spend the entire day with Peter in his hi-tech air-conditioned pickup truck. Hi-tech because he had two cell phones and a Mac PC bracketed to the dashboard and open at all times. One cell phone had a direct two-way radio line to Harold Treadwell ensuring instantaneous communication. That phone also had a GPS service to track Peter's location so Harold would know exactly where Peter was at all times.

Kevin and Cody knew not to mess with Harold's phone, but they had no trouble using the other phone or using the Mac whenever Peter left them alone in the truck. Some days he would be gone for over an hour checking on the men or running errands in town. Kevin and Cody soon began to feel they were entitled to ride around with Peter for a good part of the day.

The next few days would be different. Harold was coming in from Sonoma, California to attend Wes Ackerson's party and to monitor the first several days of planting. That meant Peter would need to be absent his sidekicks. This happened every time Harold came home to visit.

Harold let Peter run the farm as he saw fit. He trusted Peter, but he also kept him on a long leash. As long as the phone was there and he could track Peter down maintaining instant communication using the cell's walkie-talkie mode, he was content to run the farm by proxy.

Today was unusual because Harold hadn't followed the normal protocol. He chose Marco to pick him up at the airport and they went on to spend the entire afternoon together. That really bothered Peter. He was the one running the farm but Harold treated Marco like the chosen one, lauding his tobacco genetic heroics, his efforts to create the perfect bigger and better tobacco strain, which was, in Peter's mind, total bullshit.

As time went on, Peter's distrust of Marco ran deeper and deeper. Peter had examined the strain document files in the seed house. He thought Marco had done a pretty thorough job documenting each strain, but there was one piece of critical information missing from the files: the strain lineage. Each strain was the result of a pollinated pairing of two parent strains, but that information was conspicuously absent from the seed house files. This meant Marco had a second set of files somewhere - or it could mean Marco was a total fraud.

Peter was inclined to believe the latter until Kevin confirmed one day what he suspected all along: Marco was crossing strains in an offsite location, in a greenhouse facility in the basement of his house. That information fueled even more distrust and anger as Harold and Marco had obviously conspired at great expense, to build that greenhouse without his knowledge or participation. Peter was left totally out of the loop and was reminded of that again today as Harold spent the whole afternoon with Marco.

The rift forming between Peter and Marco was serious. Peter's jealousy and anger had reached a point where he would go out of his way to avoid him entirely. The polarization was so intense, he was even considering not attending the party for Wes at McLadden's.

He would decide about the party within the next 20 minutes, depending on how it went; Harold sent a cryptic cell message asking for Peter to meet him and Marco in the #4 greenhouse to review the seedling size for readiness. If the seedlings were big enough, they would move the planting schedule up by two days and begin planting tomorrow morning in a well-drained 20-acre field called the Sandy Lot.

Peter wasn't surprised Harold wanted his opinion; Marco had little practical experience in such matters and Harold relied heavily on Peter for day to day guidance. He was on the fence about moving the schedule up. They barely had enough plants ready and with the weekend coming, finishing on Friday would put the Sandy Lot two whole days ahead of the other fields in the rotation. Peter's vote was that they wait until Monday. He wasn't sure how Marco felt about it, but he was hoping to avoid a confrontation in front of Harold. If there was one, so be it.

Peter pulled his truck into the yard and continued on down the gravel path behind the parked vehicles and equipment. He glanced at the clock as he pulled up to the greenhouses; it was 6:30 so if the conversation with Harold was short he would only be a few minutes late to the party, provided he was still going.

As he parked in front of the #4 house, he could see Marco's car parked at the seed house 50 yards away. He left the truck and walked in through the small plastic covered front door. The rain had cooled the air into the low fifties so the furnaces were on, blowing warm air into the house.

Peter looked down into the cavernous space and could see Marco and Harold standing next to each other in the center of the watering track 100 yards in, surrounded by white trays sprouting the bright green three-inch tobacco seedlings.

They both looked up and Harold yelled out waving his hands, beckoning Peter to come, "Peter, great to see you. Come on in and join the fun."

Harold Treadwell was a privileged individual. As the sole owner of Treadwell Enterprises Inc., he was heir to the largest and most profitable farm in the valley. He was friendly and personable and was often thought of as a really nice guy. In excellent shape at 63 years old and taller than most men at 6' 5", he possessed a foreboding John Wayne-like façade, belied by his kind and gentle personality.

He was also filthy rich. His real estate in Sunbridge alone, was valued between 35 and 45 million dollars. His investments in the stock market, funded by years of profitable tobacco farming and commercial real estate sales were pushing 30 million. The land holdings, centered mostly up and down both sides of the two-mile-long stretch of Night Valley Road were listed as prime real estate, and even though nothing was currently for sale, commercial brokers waited at the ready to quickly pounce on any opportunity presenting itself in that corridor. Treadwell property was at the top of their list.

He was a fifth generation farmer. Some would say he was a gentleman farmer, as it appeared to the outsider he rarely got involved in the operation, but that was far from the truth. Harold was very much in touch with the day to day events and stayed connected to Peter during working hours through the use of the instant-connect cell phone. In the evenings, Harold would call Peter at a prearranged time to discuss the next day's activities. These calls would last only five to ten minutes, but the net result was always the same; Peter was following orders and the real daily operation was being orchestrated by Harold.

When Harold was in town, Peter made it a habit to chauffeur him around in his truck. This worked to both their benefits; Harold got to see and discuss the operation first hand, and Peter had Harold as a captive and could keep him away from direct contact with others. It was important to Peter his staff not learn how much oversight Harold maintained over the operation. He felt if they knew the extent of Harold's control, his own authority would erode.

In Peter's eyes, Harold's visit was not starting off well with Marco taking the lead.

Peter made his way down to the center of the house where Marco and Harold were standing. Both men were smoking cigars and the warm furnace air was disbursing the sweet smoke quickly. He reached out and shook Harold's hand with a warm friendly smile and a firm grip. He ignored Marco who stood there smiling and finger rolling a lit cigar in his mouth.

"Great to see you Peter," said Harold.

"Good to see you too Harold. I trust you had a nice flight and all went well?"

"Yes, the flight was okay. Had a layover in Denver and we managed to connect to an earlier flight, so it wasn't bad. Thanks for coming. We have just a few minutes left before we're headed over to a gathering in Simsbury to say goodbye to Wes Ackerson. Good man. He's moving overseas to teach there."

Harold looked down at the seedlings on the floor of the house and pointed to them with his cigar.

"Before we all head on out, we need your help to decide if we should plant tomorrow."

Taking a long pull on his cigar he continued, "Like I always do, I'd really like to push the schedule. Most lots are too wet except for the Sandy Lot which is pretty well drained. I know you've got that field ready; we swung by on the way back from the airport. Marco and I think we have enough plants for those 20 acres and it might be a good idea to start tomorrow. The weather will be perfect for it. What do you say, Pete?"

Peter never liked being called Pete, but he put up with it

from Harold. He was reluctant to give an opposite opinion, especially since Harold had already made up his mind. He also had no desire to pick a fight with Marco, who always agreed with Harold no matter what the topic.

Peter quickly responded with a turnaround in his thinking, "I see no reason why planting can't start tomorrow. We may have enough plants for Sandy Lot now, or will have by midday tomorrow if we have a warm day. We're getting almost half an inch per day growth on hot days. As a hedge, we can start planting on the north side and move to the south. If we're short and can't finish, we can pick up again on Monday and the southern exposure will aid the catch-up. Any fill-in we need to plant on Monday won't be far behind. I think we'll be fine."

"That's the spirit I like to see! It's settled then. Tomorrow at 7:00 a.m. we'll begin the schedule, first 20 acres. I'll get you a new plan Peter, adjusted for this."

Harold started to make his way out of the house with Marco and Peter following behind. True to form, Harold began his team lecture both Peter and Marco had heard a hundred times. The sermon always took the same format: Harold in the parental lead, not looking at either one, leaving no room for argument. He waved the cigar in the air as he talked.

"It heartens me you both have teamed up and are working so well together again for another season. Peter, Marco told me how attentive you've been to his efforts in the seed house and I saw firsthand the progress made there. I know you know how important that effort is to the future of Treadwell Enterprises. I also recognize you two haven't always seen eye-to-eye and you've had your differences in the past. I'm proud of you both for working together and keeping the hatchet buried."

They had walked to the front of the house and Harold turned around to face them. Peter and Marco turned as well, to see the small seedlings completely covering the white trays spreading before them as a vast sea of green.

"Tomorrow we start a new year and what you see here before us will be the beginning of another special season at Treadwell. Thank you both for your hard work and your best efforts.

"I think it's time to leave now for the party. Marco, would you mind if I rode with Peter in his truck? I've been with you all afternoon and haven't spent a bit of time with Peter. I need to catch up with him."

Marco responded with a smile as he puffed on his shrinking cigar, "Of course Harold. I'll be right along. There a few things I want to finish up on here and I need to lock up the seed house too."

"Okay then. We'll see you there."

Peter and Harold left the house, leaving Marco puffing on his cigar to finish up.

Alondra had never been to Treadwell farm, but she knew it would be a short trip as she'd passed it on her way to the hotel several times.

I made a sharp left turn with the Prius into the yard and headed past the equipment onto the gravel road leading to the greenhouses. As we drove up to the first house we could see Marco's car in the distance parked in front of the seed house. I stopped the car to consider the options.

"Oh crap," I said. "That's Marco's car. Fat chance we can search the house with him there. We don't want to bump into him either. He may be getting suspicious. We're so close; I don't want to blow it now. Maybe we should come back after the party. No one will be here then and we can stop on our way back to the hotel."

"Jason, I'm not exactly dressed for a night operation. We can do it, but I'll need to change my clothes and put on sneakers."

"Okay, okay, no problem."

"So we're heading to the party now? I hope so, I'm really hungry," she said.

"Yes, might as well. Can't take the chance we'll run into Marco in the seed house. Damn," I said and slapped the steering wheel.

"Do you think Becky will be at the party?" she asked.

"Becky?"

"You know, Marco's girlfriend."

"Did I mention her name?" I asked. Something was coming to me now.

Alondra responded in a defensive tone, "She introduced herself at lunch and you mentioned her name before when you told me about meeting her at the experiment station yesterday."

Now I understood what it was bothering me at lunch earlier. Alondra knew Becky's name and had mentioned it at the bar before lunch, but I never revealed her name. I had only made a reference to meeting Marco's associate who was rumored to be his girlfriend. She knew her first name before we made introductions at the table, I was sure of it.

We were parked in front of the #1 house, still pointed toward the seed house and Marco's car. I was quiet for almost 30 seconds before Alondra asked about it, "Jason, what's wrong. I know something's on your mind. Please tell me what it is."

"Okay, I'll tell you," I said. "How did you know Becky's name? You asked me about her at the bar before you were introduced to her. And I know I didn't pass you her name before that. I never learned about Marco in Jackie's presentation and neither did you, so why don't you tell me now how you knew. What's going on?"

There was a long silence before Alondra spoke.

"I'm sorry Jason, I really am. I was told you didn't know, and I didn't want to be the one to tell you."

"Tell me what?" I had no clue what Alondra was about to tell me.

"That Becky Sadler is DEA and she's been on the case for two months. I almost told you about it yesterday, but I decided not to. That's the reason you started so late in the case. That's why I asked why your involvement was delayed. You couldn't explain the delay so I knew you still didn't know about Becky. I'm sorry I didn't tell you."

I was boiling mad. "That's just fine. You had no trouble

telling me about the research team's involvement with Marco, why did you stop there? Why did you hold back?"

"The DEA doesn't know I know about the research team, so they never asked me not to tell you. I found out about that on my own, using connections I have at the FBI.

"They told me if I ran into you, it would be better if I didn't tell you about Becky because you didn't know and they wanted to keep it that way. I thought it was strange too, and I have no idea why that is. That's all I know. That's the honest truth. I'm really sorry, I should have told you."

Shaking my head in disbelief, I put the Prius in reverse and backed down the gravel road using the backup camera until there was enough room to back into a grassy turnout, and do a reverse K turn to point the car toward the exit. I selected the drive mode and slowly made my way down through the yard and out to Night Valley Road.

I was upset with Alondra, but it wasn't going to last long. She was so cute and I adored her. But the more I thought about it, I was really pissed at John.

"Let's go to the party. Not sure I'm in the mood for a party now, but maybe by the time we get there, I'll be in a better mood. We'll make an appearance and then we're coming back here to do some snooping and find that strain. Now let's go say hello to Becky, my new teammate."

"Deal," said Alondra, smiling now.

Chapter 36

My mood was improving in general and it continued to do so largely due to the second 20-ounce beer I was nurturing. I had successfully pushed away most of my negative thoughts about John and the case and how, once again I was the last to know the truth about what was really going on. I couldn't put it down entirely though and I made a vow to let John have it the next time we talked.

I grew more and more interested in the golden liquid as it made its way down my glass and flirted with the bottom. I also noticed social courage was inversely proportional to the level of beer in the glass; as the level dropped my courage took off.

This rule did not apply to Alondra, as she was and has always been a social creature and didn't need alcohol or anything for that matter, to revel in a social discourse at a party or gathering. She had the added benefit of her acute sexual magnetism and she had no problem drawing and sustaining a male crowd.

In the past she carried me in these social situations, and this time was no different except this was my show and she was my guest, but the opposite seemed true and that was fine with me. She was fully engaged with everyone and they totally bought the cousin story which was evidence to us both I was accepted and had earned legitimacy, at least for the time being.

Wes Ackerson had picked a perfect place for a party. McLadden's, fashioned after an old Irish drinking hole, had a large private back room with a low metal ceiling. We were all packed in tightly; it was a lively group of about 25 or so, half of whom I had yet to meet.

I had to remind myself not to relax too much. Individuals like Cody were here to interview and we could still make progress on the case. We also couldn't get too sloshed to make it back to the seed house later to search for the #13 strain. That would be more difficult now that we'd be searching with a flashlight in the dark. The risk of discovery was increasing and I couldn't easily explain away our presence if we were caught. Then again, if we were well-oiled enough (or acted that way) that could stand as a plausible defense.

I was watching for Marco and Becky, who were so far absent. We figured Marco would be along following us as his car was still at the seed house when we left, but it was getting late and I was beginning to believe Marco might be a no-show.

From my spot standing in the corner, I could see Peter and Harold Treadwell, whom I hadn't formerly met yet, sitting in a booth along the wall. They were both drinking Guinness, discussing paperwork of some kind spread out on the table in front of them.

Alondra was talking up a storm with Kevin, Cody and Julio, and two other men standing next to her in the center of the room. The guys were clearly taken with her looks, especially Julio and his friends. I could hear her jump into Spanish to address them then back to English for Kevin and Cody.

Her worries to me about Julio in the car on the way over

were unfounded; Julio was relieved she was my cousin and acted as if there was safety in numbers knowing he had a new friend he could confide in about the union topic.

I could only marvel at Alondra and her ability to blend in. The loud cacophony of voices in the room prevented me from hearing much of the conversation they were having but I saw her enthusiasm and passion and I was proud to hold the secret I was someone special in her life.

My attention moved to the other larger group standing on the other side of the room. There Wes was jawing with Bob and Cheryl Kingman, and with several other men and women I didn't know in their early twenties. I could only guess their ages, but they were holding drinks and that put them 21 or older.

I met Wes briefly when we arrived but it was time for me to strike up a more meaningful conversation, so I made my way across the room and went right up to Wes. There is no such thing as butting in, in a venue like this so I extended my hand, interrupting the conversation and we shook once again.

"Hey Wes, I'm the lucky guy that's taking your place," I said to him as we shook hands again. The others standing close parted slightly and Wes inched through and outside of the circle surrounding him to face me so we could chat more privately.

"I did hear that. Bob told me. Jason, I'll miss the opportunity to work with you to get to know you. Bob says you have a teaching job in the area; what town and what grade?"

Wes Ackerson looked like a 35-year-old holdover from the 60's, with longer hair below his ears and a full beard and mustache. In excellent shape and with piercing blue eyes he possessed a special quality. I could tell right away he was highly educated and carried a rare intellectual caliber to the way he spoke and with the warm impression he left me communicated by his demeanor and body language. I instantly thought he would be a great person to get to know and spend time with.

“Well to be totally honest, I have three high-potential jobs in the works, one solid offer in Windsor Locks, teaching grades 9 and 10, and two more offers on the way hopefully, in nearby towns. I’ll leave it at that so not to jinx them.”

“Well good for you. I know how difficult it is to get even one teaching offer. If you get more than one, you can consider yourself blessed. I wish you the best,” he said.

“Thanks Wes. I hear you found a teaching job overseas, in Russia? Peter told me. You must be excited.”

“Yes, very. I applied two years in a row for a position in the embassy there. They rejected me twice, but about two months later I was accepted into an even better opportunity. Strange how things work out, like I had a guardian angel this time.”

“Yeah, it appears that way sometimes doesn’t it,” I said, knowing full well his guardian angel had a name and it was Uncle Sam.

“Yes it does. So you’ve been here at the farm how long now? And what do they have you doing?”

“Just four days, mostly greenhouse work. I’ve been watering the trays and working in the seed house with Marco. You ever work with him?”

"Work with him?" Wes asked emphatically. "Is he here yet? I should make sure he's not listening before I go any further. Hey, would you like another beer? Let's go to the bar," as he grabbed my elbow and turned me around. He led me across the room and headed toward the bar which was on the other side of the restaurant. As we passed Alondra I caught her eye and she gave me a questioning look. I shrugged and kept walking with Wes alongside.

We took two empty stools at the corner of the long bar and Wes ordered a Guinness for himself and another Harp for me. We couldn't help noticing the beer-tap arrangement in front of us; it was amazing. There were more than 70 taps built into the long bar.

"Now to answer your question, I didn't work *with* him. I did *all his work for* him. The man is a genius, but he's one very lazy one."

"Why is he a genius?" I asked.

"You haven't really spent much time with him yet, have you?"

"No, not really; about a day and a half. I worked with him seeding some strains in the pink trays and stripping seed pods from the plants in the seed house."

"Well let's just say he does all his really important work in a greenhouse in the basement of his house. If you met him on the street, he'd give you the impression he's a bumbling idiot, but that's not the case at all. His basement is where you'll learn he's a genius."

"Kevin told me about his basement. Do you know firsthand the kind of work going on there?"

"Drink up my friend, before your beer gets warm," and we both took long hits on our beers.

"I shouldn't tell you all this, but it really doesn't matter anymore. I'll be on a plane to Moscow in three days.

"Where was I? Oh, Marco in his basement, right. There are two; sorry, I mean three kinds of plant genetic work going on there.

"One is the tobacco straining. He's on a quest to create the best shade tobacco in the universe. Shade tobacco is cigar wrappers, but maybe you know this by now. This is all being done for Treadwell. He crosses this strain with that one, leaf size with leaf thinness; leaf color with leaf shape, he even had some seedless strains growing. That one didn't get too far, too hard to produce in quantity. Works for tomatoes, grapes and watermelon, but not for tobacco. He has this elaborate database tracking all the parents and child outcomes. It's quite impressive I must say."

"Sounds interesting. What else is he working on?" I asked as we both took long pulls from half empty glasses.

Wes was purposefully quiet as the bartender wiped the bar down with a wash rag in front of us. As soon as he was gone he continued.

"Don't repeat this and be kind not to rat the guy out, but Marco is what I would term a 'future thinker'. He thinks at least three to five years out."

"What's there to rat out about that?"

"Hold on, I'm not finished."

"Sorry, my bad. Go on."

“Marco sees a clear path into a future where recreational marijuana will not only be legal, but it will be thriving in the Connecticut River valley, just like shade tobacco used to, many years ago.

“Did you know shade tobacco output in Connecticut is down below 10 percent of what it once was, 50 years ago? So now we have a void to fill. Marco is all into the thinking opportunity awaits the brave and daring who can step up to grab the brass ring, march forward with new ideas.

“His idea is to fill the void with the mass cultivation of legalized marijuana. So about a third of his basement is devoted to perfecting marijuana strains. That’s the part you can’t rat out.”

“How do you know so much about all this?”

“I spent weeks working with him in the seed house, doing grunt work. Then one day we got into this huge discussion about legalizing marijuana. He has some pretty strong views about it. He invites two of us over to his house for beers afterward, me and Cody Mason, he’s here tonight. Maybe you know him.”

“I do. We’ve worked a bit together already.”

“He has a really nice house, post and beam. We end up in his basement where he has this incredibly expensive hydroponic setup for growing tobacco and marijuana. I think he hooked into some kind of university research grant to pay for it all. Anyway, he wants us to try some different strains of weed to see how potent they are. So he sets up six different strains for us to try. I was more stoned that night than ever before.”

"Did he partake?"

"That was the strange thing. He didn't. He's not a user. He drank wine the whole time."

"You mentioned there are three kinds of genetic work. Tobacco, marijuana and what's the third?"

I was sitting with my back to the room, but Wes had taken the corner stool to my right so he had a side view of the room and the entrance way. He was looking past me into the room.

"There's Marco now. He has a woman with him. Not so bad looking either; reminds me of Jennifer Aniston. We'll talk later."

I turned around on my stool to see Marco and Becky walking straight over to us. They were holding hands which looked a little odd for two adults their age. Now that I knew who Becky really was, it looked even more strange.

Wes jumped off his stool and was the first to greet Marco, reaching out to give him a warm handshake.

"Marco, so really great to see you again. Who's your friend?" Wes asked.

"Hi Wes. It's good to see you too. This is Becky Sadler, I work with Becky at the experiment station and she's a very good friend of mine. Becky this is Wes Ackerson, this is his party tonight. Jason, you know Becky so introductions aren't necessary."

I had Becky's attention now so I gave her a forced smile, "Hi Becky."

"Nice to meet you Wes," as they shook hands. "Hi Jason. Nice to see you again so soon."

Marco took to acting like the MC, "Ladies and Gentlemen, let's go into the back room where the party is. The whole team is there so let's not be rude."

We all agreed and headed for the party crowd. Marco looked back at me as we made our way across the floor and into the back room, "Jason, is your cousin here tonight?"

"Yes she is Marco. She's here."

His question prompted a frown from Becky Marco couldn't see.

As we walked Becky and I were lagging a few steps behind Marco and Wes. I leaned over and spoke softly into her ear, "I know who you work for. Do you really care for him or is this part of your scam?"

She ignored me with no reaction and kept walking.

Marco entered the party room first and went right over to Harold who was still sitting in the booth with Peter. He leaned over and spoke only to him. Harold nodded in agreement and stood up from his seat, grabbed Wes to follow him and they walked quickly to the center of the room, next to where Alondra was standing.

"Can I have your attention, please? Quiet now, please can I have your attention?" Harold bellowed out loudly in his deep voice. The room quieted down instantly as soon as everyone realized it was Harold.

"Thank you all for coming tonight to say goodbye to Wes Ackerson. I'm not an experienced speaker, but I want to say just a few words tonight about Wes. You all know him, his quick wit and caring personality. He gave us five years of extraordinary service as a tractor driver and a straw boss in the fields. We'll miss him, but we can be proud to know he's moving on and up into his career as a teacher.

"Wes, I know where you're going, they don't grow shade tobacco," everyone chuckled. "But if and when you come back to Sunbridge and you want to work in tobacco again, remember we'll always have a place for you at Treadwell Enterprises. Let's give Wes a round of applause for a job well done and wish him the best as he embarks on the next phase of his career!"

The room erupted with applause and whistles and repeated calls for a speech.

Wes looked humbled. He raised his hand to quiet the crowd. Once again the crowd quieted down, this time for Wes.

"Thanks Harold, for the kind words. Thanks everyone for coming, it means a lot to me.

"Earlier today I was thinking about what I could take with me to Russia to remind me of the farm. That's both a hard one and an easy one. It's not like we have material things to remind us, except a cigar or two if I could sneak them in my bags and get them through customs."

That got a quiet laugh from the crowd.

"But what I will take are all the fond memories of hours spent on the tractors and in the trucks and of hot work in the greenhouses and under the nets in the fields and in the sheds. And all the experiences and friendship we shared along the way. I will take a piece of each one of you with me. I will keep all of you very close through all those cherished memories. I wish you all the best."

The room had quieted so you could hear a pin drop. The smiles were gone and replaced with a subdued sadness. It was clear that Wes had been a good friend to all in the room and everyone would miss him.

"Thank you all for coming and Harold wanted me to tell you the bar is on the other side and don't be bashful because he's paying tonight."

For a second time the room filled with loud applause and whistles. Several people went over to greet Wes and he was soon engulfed in the crowd again. The noise in the room returned as the party moved back into full swing.

There was little likelihood I would continue my conversation with Wes, but I knew what he was going to tell me anyway. Marco's third effort in plant genetics was his attempt to cross marijuana with tobacco. The real question was, where was the strain now and what was Marco's long term plan for it?

The party was in full swing again and Marco and Becky had parked themselves in a booth across the table from Harold. I could see they were holding hands again. Peter had left the booth earlier and was nowhere in sight.

As I watched Becky from across the room I tried to imagine how much she knew about the strain's whereabouts. She'd been on the case for two months and was probably sleeping with Marco by now. The case was still active so she hadn't made any real progress in that time which I found hard to believe. It made better sense to think she was seriously involved with Marco, loved him and was protecting him. If that was the case, she was protecting him from me now. I wanted a conversation with her and John as soon as possible.

I could see Alondra standing along one edge of the room engaged in conversation with yet another small group of young men. They were listening and watching intently as she spoke. Cody appeared from somewhere behind holding his beer and a glass of white wine, which he politely presented to Alondra.

Winding through the room I saw the bartender from the other side going from person to person with a note in his hand. He saw me and then made a beeline right to me, handing me the note.

"I think this is for you; is your name Jason? You're the only guy in the room who looks like Matthew McConaughey so it must be you."

"Yeah that's me. Thanks." He turned and left.

It took me a few seconds to open the note as it was taped shut on three sides.

It was a handwritten note and it read:

> *Jason,*
>
> *New developments. Meet me outside in front of the restaurant in 5 minutes. Bring your cousin.*
>
> *John Trane*

Chapter 37

Holding the note, I went right up to Alondra and told her to excuse herself from the group and follow me out. She read the urgency in my tone and said a few words in Spanish to Julio who took her wine glass. She then quickly followed me through the entrance way, out into the outer vestibule of the restaurant. When we were alone there she immediately asked what was going on. I passed her the note.

"Wow, John Trane's your handler, right? He's here and wants to meet us. Did you know he was coming?"

"Of course not. I would have told you."

"Something big is going down Jason. Handlers don't fly in unannounced for Thursday night status meetings."

"Yeah, I know. Let's find out what it is. I'm assuming you've never met him?"

"No, never."

"This ought to be good."

We walked outside through the doors to the front of the restaurant and found John standing there next to a black Jeep Grand Cherokee parked in a handicapped spot. In true spy fashion, he was wearing a light beige trench coat. It was almost 9:00 p.m. and was already dark.

I walked up and shook his hand.

"John, what are you doing here? This is Alondra Espinoza, FBI."

"Alondra, please to meet you," as they shook hands. "Nice cover, standing in as Jason's cousin."

"How did you learn that?" I asked.

"Never mind. It's not important. Please get in the car. Back seat for you both, there's someone I want you to meet."

We climbed into the back of the SUV and John got into the driver's seat. It was dark, but the dome light was on, and there was enough light where I could see everyone's face.

"Jason and Alondra, I'd like you to meet FBI agent Helmut Bergmann."

Helmut was a tall man in his fifties with light gray hair and a mustache. He reached back and shook both our hands.

"Very good to meet you both," he said in a thick Austrian accent. "I wish it were under more pleasant circumstances."

John continued talking as he started the car, "I'm sure you're wondering what brings me to Hartford to track you down with no notice."

He proceeded to back out of the space and drive out of the parking lot.

"We're not going very far, but we can't stay here in front of the restaurant."

He drove about a half-mile before coming to a stop into a parking space in front of another line of small stores in a strip mall. All the stores were closed. He put the Jeep in park and turned off the ignition.

"Go ahead Helmut. Show them the picture on your phone."

He took out his iPhone and swiped it on to show a picture of a woman in dark glasses wearing a peach colored blouse sitting at a table. The shot was from below looking up and it was of excellent quality.

Helmut started in, "This is a photo I took this morning of a woman I met with at the airport bar. Her name is Gretchen Feinman. Do you recognize her?"

We both looked at the photo and we knew immediately we were looking at Becky Sadler. Her hair was fixed differently, but it was definitely her.

"Yes, that's Becky Sadler, Marco's girlfriend," I said.

Now was a good time to let John in on the secret that I knew about his secret, that Becky was DEA. If I told him, I'd be compromising Alondra, so I kept my mouth shut. I was more interested in what this was all about and if it centered around Becky, he'd be telling me the truth soon anyway.

John started in, "Jason, maybe you know this already," he said as he glanced at Alondra, "but Becky Sadler is DEA and she's been covert on the TobaccoNet case for two months now. I'm sorry we didn't tell you, but we felt it was necessary to keep agent separation and both your covers secure."

"That's just great John. Then I assume she didn't know about me either? Right?"

"Yes, she knew about you. She was the initial lead on the case Jason. That she knew about you is of no consequence."

I couldn't just sit back so I poked at him, "Nice double standard John."

He continued, ignoring my comment, "What I'm about to tell you now must remain strictly confidential.

"Becky has decided to take matters into her own hands, and go into business for herself. Helmut can you give us some background here?"

"Certainly John. About three days ago a representative from the European American Tobacco Company contacted the FBI about some calls they were getting from a woman who was peddling a unique strain of tobacco. This tobacco reportedly had a high THC content, like marijuana.

"European American Tobacco is on probation in the states for a number of egregious tax and accounting violations so rather than be involved in something potentially illegal, they felt inclined to contact the FBI. This woman's sale's pitch rang a bell in our organization relating to your TobaccoNet case, so we decided to play along. We set up a call trap and routed her calls into my office in D.C. I became Randolph Haussmann for the purposes of dealing with this woman.

"This morning I flew into Bradley International and met Gretchen Feinman, attorney, acting as an agent on behalf of a nameless client at a bar at the airport. I purchased a small sample of this tobacco," as he held up a small glass pill bottle holding a few strips of brown leaf so we could see it, "for 5,000 dollars in small bills."

I was dumbfounded. Becky and Marco had the strain and they were selling it. I just couldn't believe where this was going. I looked over at Alondra and she looked back at me just as perplexed.

John interjected, “Tell them what’s happening next.”

Helmut continued, “The 5,000 dollars bought us the right to examine the strain, to verify the THC content, and to prove we were seriously interested. I couriered half the sample she gave me to D.C. today and our lab confirmed this is a high THC product.

“The next step is for Gretchen, I mean Becky, to provide us with a more substantial uncured sample of this tobacco.”

“Do you know what the terms of the final deal were?” I asked.

“We only gave her ballpark figures, but it was thought to be something like a million dollars for 500 acres of seed, provided the quality was there and all the samples checked out. The payment was to be paid half up front and the other half over the following six month period.

“The original plan I had with her was for me to courier this sample back to a Washington lab today for analysis and to have another pickup of a larger uncured sample from her within a day or two, ASAP.

“We decided to push this schedule somewhat. We told her the sample checked out and I had a new assignment to secure the larger uncured sample from her right away. We were hoping she had the larger sample in her possession to give to me all along.

“We were right; I contacted her about an hour ago and scheduled a pickup for tonight. We’re meeting her in,” as he checked his watch, “15 minutes inside the mail drop at the Simsbury post office about a quarter mile from here. We’ve asked the Simsbury police to meet us there.”

"That's unbelievable," I said. "How will this play out when you meet?"

John answered, "She'll be arrested for selling government property or critical case evidence and we can probably get her on conspiracy charges as well, but our primary focus is to acquire the strain. Obviously Marco's involved but we can't arrest him until we have more evidence."

"What if you're wrong and this breach is all part of her plan to pry the strain away from Marco?" I asked.

"That's a stretch," John replied. "We've had our suspicions something wasn't right with her for a while. I won't get into it right now but let's just say we had indications.

"She'll have her day in court, no doubt, and this won't be easy on any of us. I've known Becky for a long time. This isn't the first case we've worked together, but I'll bet it'll be the last.

"I'm going to drop you both off back at the party now." John started the SUV and backed out of his space, shifted into drive and headed back toward the restaurant.

"There's no reason you need to be with us for the pickup. As far as the case goes, for all practical purposes the case might be over for both of you, but it won't be formally over until we have the strain in hand. The way I see it, that will be tonight or tomorrow morning. We also obtained a search warrant for Becky's apartment and her office.

"Oddly enough, the agricultural experiment station where she works has the closest lab where we can do analysis on the uncured sample. We've arranged to have the analysis done tonight. We'll get a confirmation in a few hours. I'll call you with the results."

We could see the restaurant lights ahead on the left and John pulled up to the curb and stopped to let us out. He reached back to shake my hand.

"Thank you Jason. I think indirectly you can take some credit for this. Without you here, Becky might have dragged this out for a long time. I think she probably felt you closing in and she had to do something.

"Guess we also have to credit European American Tobacco for not falling asleep at the switch when her calls came in."

"Yeah, well thanks John, and good luck tonight. Helmut, nice work. Take care," I said and patted him on the shoulder.

Alondra said nothing as we climbed out of the back seat of the SUV onto the curb side of the street and shut the door. He made a quick U-turn and headed back toward the post office. We stood there in front of the restaurant, both still in disbelief.

"Let's go in. I need a drink."

"Me too," said Alondra, as I put my arm around her and we started back into the restaurant building, both of us in mild shock.

Alondra added, "Jason, I can't believe Marco actually had the strain and we caught them trying to sell it. I was hoping for an end to the case but I didn't expect it to end so suddenly like this."

"Nothing surprises me anymore."

We walked into the outer vestibule and we made our way to the restaurant entrance, which, from this entry point was up a set of small stairs. As we made our way up the stairs I reached for the door and it opened suddenly from someone pushing it from the inside coming out. It was Becky and she was holding a manila envelope.

"Hi Becky."

"Oh hi Jason. I'm just running to the post office. I know they have an evening drop-off and it's open till 9:30. I'll be back in a few minutes."

She pressed by us both in the small space at the top of the stairs.

"Hi Alondra," she said as she made her way down the stairs headed toward the parking lot.

"Hi Becky," Alondra said back, as Becky went through the door and out the building.

"That is really sad. I feel sorry for her," Alondra said sadly.

"Can't say I do," I said. "It is what it is. Let's go in. I know they have a great selection of scotch here."

"I don't even like scotch."

"Maybe you should start liking it. You know this could be my last day at Treadwell; I want to make the most of it. I've been here for only four days and the case is over. That really sucks."

"Why does it suck?" she asked.

"Well for one thing we have to leave here and we can't be

together. That sucks. And plans you had to establish unions here will fade away. That sucks too. Not to mention all the good people here and the friends I was making. I'll miss that. Kind of dig the farming thing too, brings me back to my days on the potato farm with my dad."

"Yeah, I can see why you're disappointed. I am too; we had a great opportunity to make a real difference in the lives of so many. I'm not sure I'm ready to give it all up."

"We really don't have a choice in the matter do we; shortest scam ever for me."

"I guess you're right. But it's not all bad, you can move into my apartment with me in D.C."

"Wow you switched topics and made a fast turnaround. Really? You'll let me do that? Last time, that was a flat NO," I said.

"Yeah, that was before I knew you drove an electric car and were such a good farmer," she said smiling now.

"Yeah right," I said. "Come on, let's go in. I'm not working tomorrow, so let's have one more party time."

"Okay, then back to my hotel, not yours."

"Why?" I asked.

"Clean sheets."

"Right," I replied.

As we started into the restaurant through the entrance door, my phone chimed with a text from John. I read it out loud: *"Mission accomplished. Sample secured, person in custody, analysis pending."*

I looked at Alondra and said, "She'll have to cut a deal now and tell us where the strain is. So it's all over for Becky and Marco now. The DEA has two big black eyes over this one. It was their making in the first place and a bad agent caught in the act. Hard to believe. And it's all over for us too."

"I hope it's not over for us Jason," she said.

"I mean the case is over for us. You and I have just begun. Let's go in and get that scotch, and something to eat."

"Good deal," she said as we walked arm in arm into the restaurant and made our way through the crowd to the bar.

Chapter 38

5 days later...

A case wrap-up was not the same thing as a case post mortem.

The post mortem was an analysis of what went right and wrong in the case. We were not here for that.

The wrap-up was an informational recap of case outcomes. This was almost always held onsite in the training center in Quantico, Virginia. This time was different; the TobaccoNet wrap-up was being held offsite in Scottsdale, Arizona. Bill felt it was warranted to spend the money and give us all a few days in the sun at the Fairmont Resort where he was finishing up his annual two-week vacation. He could justify the spend because the case had a positive result and ended so quickly. I was always amazed how easy it was to justify spending taxpayer funds.

This was a beautiful spot for a wrap-up. I had only one complaint: the heat. We flew in the day before and fortunately the plane landed before noon. It was so hot at 117 degrees, the Sky Harbor airport closed at 2:00 p.m. It was explained to us that in extreme heat, the tires on the plane could suffer a blowout. Not a comforting thought the temperature could rise to 117 in late May enough to impact air travel. Then again the whole country and probably the world was affected by the climate change phenomenon.

I was an independent and I couldn't decide if climate change was real or not. More and more days like this provided evidence the Democrats were right and global warming did exist. More to the point, I was sure tornado alley was politically agnostic. Or was it?

The case was officially closed now and we were all here. There were seven of us pressed into a small windowed meeting room overlooking this beautiful resort in the desert. Bill, John, Alondra and I, Patrick Bobka whom I met for the first time, Helmut Bergmann and Jackie were in attendance.

Jackie was one of the original case architects. It was standard procedure to bring back in an architect for the wrap-up. She was here to provide any case background or details if needed.

I could tell Jackie was a bit uncomfortable and I could imagine why; someone had filled her in on the true nature of the case: Treadwell farm was involved not with marijuana growing, but tobacco straining. The DEA knew all about it as it was their idea to begin with. This information had been kept from her and I could tell by her attitude and body language this was not sitting well with her right now.

DEA's involvement was kept from me too, but I had the benefit of a spy who filled me in and I had more time to think about it.

As usual, Alondra was a standout in the room but I was biased.

We'd moved out of our hotels on Sunday and back to Washington. She was serious I should move in with her, so I did. I would still hold on to my apartment, just long enough to be sure our relationship was showing elements of permanency. You never know.

The meeting was to begin promptly at 11:00 a.m. and we had five minutes to go, but we were all at the table so John launched the meeting early. He had the floor first and started up.

"Thanks everyone for coming. Please thank Bill for recommending and paying for this incredible venue for our meeting today."

We all smiled and acknowledged Bill's generosity.

John continued, "I don't think this will take too long. The interview with Marco is a good place to start. I hear it went well. Patrick, can you fill us in on that?"

"Sure," Patrick said as he looked down at his notes. "Marco cooperated fully and opened up his basement for a thorough examination. He maintained what we fed him all along, that his program was funded by a UCLA grant. He said he worked for more than six months, but he was never successful in creating that strain.

"We treated him as an innocent party, as Becky freely admitted Marco had no knowledge of her plan, and subsequent interviews with Marco proved that to be the case. He knew nothing about what went on under his nose with Becky and we saw no reason to tell him.

"He admitted he knew from the onset the UCLA goal was impossible, but he went along as a willing participant to acquire the hydroponics in his basement and continue his tobacco strain research at Treadwell.

“As you know, the TarLight project closed over a year ago. For those of you who are unaware, TarLight was a DEA-funded project to create a THC-potent tobacco. Marco didn’t know it, but he was actually working for the DEA. He still doesn’t know and he will never know.”

I was glad to hear Patrick admit DEA involvement to the group. Judging by the look on Bill’s face, I’m not sure he was authorized to talk about it so openly, but it was too late, the cat was out of the bag.

“As we indicated all along, there was no special strain, and Marco was never successful creating one. The examination of the questionable #13 strain revealed only straight tobacco, with no THC content.

“Leaves on that strain matched the leaf Becky provided for the uncured sample. Later, Becky confirmed she never tested the uncured sample and had planned to do so the next morning, but the call came in that evening and she never had the chance to test it. She made the assumption it was the TCH strain from the #13 label and the placement in the marijuana bed.”

Patrick glanced at his notes and continued, “We asked Marco how the strain came to be labeled #13. He claimed Cody Mason, one of the college boys he worked with, came up with that number on his own as a joke, knowing Marco would never use #13. That strain was a cross of a shade tobacco strain with a different kind of tobacco called ‘broadleaf’.”

Jackie interjected, “For those of you who don’t know, broadleaf tobacco is an open field tobacco used as the tobacco inside a cigar, not the wrapper. Plants are totally different, usually smaller in height with less leaf count. This type of tobacco is never grown under the nets."

"Thanks Jackie." Patrick continued, "Marco said he planted that cross in the marijuana section away from the other tobacco intentionally, just to separate it from the normal shade tobacco. Treadwell has designs to grow more broadleaf; they even have an open field designated as the Broadleaf Lot."

That made perfect sense to me as that strain was labeled 13BL, the 'BL' clearly stood for BroadLeaf.

But I still had a question so I asked, "So you're saying Becky only thought she had the THC strain, and it doesn't exist?"

John answered, "That's right Jason. Not only that, the small bottle sample checks out as pure cannabis, a.k.a. marijuana. It's a highly potent strain too, with a THC content almost 30 percent higher than average. One thing we're sure of, that sample is definitely marijuana and not tobacco."

"Does this sample come from the original weed sample from the man they arrested in Puerto Rico?" I asked.

"Yes," John replied. "In fact it's all that's left of that original find. Much of it was eaten up in the lab testing and Becky started with a bigger sample too, but some was used by her in the comparisons she was making with the seed house strains at the farm."

I saw this more clearly now so I said, "But that implies the labs were wrong. All three labs, the quick lab at the Maria station in Puerto Rico and their main lab returned two weeks later and our own lab in D.C. What are the chances of that?"

"You've got a great memory Jason, but we know that don't we."

John continued, "That's the other interesting thing; all the lab results in Puerto Rico are missing. They only have a record of checking in a sample, and mailing a completed report. The actual report itself is nowhere to be found. Copies we had are gone too. We have no reports and we don't know who ran the tests or signed off on them.

"Our lab is a different story. We still have our lab report, but we only did a THC test and not a burn test. There wasn't enough sample left to register a proper test so they skipped it.

"In our report there was also a reference to the microscopic cell pattern being similar but different than shade tobacco, and they expected that because it was labeled from the Puerto Rico lab as 'special tobacco'. Had they gone further and compared the sample against marijuana, they would have seen a very close match, but our lab never checked the cured sample against marijuana. They never made that connection."

"So what you're telling us is the original sample identifies as marijuana, and we can't prove the original find was anything but that. There were lab reports in Puerto Rico stipulating the sample was like shade tobacco and not marijuana, but they're mysteriously missing. Fascinating."

I continued, "What did Marco say about the possibility of pure marijuana finding its way to the cigar plant in Puerto Rico, his marijuana?"

"He said it was possible some of the boys he worked with had attempted to cure marijuana by hanging it in a shed. He found some tending to last year's harvest."

Jackie jumped into the conversation again, "Remember shade tobacco makes its way to the Hartford Shade Co-op for processing first. Chances are cured marijuana wouldn't look anything like tobacco and it would easily be discovered there at the co-op. I highly doubt marijuana would make it all the way down to Puerto Rico, unnoticed from Treadwell farm."

"That's an excellent point Jackie," I said. "So we can logically assume the marijuana found in Puerto Rico didn't come from Treadwell."

Bill spoke up for the first time, "Then where did it come from?"

I replied, "Doesn't really matter does it? It's probably a local issue and was all along. We'll never know. What we do know is there is no THC tobacco strain hitting the street and TarLight and TobaccoNet are both closed and we're moving on.

"What's going to happen with Becky?"

John answered, "She'll lose her job and plead guilty to evidence tampering or some other small charge. She'll give the money back, pay a hefty fine, get a suspended sentence and probation, maybe retire early on her savings. Not too bad really.

"I think she really loved this Marco guy and believed she had an opportunity she couldn't pass up. Too bad it ended the way it did. You shouldn't feel too bad about Becky; Marco posted her bail. I think they're still together."

Bill chimed in to break a ten-second silence. "Well, I think that about does it. Do we have anything else to share in the wrap-up?" He looked around the table, but we were all satisfied and no one talked.

"I'll take your collective silence as a no.

"Thank you John, Jason and Alondra for your efforts. I see this as a positive result on balance. Jackie, excellent work on the case, Patrick nice job and thanks for not saying 'I told you so'. Helmut, thank you for coming and playing your critical role in the case.

"Let me suggest a swim this afternoon in the South Pool. It will be hot today again but it's a dry heat and a dip in the pool is really quite nice."

Watching other men watch Alondra walk to the edge of the South Pool and down the stairs into the water wasn't doing much for me. She just had to wear the most provocative thong she could find and a string top with cover-ups the size of postage stamps. The combo feeling I was having of pride and protectionism was a strange mix. I guess that was her thing, always pushing the edge; I suppose it was something I would have to get used to.

The umbrella over me was blocking nothing because the chaise lounge I was lying on was under a group of tall palm trees blocking the hot midday sun. It was a dry heat as Bill had said earlier, and 109 degrees didn't really feel like 109 degrees.

The waitress had just taken my order for two margaritas Alondra had agreed to pay for. I was holding her wallet; she told me to use the red card to pay for the drinks. At 16 dollars each, I thought that was a good idea.

I had to admit this resort was incredible. We were leaving tomorrow and it saddened me. Only two days here in this paradise and we'd be flying back to Virginia to start all over again with another case. Chances of us working together again right away were small, but we were finally living together and that thought gave me comfort.

I still had some trouble dealing with the closure of TobaccoNet. What was bothering me the most was the disappearance of the lab reports in Puerto Rico. In fact, reports from two different labs had gone missing.

Without the physical reports in hand, we couldn't ask the lab staff tough questions about why (or if) they were falsified. It really didn't matter now, but it was a loose end and I hated loose ends.

We'd discussed it some at lunch after the meeting. John's theory was someone got to the lab personnel and paid them to change the reports in both labs from marijuana to shade tobacco. Simple enough; Puerto Rico is a close-knit community where everyone knows everyone else. Corruption is high there too. Entirely possible someone stepped in with some cash to make sure the man's record would be clean; they could never get him on a possession charge if the substance was only tobacco.

I was still bothered by it all and I couldn't shake it. We didn't have the reports, so we'd never know if the language was specific enough to point to a TarLight-like strain. There were probably elements of the initial report that couldn't be altered, THC content for one.

The original case in Puerto Rico was bizarre enough to warrant the attention of the DEA, where there was already a hypersensitivity to a tobacco-THC theme due to the TarLight case. I just didn't see how the Puerto Rico case could align itself so perfectly to TarLight, but it was probably all a coincidence, with the DEA creating the connection out of their own paranoia.

I personally believed the DEA sequestered the original lab reports after the fact to keep it all quiet. That would have been the smartest thing to do. Of course we'll never know; that was hardly something anyone at the DEA would ever admit to.

Only one thing I was sure about, the guy in Puerto Rico, Roberto Martell-Valentin, had some luck that day, and maybe some help too.

It was time to let it go. I'd thought about it enough and gone round and round with it, and it didn't matter now anyway, both cases were closed.

The waitress arrived with the Margaritas and placed them down on the small table next to our chaise lounges. Alondra was still in the pool swimming laps; I could see her long black hair flowing down her back, tied in a ponytail.

I still could not believe her lack of modesty; everyone watching this beautiful woman swimming laps in a thong was getting quite a show. I'm sure she knew.

I opened her wallet to find the red card and gave it the waitress to pay for the drinks. She swiped the card and returned it to me with the receipt. I added in the tip; she thanked me taking the receipt, turned and walked away. I took the card and slid it back into her wallet.

Inside her wallet on the top flap under plastic, was her FBI ID. I looked at her picture, a really nice one; it read FBI in large letters in the center, and underneath: Ms. Alondra Espinoza, Special Agent.

Below that ID was her driver's license, also in plastic. Nothing special until I saw her name.

I looked up and watched her again swimming in the pool. I couldn't help smiling; Alondra Martell-Valentin Espinoza, you are something else.

The End

About the Author

Keith Bombard lives in rural Connecticut and has a career as a System's Architect in the health services industry. He lives with his family near the tobacco fields where for 12 years as a youth, he learned all there was to know about raising shade tobacco as a summer laborer.

A huge fan of authors Nelson DeMille, Michael Connelly, James Patterson, Author Conan Doyle and John Steinbeck, he is hunkered down, planning his next Jason Kraft novel.

Made in the USA
Charleston, SC
21 November 2015